PRAISE FOR LUCY BLUE'S PREVIOUS BOUND IN DARKNESS NOVELS

THE DEVIL'S KNIGHT

"Blue cleverly crafts [*The Devil's Knight*] so that readers not only feel they are living, breathing, and seeing medieval England, but are part of the world of the vampire. She ensnares you in a delicate, yet powerful web of suspense, passion, and the paranormal so that you become a willing captive and a true believer in the world she has created."

—*Romantic Times*

"A fabulous medieval vampire romance. . . . The changing relationship between Siobhan and Tristan is cleverly devised to enhance the powerful paranormal tale while the audience anticipates the confrontation between the two men in her life. . . . A fine fresh historical."

—Harriet Klausner, The Best Reviews

DARK ANG … as an eBook

MY DEMON'S KISS

"Taking her cue from the original vampire legends and adding bits from TV series *Buffy the Vampire Slayer* and *Angel*, along with a touch of Van Helsing, Blue pens a fascinating re-imagining of a vampire's search for salvation. Once you're hooked on this first glimpse of Simon and Isabel, you'll be thirsty for more."

—*Romantic Times*

"Blue's pacing is fast and furious, but the personalities of her characters shine through, and Simon and Isabel's conflicts are believable and just unresolved enough to leave readers eager for the next in the series. Blue's noble vampire who fights to retain his humanity and heroine who fights for what is hers make for an unusual and compelling paranormal romance."

—*Booklist*

"A terrific tale with an intriguing final twist."

—Harriet Klausner

"A stellar story . . . the first stunning book in the alluring new medieval series, Bound in Darkness. Blue compellingly sucks readers into a bygone but thrilling world of knights and vampires, romance and terror. . . . Utterly captivating. . . . An absolute must for fans of paranormal romance."

—Road to Romance

"A fine medieval vampire romance. . . . *My Demon's Kiss* [is like] taking Angel and placing him mostly in eleventh-century England. The story line is action-packed . . . and never slows down."

—The Best Reviews

ALSO BY LUCY BLUE

The Devil's Knight

My Demon's Kiss

Dark Angel

LUCY BLUE

POCKET BOOKS
New York London Toronto Sydney

An *Original* Publication of POCKET BOOKS

POCKET BOOKS, a division of Simon & Schuster, Inc.
1230 Avenue of the Americas, New York, NY 10020

ISBN-13: 978-1-4165-1196-0
ISBN-10: 1-4165-1196-2

This Pocket Books paperback edition January 2007

10 9 8 7 6 5 4 3 2 1

Illustration by Franco Accornero

Manufactured in the United States of America

For Kathryn and Nico,
far and away the most gorgeous people I know

Acknowledgments

As always, the following are worthy of more gratitude than I could ever express: Timothy Seldes and all his kind colleagues at Russell & Volkening; Lauren McKenna at Pocket Books and her lovely and talented assistant, Megan McKeever; Michael Wertz of Wertzateria; Isabel Samaras; W. Michael Hemlepp, Jr., Esquire; and most of all, my beautiful family, Addison's always included.

Dark Angel

Prologue

Orlando bathed Isabel's forehead, trying to cool her fever. "Brave little girl," the dwarfish wizard murmured, smiling down on her. "Do not lose faith." She made a sound that could have been laughter or a sob. "All is not yet lost."

For more than a week they had traveled north into this land the Britons called Scotland. But he had known it by another name. A thousand years ago or more, he had made his way down from these highlands in pursuit of the creature Lucan Kivar, his cursed demon father. But now the creature had captured him, along with this innocent young woman, a descendant of their ancient blood.

Isabel's hand closed around his wrist. "He will come." Her red hair flamed against her death-pale cheek, and her dark green eyes were bright. "My love is not dead, Orlando." Her touch was like a burning brand against his skin, so racked was she with fever. Kivar now possessed a living man, a brigand captain named Sean Lebuin, and in this form, he could move in sunlight. But he still hungered for mortal blood. He had fed upon Isabel steadily at intervals for days, weakening her as he made himself stronger. "I would know."

"Of course you would," he promised, stroking her hand, though in truth he could not believe it. After so many centuries, the last of his hope was finally lost. Too many had died. He rose to look out of the tent flap. The sky was beginning to lighten over the mountaintop. Soon Kivar would awaken and come for her again. How much longer could she last? Would she make it to their destination, to the lands of ice? Orlando knew where they were going, had known as soon as he had seen these mountains. He knew Kivar's design. The creature meant to take the Chalice, the only hope of salvation for every vampire he had cursed. But Orlando was powerless to stop him, powerless to save this woman from her fate. For all his learning, all his study, all his immortality, now at the end of his quest, he could do nothing at all. The Chalice was all but lost. His hand strayed to his pocket, to the ice-cold bottle of ruby-colored glass that was all he loved distilled. He drew it out and clutched it tightly in his fist, tears stinging his eyes.

"Who is she, Orlando?" Isabel said softly as he brushed his lips over the glass. "You have never told me." Her voice was weak, barely more than a whisper. "Is she your true love?"

He went back to her, touching her cheek as he looked into her eyes. "She is my daughter." Her eyes widened, and he smiled. "My Roxanna." He tucked the bottle back into his pocket. "But you must rest. Kivar will be ready to travel again soon."

"Ready to murder me some more." Even now, her wit was sharp, but her gaze was losing focus. A thin sheen of sweat had risen on her skin, and her breathing was more labored. Her next words came out broken, as if it were a struggle to remember what she meant to say from one word to the next. "I did not know . . . you had a daughter."

"She did not know herself," he answered. He bathed her brow again, and her eyes fell closed. "She believed she was a princess, a useless, beautiful thing." He drew the bottle out again, his heart clenched tight and aching in his chest. "And now she is a vampire, trapped inside a bottle for her own protection." He looked back at Isabel to find her eyes open and lucid again.

"You should release her," she whispered, her voice now gone.

"No." He cut her off, shaking his head. "I cannot. I will not."

She looked as if she would argue, then she closed her eyes again. "Foolish man," she whispered, turning her head slowly on the pillow. "All of you . . . so foolish."

"Perhaps." He caressed her cheek with the back of his hand, but she did not stir. "My lady? Isabel?" He put his fingertips against her mouth and felt the lightest brush of breath, but she was completely unconscious.

He went back to the tent flap and held the bottle up

to the tender, misty light. Flashes of muted fire played along its facets as from a precious jewel. "Let me go," his child had begged him, believing all of her blood to be destroyed, that she was at last alone. "Let me die," she had begged, breaking his heart. If he released her now, surely Kivar would destroy her easily. She had been idle for so long, sleeping in the bottle. She would have so little strength; she would know nothing of what the monster had become. But she would fight. A beautiful, useless thing, she had called herself. But he knew better.

As the sun broke free of the Highlands, they rode along a jagged mountain ridge, Isabel held limp as a rag doll before Kivar on his horse, Orlando bound to his pony. His free hand strayed to his pocket and closed around the bottle, cold as a gem kept in ice. The mountains around them seemed much like the Urals in this light, their jagged, snow-capped peaks like the stony crown that had surrounded the palace of the caliph. His child would think herself at home. Forgive me, beloved, he thought. If he kept her safe inside the bottle, she would likely stay forever, trapped between her curse and death. But if he released her, how would she survive? What choice did he have?

"I give you to the gods," he whispered, letting the sealed bottle fall.

1

The abandoned camp was fresh, no more than one day old. "It was probably a hunting party," Gareth said as he climbed down from his horse. "My grandfather's men often came down this far to hunt."

"To prey on travelers, you mean," his tutor, Sir John, corrected, still safe on his mount, his arms crossed on his chest.

"My grandfather is laird of his clan," Gareth said mildly, barely expecting to be heard. Sir John had once served Gareth's English father, and his ill opinion of his Scottish mother's people had never wavered.

"Don't let him fool you, my lord Marcus," the aged knight scoffed now. "These Highlanders are no better than bandits, no matter what titles they may make up for themselves."

"This was no hunting party," Gareth's cousin Marcus said, brushing his boot over another pile of ashes. "Nor bandits neither. There were too many of them." His English cousin was the best tracker in their liege lord's army; Gareth was lucky to have him.

Gareth had been born in the Highlands, had loved them as a child. But the last time he had traveled this road, he had sworn he would never return, and for fifteen years he had kept his oath. Now he had no choice, though, and his cousin had sworn to come with him.

"How many?" Sir John asked, looking around the clearing.

Marcus bent down to examine some bit of rubbish on the ground that would have meant nothing to Gareth. "An army." He straightened up again. "Why would an army travel so far north?"

"They wouldn't," Gareth answered. "But the clans make war on one another—"

"For sport, like as not," Sir John finished for him.

"For grazing rights, most of the time," Gareth corrected. His grandfather's letter had sounded desperate, he thought. "Old sins have come to light," he had written, the creased and grimy letter finding the young knight on the fields of France. " 'Tis time, ye must come home." Could a war between clans have been the cause? It seemed unlikely; the laird he remembered had feared no man in the Highlands. But he would be old now, more than seventy, with no heir but Jamey, Gareth's uncle. *Old sins have come to light.*

"What is this?" Marcus said, breaking into his thoughts. He bent down again at the edge of the clearing. "Where could this have come from?" He held up a tiny cut glass bottle, red as blood.

"Some charlatan's potion," Sir John said. "Mayhap your army is no more than a caravan of gypsies."

"No," Gareth said, taking the bottle. "No gypsy could afford to let this fall." It was exquisite, heavy for its size but delicate. "Does it feel cold to you?" He handed it back to Marcus to strip off his leather glove. "Like ice," he said, taking it again.

"And so shall we be soon, if we don't make a camp of our own," Sir John grumbled, climbing down from his horse at last. "Keep it then, if you think it worth a penny."

"Who would leave this behind, do you think?" Marcus said.

"I couldn't guess." Gareth turned the bottle slowly in his palm, entranced by the play of the light on its facets. His guess was that it was worth very many pennies. "Here," he said, offering it to Marcus again. " 'Twas you who found it."

"Nay, cuz, you keep it," Marcus answered with a grin. "For luck." As his lordly father's only son, Marcus had no need for such trinkets. He clapped Gareth once on the shoulder. "Come, let us make camp."

Later Gareth lay on his back by the fire, listening to Sir John snore and gazing at the stars. In truth, he hadn't slept soundly since they'd crossed the border into Scotland, his restless memory returning again and again to the day he had left long ago. In his mind, he saw his father's broken body lying in a wagon, covered with a blanket, surrounded on every side by his own

English knights. "'Twas an accident," his grandfather the laird had promised, kissing his daughter's cheek.

"Aye," she had answered, but even as a boy of twelve, Gareth had known she did not believe it. Her face had been pale, but her blue eyes had been dry. Gareth had her eyes and her resolve; he had not cried for his father. Only the weird woman had wept, the misshapen, dirty creature his mother had pitied and protected all her life. She had clung to his mother's skirts and howled like a beast caught in a trap as their belongings were packed up to go. Kyna had been her name—'twas strange that he should remember her so clearly when so much else had been forgotten.

"You should sleep," Marcus said, leaning back against a tree on the other side of the fire. "Your watch is coming soon."

Gareth turned his head toward him and smiled. "I have to make certain you stay awake." As a squire at his uncle's manor, he would have been lost without Marcus. The boys his own age had looked down on him because of his Scottish birth, no matter how well he could fight. Sir John's excellent lessons in combat had kept him alive—any English lad who challenged him was quick to regret it. But he had no friends; the easy humor he had inherited from his father quickly curdled to a sharp-tongued bitterness that turned aside even those few who would have accepted him.

Then Marcus had come home a knight. Taller, stronger, and more handsome than any man at the castle, his cousin had taken Gareth entirely under his wing, making certain all knew they were kin and making him his own squire. With patient attention, he had taught him to soften his rough brogue to something more like an English noble's tongue, taught him which minstrel's tales he ought to admire and which he ought to scoff at, taught him how to wear a velvet doublet as casually as a peasant's shirt and a maiden's wreath of flowers as grandly as a crown. He had blossomed in Marcus's shadow, so much so that by the time he was dubbed a knight himself, Gareth had a place in a noble lord's house any English lad would have envied and friends enough who liked his jokes to make him feel content. And if he sometimes wearied of being called Marcus of Lyme's Scottish cousin rather than by his own name, he counted the price small enough.

"Sing me something, then," Marcus said now, laying his sword across his lap to settle back more easily. "One of your mother's songs."

Gareth grinned. "That's more likely to set you dreaming." Marcus had been dazzled by Gareth's mother at their first meeting and never truly recovered—the true root of his tender care of Gareth himself, no doubt. When she had finally entered a convent to be alone with her grief for her husband on the day of Gareth's knighting, Marcus had drunk himself into a stupor. "What shall it be?" He sat up and took out his lute, glad for the distraction. "A romance?" He plucked at the strings, testing and tuning the notes.

Marcus took a sip from his wineskin. "The one about the princess."

"Oh, aye . . ." His fingers found the melody, the music lifting his heart. The song was a silly thing, his own translation from his mother's Gaelic of the tale of an ancient warrior princess. But the tune was pleasing and well suited to his voice. He sang the story of the red-haired beauty who gave her heart over to a wolf, suppressing a smile at the dreamy expression on his knightly cousin's face. The tale did not even have a proper end—in the last verse, the maiden went off into the snow-capped mountains in search of her lost lover, never to return. "Perhaps she died of frostbite," he finished with a purposely dissonant chord.

"Soulless ass," Marcus muttered, passing him the wine. "In faith, you're as bad as Sir John."

"Surely not as bad as that." He set the lute aside, suddenly noticing the old knight's snores had stopped. "Sir John, did we wake you?" He turned toward the lump of blankets where he lay. "Here, have a drink and forgive us." He gave the lump a gentle kick. "Sir John?" But still he did not stir.

"Is he ill?" Marcus said from behind him. "He should not have come—"

"Don't be daft," Gareth cut him off, getting up without looking back. "Sir John is as hale as I am—here, old man, stop jesting." He rolled his tutor over on his back. "Sweet Mary—Marcus!" The old man's eyes were staring, his blankets soaked with blood. "Marcus!" He turned to find his cousin lying face down by the fire, his limbs still twitching, a lance protruding from his back.

"Not that one," a voice snarled from the shadows to his left. Turning, he caught a glimpse of a face half masked behind a cowl. "This one." Something heavy struck his skull from behind, dropping him to his knees. The face above him smiled. "You should never have come back." A barbed mace crashed into his chest, crushing the air from his lungs. He tried to stagger to his feet, but the villain struck again, knocking his sword aside. A blade plunged into his back through his stomach, and he fell indeed.

The ground seemed to roll beneath him like the back of some great beast as hot blood pooled around him. His right hand clutched his sword hilt; his left clutched the grass, but he could not move, could barely see. Painful points of hot, white light danced before his eyes, and his body felt heavy as stone. Someone said something, but he couldn't understand the words—they seemed to be speaking too slowly, the sound dragged out and torn. A sharper word from the other side, like the bark of a dog, and the first voice fell silent.

A boot levered under his shoulder, kicking him onto his back. A face leaned close—red beard, bloodshot brown eyes, breath that stank of sour wine. Hands rummaged through his clothing, searching him for coin, and he tried to strike back, to lift his sword and fight. But his arms were too heavy; he could not move. The man searching him drew in a sharp breath and grinned, yellowed teeth bared to the firelight as he straightened up again, his fist held aloft. The bottle . . . he had the bottle Marcus had found. Gareth's vision clouded as if in a red mist, and blood foamed at the corner of his mouth. *For luck,* Marcus's voice echoed in his memory. *Keep it, cuz, for luck.*

The villain drew the stopper from the bottle with his teeth. A cloud of sweet perfume enveloped them, some spicy, exotic scent. Gareth fought to draw another breath, and the sweetness filled his nose and mouth even as his eyes grew darker still, his sight all but lost. A vision seemed to rise before him, a beautiful woman with ebony hair, her back turned to him. She wore a gown of ruby red, the color of the bottle, and her skin was creamy white.

The villain's eyes were wide with shock, but a drunkard's smile twisted his mouth—he saw the woman, too. She turned toward him, and a strange, guttural growl rumbled in her throat. Her lips drew back into a snarl, beautiful, rosebud lips over the fangs of a wolf. The villain swore an oath, and she attacked him, driving him backward to the ground with no weapon but her strength alone as her fangs tore out his throat. As Gareth lay dying, he watched her, helpless, as she moved among the villains who had killed him like a whirlwind, her black hair and ruby red gown whipping around her as she struck. The man in the cowl raised his mace. She grabbed his wrist in both delicate hands, wrenching the arm from its socket and tossing it away. As he fell to his knees, she grabbed him and drew him up to her again, bathing her beautiful face in his blood, and Gareth swooned, pure, blessed darkness taking him at last.

Roxanna let the corpse fall from her grasp, raising her face to the moonlight. The air was cool and thin, rich with the scent of evergreen beneath the stench of blood. "Orlando!" she called out, turning in a circle. How long could she have slept within the bottle? "Orlando, where are you?" The mountains rose around her, the snow that capped the distant peaks glowing white against the darkness of the night. "Where am I?"

The man whose arm she had ripped off grabbed for her leg with the hand he had left. "Devil," he rasped in the language of the Crusaders, his lips drawn back into a snarl.

"Murderer," she answered, unconcerned. She drove her boot down on his face, crushing his skull and snuffing out his life. She had heard singing, a beautiful masculine voice calling to her through her dreams. Where was that man now? The corpses of the brigands she had killed were scattered all around the clearing—four, she counted; no, five. She must have been starving indeed. But those men had all been evil; she had smelled the stench of it on them before she had tasted their blood. None of them could have been the singer.

The corpse of a man dressed in the armor of a Christian knight was lying facedown near a fire, a lance protruding from his back. She knelt and removed it, rolling him onto his back as gently as a mother tucking in her child. Even in death, he was handsome, and she trailed her hand along his bearded cheek before she closed his eyes. "Allah see you safely home," she murmured, the name of God burning for a moment on her vampire's tongue. As a mortal woman, she had doubted the faith of her father, the hypocrisy of the caliph's luxurious life making his belief seem almost comical. But now, as a demon, she knew better. God was real, whatever His name might be.

This man had been good, she thought, looking down on the Christian before her. He reminded her of Simon, the poor knight Kivar had damned on the night she went into the bottle. Where was he now? He and Orlando had meant to find the Chalice, the relic the wizard was so certain held her salvation. She had gone into the bottle, unable to bear another moment as a creature of the dark after the death of her small mortal brother that night. Orlando had sworn he would keep her safe until the Chalice was found. But where was he now? Surely he would never have willingly abandoned her.

A small sound from behind her broke into her thoughts—a groan of pain. Someone was still alive. She closed her eyes, listening for the pulse, faint and weakening. Taking the fallen knight's sword, she followed the sound to another man lying nearby. This one was on his back, and his eyes were closed. Leaning closer, she could sense his failing breath, warm and sweet in spite of the blood that stained his lips, and with the strange, unfailing senses of her demon state, she could feel the goodness in his heart. "You," she said sadly, wiping his mouth with her fingertips. "It was you I heard." He clutched a sword, but a broken lute lay beside him. He was handsome, too, but younger than the other knight, with the faintest shadow of beard on his chin. She started to rise and turn away, but he moaned again, plaintive but masculine, a warrior's despair, his brow drawn in pain. She touched the crease in his forehead without stopping to think, smoothing it away. "Hush, love . . ." She brushed back his hair, light brown and soft as silk. A smear of dark brown blood stained his cheek where she touched him—her hands were filthy with gore. She recoiled from the sight, feeling sick, but she smiled, a bitter grimace. She was a monster, a demon loosed from hell. Who was she to comfort him? Still, she wiped her hands clean on her skirt, even scrubbing at her nails until every trace of blood was gone. Then she wiped her face as well, licking the last trace of blood from her fangs and lips.

The sky on the horizon was barely beginning to lighten—the dawn would come ere long. "Orlando!" she shouted angrily, starting to feel afraid. The death of this knight might be a tragedy, but she had problems of her own. There was no sign of the wizard among the dead or of Simon, no answer to her call. Orlando would have died before he let her be taken from him; she was certain of it. If she was truly alone, he must be dead. The quest for the Chalice must be lost.

A sob rose in her throat, but she forced it back, pressing the heels of her fists to her eyes to stop her bloody tears. She had known this night would come, that Orlando's Chalice was no more than a child's fairy tale. The wizard had loved her like a father, as dearly as she had loved him. He had wanted to save her long after she had known she was lost. "My poor Orlando," she murmured, remembering his face. "Poor fool." If he were dead, she had no more reason to continue in the dark. On the night of Simon's making, she had begged him to destroy her. Only Orlando's pleading had convinced her to take refuge in a bottle like a djinni in a jester's tale. She had never truly believed he could protect her, but she hadn't been able to bring herself to hurt him by telling him so. *Let me go,* she had begged him. *Let me be free of this curse.* When he had refused, she had not had the strength to resist him.

But now Orlando was gone. She could face the sun in peace.

She walked to the crest of the ridge to look to the east for the dawn. But looking down into the valley below, she found it green and lush instead of the desert she expected. The sun was rising on the wrong side of the mountains, she realized, behind her instead of before her. How far had they traveled? Could they have made it back to Simon's Britain? How long had she been asleep?

"It doesn't matter," she said aloud, straightening her shoulders. The sunlight would consume her entirely, she knew, from wherever it came. She had seen it happen. As a new-made demon, she had experimented on Kivar's other "children," chaining them to the rocks at the foot of her dead mortal father's castle to face the dawn as she watched through a catacomb grate. Standing at her shoulder, Kivar had laughed at her cruelty. The vampire king who had made her what she was had offered her every indulgence but life. He had even hoped she might come to love him for it. Or so he had said.

"It doesn't matter now," she said again. Soon the sun would rise to burn her to ashes, and at last she would be free. A chill wind stirred her hair against her brow and rippled through her red silk gown. She closed her eyes, breathing deeply. In her mind, she saw her mortal father's hall with its golden columns studded with jewels, the court assembled before them, the beautiful young soldiers she had taken to her bed, the beautiful young women who had been her friends. She could hear the music they had made, the laughter that had surrounded her before Kivar had come and murdered all and damned her to the dark.

A familiar smell wafted to her nose as if conjured by her memory—the smell of Lucan Kivar. She snapped her eyes open, instantly alert. The monster was here.

She turned back toward the clearing, but the scent faded—the killers she had slaughtered in her hunger had been mortal, no creatures of Kivar. Turning again, she walked along the ridge, sniffing the air like the cat she could become. As the underbrush thickened, the scent grew stronger, more rank, less alive. Kivar himself had passed this way less than a day before. He had killed among these trees. Snarling in fury, she tore through the brush until she found the body, a man dressed in green and black livery with the telltale gouges in his throat. She bent close, ignoring the stench of the dead flesh to find the lingering smell of her vampire father.

"The monster lives," she murmured, feeling sick. Simon had driven his sword through Kivar's heart, splitting him open and draining him dry as a husk. She herself had stabbed him again with a stake and decapitated the body. He had dissolved into nothing, a vile, green fluid that steamed to a vapor before it disappeared. But Orlando had been certain the creature had escaped somehow, that only the Chalice would destroy him. And now she knew he was right. She sat back on her heels, her fists clenched so tightly that she could feel her nails digging into her palms. Now Orlando was dead. The wizard who had never shown anyone anything but kindness, who had loved her mother with all his heart, had loved Roxanna herself even when her soul was dead, was lost. But Lucan Kivar was alive.

"I will find you," she promised his lingering shadow, rising to her feet. When Kivar had first come to her palace, she had been frightened, in despair—what could a helpless woman hope to do against such evil? But she was not a helpless woman anymore. She was a demon, a vampire, as wicked as the monster himself. Why should she fear him anymore? He had called her daughter, had offered her hand in marriage to his English prey as such. She was his creature, or so he believed, and she had believed it as well, had longed for nothing better than escape. But escape was no longer enough. "Vengeance," she whispered, the cold, cruel smile Kivar had found so beautiful curling the corners of her mouth. "Your daughter will destroy you."

She went back to the beautiful knight who lay dying on the ground. "Forgive me, dear one," she said softly as she knelt beside him. "I cannot let you die just yet." Once again, her heart went out to him for reasons she could not explain. Something about his song had reached out to her even in her enchanted sleep inside the bottle. Something in his handsome face touched her heart.

She lifted his head to her lap, so tenderly he barely stirred. The front of his tunic was soaked through with blood, and when she tore it back, she saw two wounds, one crushed into his chest, another stabbed through his stomach. Either would have been enough to kill him. "You are strong, warrior," she said. "Are you strong enough?" She had fed like a glutton from the others, but come another nightfall, she would need to feed again. "I need you to live for me." Even pale as death, his lips enticed her. She found herself longing to kiss him, to see his eyes open in surprise, to see him smile. "You must be my food." She had no time for lovers, she scolded herself inside her head. This man could mean nothing but blood to make her strong, no matter how pretty he might be.

The sky was growing lighter. She was running out of time. "Come." She caught him under the arms and hauled him upright, wincing at the sight of his blood-soaked back. He might well be too far gone to save, even with the physic Orlando had taught her. She had to find shelter from the daylight and move him there, and while her vampire strength might be equal to the task, his own will to live might not.

"Look at me." She moved in front of him, straddling his legs and catching his tunic in both fists to hold him upright. His head lolled on his neck, but he moaned, blood rising to his lips again. Using her demon's persuasion, she spoke to him again. "Open your eyes and look at me." His eyelids fluttered open, and she took a sharp, shocked breath. His eyes were clearest, brightest blue. "You must do as I say, warrior," she ordered, holding his gaze with all of her vampire's will. "You must live."

Gareth felt air rush into his lungs without his ever meaning to breathe in, and sickening pain twisted through him, making the world spin around him again. But all he could see was the woman before him. Her face was even more beautiful up close. Her features were so delicate and fine, she hardly seemed real, her nose tilted upward at its tip, her ruby-red lips full and soft. "Who . . . ?" he began, the words catching in his throat, his chest heaving with the effort of trying to speak.

"Shhhh," she whispered, leaning closer still, touching her forehead to his. "Save your strength." She drew back, and a glimmer of moonlight was caught by her ebony eyes, flickering like flame. Suddenly, he remembered what he had seen her do, the flash of wolvish fangs in her mouth as she struck, the screams of the villains she had slaughtered.

"You . . ." She saw recognition flicker in his eyes, heard his dying heart beat faster.

"No, warrior," she said urgently. "You must not remember that." Even sated, she could smell his blood and hunger for it, another, darker attraction she could not help but feel for him. But if he was frightened, he would surely die. "You must not fear me yet." She brushed her lips to his.

She kissed him, and the panic he felt disappeared, the memory dissolving like mist in his mind. His body was in agony; he was dying. But she was close to him, kissing him, his own angel of death. He reached for her, his hands, which had been frozen and too heavy to move a moment before, coming alive to take hold of her shoulders. She sighed as he drew her closer, but he felt no warm breath from her mouth. "Angel," he murmured as he broke the kiss, the words coming easier now. "You are my angel."

"Yes." Her smile was exquisitely sad as she looked down on him, and a single, scarlet tear slid down her cheek. "I am yours." She kissed his cheek as she lowered him back to the ground, and the dark overwhelmed him again.

2

The cottage was really no more than a hut, a round stone wall dug deep into the foot of a steep bank, and it had obviously been deserted for years. But it was sheltered from the sun by the hillside on the east and the forest on the west, the roof was still thick enough to block out any stray beams, and the door and the window shutters were solid. As soon as she had carried the wounded knight outside, Roxanna blocked the cracks with rags torn from his clothes and built a fire in the hearth. At the spring outside, she filled three wooden buckets, and only one leaked. She emptied this one into a copper basin, then hurried back to the camp where she had awakened.

The last of the horses fled at her approach, knowing her for a demon. But she found ample supplies in a knapsack near where the knight had fallen, everything from food and drink to weapons. She pulled out a long woolen mantle and threw it over her head to shelter her from the dawn, then shouldered the pack and hurried back to the cottage, slamming the door shut behind her just as the first rays of sunlight broke over the hill.

The knight had not stirred, but she could still make out the faint, irregular thud of his heart. Fighting the thick drowsiness that always took hold of her and every other vampire in daylight, she worked quickly, ripping the rest of his garments away. The wound in his chest was not so bad as it had first appeared, the flesh scraped and bruised rather than pierced—a blow from a spiked bludgeon instead of a blade. Luckily it had struck off-center, crushing his ribs instead of his breastbone—painful, but not necessarily fatal. The wound in his stomach was more worrisome. Someone had run him through from behind. "Coward," she muttered. "I hope I killed you first." The blade must surely have damaged his intestines—a long, painful, and almost certain death. If she were merciful, she would kill him now and release him from his misery, and for a moment, she considered it. But she could already feel the first pangs of hunger in her own belly in spite of her massacre back at the camp. Her long sleep had made her ravenous, and there was no telling how far she would have to travel to find other prey. If she meant to keep her wits about her and find Lucan Kivar, she must keep this man alive.

She washed the wounds with wine from his pack and sewed the gashes in his back and stomach closed with a needle and thread she found there as well. He swore a slurred but unmistakably blasphemous oath as she heaved him up to bind his ribs, but he was dead weight against her shoulder and made no move to fight her. "You're lucky I'm a demon, dear one," she muttered, tying off the bandage at his side. "I'd never be strong enough to hold you otherwise." On his feet, he would not be quite as tall as Simon, the only other Briton she had ever known, but he was apparently solid muscle. She shivered with a flutter of purely feminine desire, brushing a palm down the hard curve of his back. "Too bad you're unconscious."

He mumbled something as she let him down again as if to answer her, but she couldn't understand the words. "Never mind," she said soothingly, stroking his brow. His skin felt hot—he was already feverish. Still fighting her own need for sleep, she bathed him with the water from the basin to cool him, then covered him first with a blanket, then a heavy fur rug she found in the corner. "Sleep now," she said softly, kissing his brow. She should probably try to make him drink some of the water, but she didn't trust herself to have that much strength left.

Gareth tried to open his eyes, to focus and lay hold of some sense of where he was and what had become of him. The beautiful woman was still with him—his angel, he had called her, and so she seemed to be. But somehow, he could no longer remember how she had found him, how they had come to be together. He remembered finding Sir John lying dead, remembered turning to find Marcus murdered as well. He remembered the man in the cowl, the one who had seemed to be the leader. *You should never have come back,* he had said as he struck Gareth in the chest just before someone else had stabbed him from behind. Then something else had happened, something about this woman . . . a chill passed through him, making him tremble. But he couldn't remember why. The next image his memory would give to him was of her face as she leaned over him, the sadness of her smile.

His eyelids closed for a moment, too heavy to hold open, and when he looked again, she was naked on her knees before the fire, her back half turned to him. She was washing herself, holding back her dark brown hair to bathe the back of her neck. Her skin was dusky cream all over, utterly flawless, and even in his sorry state, he felt his breath catch short. She was slender, but her hips were amply curved, and as she twisted slightly, sluicing water down her back, he saw one plump breast, full and rounded as a peach and tipped with a coral-colored nipple. She was beautiful, a creature from a dream. Why did the sight of her make him feel afraid? Again, he struggled to remember, the effort making him feel faint and sink back into the dark.

Roxanna dressed herself again in clothes from the knight's knapsack, a soft tunic that fell to her knees and hose she had to double-knot at her waist. She laced her own leather shoes up her ankles, yawning as she did it.

Her red silk gown was utterly ruined. Picking it up, she remembered when she had put it on—how long ago had that been now? She had awakened at nightfall on a couch of gold, surrounded by vampire servants, just as she had every sunset for years. "A very special night," one of them had whispered as she slipped the gown over her head, but Roxanna had barely heard her. She was a cursed vampire, doomed to an unending banquet of blood, an undying revel of slaughter. What could be special in that? Little had she known. . . . Kivar had lured the Christian duke and his knights to his jeweled slaughterhouse with the promise of a royal bride. "I will not!" she had screamed, dooming her little brother, Alexi, still a mortal child, to death by her defiance. But it had done no good. She had killed her offered husband, the English duke, with her dagger, sparing him the vampire's curse, but his knights were slaughtered by the cursed court like cattle. Only the Irishman, Simon, had escaped the grave by attacking Kivar himself, and his reward was a curse of his own. Kivar had made him a vampire, imbued him with what had seemed to be the last of his own strength. Drunk and blind with a newborn demon's power, Simon had struck Kivar's head from his shoulders, and Roxanna had driven the stake through the monster's heart. But even then, she had known he was not truly gone.

"I will find you," she repeated in her mortal father's tongue, her oath of vengeance. She should never have gone into the bottle. She should have joined Simon in his quest, should have helped him protect Orlando and search for the Chalice. But she had played the princess, too delicate to be of any use.

In his swoon, Gareth heard the mysterious woman say something he couldn't understand, and he forced his eyes open again. She threw a bundle of red rags into the fire, and the embers blazed up, illuminating her face. She looked sad again, ready to weep, and his heart went out to her, the fear he had felt only moments before dissolving like a mist before the sun. Who was she? Did she grieve for him? He tried to hold his eyes open as she got up and moved toward him, but he didn't have the strength. He felt as if some monstrous weight had been set upon his chest, and every breath he took was agony.

Roxanna saw the knight's eyelashes flutter as she bent down over him, but when she touched his cheek, he didn't stir. "So handsome," she murmured, sitting back again. She had to sleep now; she couldn't fight it any longer. For a moment, she considered moving away from him. But why should she deny herself what little comfort she had? She was damned for his murder already. Looking around one last time to check for cracks that might let in the sunlight, she lay down beside him with her head on his shoulder.

Poor lamb, she's freezing, Gareth thought, shuddering under her delicate weight. She slipped a hand that was cold as ice under his blankets against his bare stomach, and he shivered. He tried to hold her to warm her, but he was still too weak. As if reading his thoughts, she reached behind her and laced her hand with his, drawing his arm around her.

So warm, Roxanna thought, half dreaming already. He's so warm. Thoughtless and contented, she let herself sink into sleep.

She awoke to find him burning up, his skin stark white with glowing spots of red on either cheek. His breathing was shallow, and his lips were cracked and dry. "Come, dear one," she said softly, kneeling beside him. "Drink for me." She raised him up against her and held the cup to his lips. "Obey me," she ordered, sharpening her tone and using her vampire's voice of command. "Drink." His heartbeat was stronger than it had been the night before, but the rhythm was irregular, racing one moment and thudding the next. His head lolled on her shoulder. "Please," she murmured, pressing a kiss to his temple, the heat of him burning her mouth. "Please, love. You must drink." She tipped the cup, and most of the water poured over his chin. But his lips parted, and some of it found its way into his mouth. "Good," she said, filling the cup from the bucket again. "Again." She stroked his throat as she tipped the cup against his lips, feeling him swallow. "Very good." She held him upright until she was fairly certain the water would not come back up, then lay him down again.

Her hunger was strong again, not painful but impossible to ignore. She should feed from him, be done with him and move on. Kivar would be at least two nights away from her now, and only God or the devil could tell what evil he had planned. But with the knight so weak, he would hardly have enough blood to sustain her, even if she drained him. She touched his cheek, remembering the sight of his blue eyes. She wanted to see them again, to talk to him. She wanted to hear him sing again, to hear what he would sing to her. It seemed a shame to have wasted so much time in nursing him only to murder him now, particularly if his death would hardly help her at all. Surely she could find better prey in the forest.

"Rest, dear one," she murmured, kissing his forehead. "I will be back soon."

She smelled the stench of the encampment as soon as she stepped out of the hovel. If she truly meant to stay another night and day on this mountain, she would have to dispose of the bodies. No demon slaves would come to do her bidding here. "Lovely," she grumbled, heading up the hill.

She dragged the corpses of the brigands she had killed herself into a mound at the center of the clearing and set them on fire. But she took the time to dig true graves for the others, the young knight who had fallen near the one she had taken and an old man who wore the same badge on his tunic. The moon was high above her by the time she was done. She drove the young man's sword into the earth at his head to mark his resting place and knelt beside it, wiping her hands on her tunic. "Forgive me, my lord," she said with a sigh. "I have no prayer for you." She replaced the turf as best she could, a gesture of respect. The knight she had taken would have done the same if he were able; she would owe him that much at least. When he was dead, she would bury him beside his friends and mark his grave with a demon's tears. "I am sorry." She hated that she was a killer, that her soul was so broken she could do nothing but evil. Her father the caliph had not been righteous, but he had not been cruel, and her mother had been pure and kind as any angel. How had she come to this?

From behind her, she heard a low, guttural growl, an answer to her thoughts. Looking back over her shoulder, she saw a wolf emerging from the trees, head down and hackles raised.

She rose slowly to a crouch and turned to face him. His pack would be somewhere nearby, drawn by the fire. But they would know she was no easy prey, would smell the demon inside her. Only the leader would be brave enough to attack. "Come then," she said softly. "Come and fight." The blood she needed could be taken from a beast as easily as a man. Her knight could live a little longer.

She returned to the hovel an hour or so before dawn, another small pack of provisions flung over her shoulder and a brace of freshly dressed rabbits she had caught on her way dangling from her hand. The knight was still sleeping by the fire. She knelt beside him and leaned close, sniffing his flesh, but his wounds were still clean, and his skin, though pale, showed no sign of poison or decay. His brow was drawn in a frown, and she smoothed it gently, whispering comfort until he seemed to relax again.

She set the rabbits to stew in a copper pot over the fire and flung in a handful of herbs she'd found in one of his packs. If he was going to live, he would have to eat. She turned back to him, wishing he would wake. She was not accustomed to being alone for so long—indeed, she doubted she had ever been before. In the caliph's palace, she had been surrounded by servants and courtiers at every moment, even as a vampire. "What is your name?" she asked him, using the language that she guessed was his, the French of the Christian crusaders. "Where do you come from?" The wolf's blood she had taken warmed her, making her restless. "Is this place your home?" If Kivar had brought this man to her as prey, he would have been alive, able to fight. But she would have seduced him, made him want her so badly he welcomed her bite. "You are so beautiful." She pressed her open mouth to his, tasting his breath, warm and sweet. He was healing. He could live.

"I don't want to kill you." She kissed his jaw, nuzzled her cheek to his. "I want you to live." She felt him stir beneath her weight, and a shiver raced through her. "Yes, my dear one," she whispered, slipping under the blankets, caressing his arms. His skin was smooth and warm, and the smell of him was irresistible, making the blood of the wolf she had stolen burn inside her, making her feel reborn. He turned his face to hers, his eyes still closed, and she kissed him again, framing his face with her hands. "I saved you," she said softly, and his eyes opened, beautiful blue, so different from those of anyone else she had known in all her cursed life. "You are mine." He frowned for a moment in confusion as if trying to focus on her face. "Mine," she repeated, kissing him again. She sucked his lower lip into her mouth and gently bit, careful not to break the skin with her fangs, and he groaned, a low, lusciously masculine sound that made her tremble. His arms closed around her, surrounding her with warmth, and tears rose in her eyes. She had been freezing so long. He kissed her, rolling her over with strength he should never have had. All of her strength seemed to leave her, dissolved into want. She had been so horribly alone.

His kiss was tender, brushed over her mouth as he murmured sweet words she couldn't understand, but his body above her was demanding, powerful and strong. She ran her hands delicately over his shoulders and down, careful not to touch his bandaged wounds, but his touch was possessive and rough, pushing up her tunic to find the soft flesh underneath. He covered her breast with a callused palm, and she gasped, moaning softly as the pad of his thumb pressed the nipple. He did not fear her, did not treat her as a princess, did not know her at all, only wanted. His mouth on hers turned hard, his tongue pushing inside, teasing and sweet, inviting her to play. She rose to meet him, wrapping her arms around his neck, and his hands circled her waist, caressing her back then pushing the hose she wore down to shift her closer, half naked, his sex a hard and prideful threat against her thigh. She made a happy sound, a sigh and a laugh intermixed, and he drew back, smiling down on her.

"Sweet Allah," she murmured in her native tongue, her heart melting at the sight. How could she bear such a beautiful smile? The blue eyes twinkled with mischief and joy; his whole handsome face was transformed. "How can I let you die?" His brow wrinkled again; he didn't understand her, of course. He opened his mouth to speak, and she kissed him, capturing the words. Death was for later; tonight they would both live.

She closed a hand around his sex, drawing him toward her, and he moaned against her mouth, pressing her hard to the floor. He entered her gently as if he feared to hurt her, and she held her breath, sweet pleasure making her feel faint. She splayed her hands across the small of his back, urging him on, and a low, soft sigh escaped her as he filled her up. He bent and kissed her briefly on the lips, arms braced on either side of her, and she caressed his bicep, delighting in the power she could feel beneath her fingertips as she arched up beneath him. He rocked deeper inside her, finding an easy rhythm, and she let her eyes fall closed, giving herself over, all else forgotten but the feeling of this stranger in her arms. She felt the first waves of her climax swell inside her, and she held him more tightly, her open mouth pressed to his throat. He quickened his pace, brushing a kiss to her brow, reading her perfectly, this stranger from a mountain she had never seen. She cried out as she came, and he let his full weight sink to her, cradling her in his arms, kissing her cheek as he drove himself harder into her sheath and exploded himself.

He was talking again, murmuring sweet lover's words that meant nothing . . . she was beautiful, his angel. She buried her hand in his hair, caressing him as she kissed his cheek, and she felt his heartbeat slow. He was still so weak. She tried to push him back to make him rest, but to her shock, she could not. But that was madness; he was but a mortal man and mortally wounded at that; she was a demon. How could he be so strong?

"Rest," she ordered in his language, pushing his shoulder again, and this time he gave way, letting her roll on top of him. "You must rest." She looked down into his face and saw him smile again, the smile that made her melt. "I will stay with you." She touched his cheek, her heart aching. She would carry this image the rest of her immortal life, the perfect sweetness of his smile. "Close your eyes and sleep." Would he wake again? she wondered. His fever still burned, but his heartbeat was strong. How long did she dare stay? "I will wait for you." She slipped from his arms but kissed his mouth, and he obeyed, letting his eyes fall closed. She covered him again, tucking the blankets close around him before she backed away.

3

Gareth woke slowly, rising back to life like swimming to the surface of a muddy pond. He was hungry, he realized first, smelling the stew simmering nearby. He was in pain, the wounds in his chest and back and stomach burning. He was sweating, but not shivering—his fever had broken. He was alive.

He shifted in his cocoon of blankets, and the pain in his back sharpened just a little. He touched the bandage at his waist that bound his ribs—broken, he realized, breathing in sharply as he tried to move again. The wound in his chest was bare but clean and neatly stitched. He tried to remember how it had come to be so, but everything from the moment the brigands had attacked him until now was a kind of fog-bound blur. Marcus and Sir John were dead; that much he could remember. They had been ambushed by half a dozen men or more. How had he survived? He tried to remember fighting back, the blows that had brought him his wounds, but that was where the fog began. He had fought, but there were too many—he had been dying, helpless on the ground. Then . . . but it was useless. The memory wouldn't come.

The room where he lay now was dark, the only light coming from the tiny fire on the hearth. Gritting his teeth against the pain, he made himself sit up and dragged himself closer to its warmth. The stew was bubbling in a small iron pot, and luscious-smelling steam rose up when he opened the lid. Using the corner of his blanket, he slid it from the coals, then burned his fingers anyway picking out chunks of meat from the steaming broth, too ravenous to wait.

The pot was empty long before he would have called his belly full, but the sharp edge of his hunger was gone. He found a bucket of water with a dipper near his makeshift couch and took a long drink. *Come, dear one,* a sweet voice murmured in his memory. *You must drink for me.* He dropped the dipper in shock, splashing himself with water. He remembered the woman, his angel.

She was sleeping on the far side of the rounded room, huddled in a lump he had taken for an empty bundle of blankets. Her face was turned toward him, pillowed on her arm, innocent and pretty as a child's. "Lady," he called softly, loath to frighten her. Her blanket was pooled at her waist, and he saw she wore his own spare tunic. The neck was unlaced, and he could just see the swell of one perfect breast at the opening. Her lips were slightly parted, plump and pink, and her lashes were long and black against her pale gold cheeks, dark as her ebony curls. The sight of her made him feel dizzy again, as if his fever had returned. Another tantalizing flash of memory passed through his mind, sharp and sweet. She had kissed him, he thought. *I saved you,* a voice whispered inside his mind. *You are mine.* But surely that was a dream. He tried to make sense of the images in his mind, but nothing would come clear. He had been delirious, dreaming of her. He had only just come to himself enough to wake; he could not have kissed anyone, much less. . . . He shook his head, shaking off the memory of the dream. Even if he had found the strength to do what he thought he remembered in scattered fragments, surely she would not have allowed it, whoever she might be. But how had he come to be here with her in the first place? How long had they been alone?

He climbed carefully to his feet, holding his blanket around him like a robe. Someone else besides this girl must surely have carried him here, he thought, moving around the room like a limping old man, his ribs aching with every breath. She was a tiny thing, much too delicate to have managed such a feat alone, even dragging him. But he could find no evidence of any other man in the tiny house. The only weapons were his own, cleaned and set neatly by the door, along with two of the packs he and his friends had carried. He smiled to see his broken lute laid on a bench—his angel's work, no doubt. Only a woman would have thought to save such a trifle. When she woke, he would have to question her closely. He had to know who had attacked him and, more curious, who had cared enough to come to his aid. The men who had killed Marcus and Sir John could have been common bandits, but whoever had saved him must have surely had a more particular purpose. His grandfather's people would have taken him home; no one else had any reason to think of him at all.

He had thought it must be night, the room was so dark. But standing at the door, he saw a tiny beam of daylight peeking through a chink in the upper corner. Someone had blocked up the cracks with rags as if to keep the hovel warm, and they had blocked out the light as well. Glancing back once at the beauty sleeping behind him, he opened the door.

"No!" She screamed like some wild thing, scrambling to cover herself. "Close it, please!" She was obviously terrified, and he slammed the door shut, his heart racing with shock. One moment she had been sound asleep; the next she was hysterical. "Are you mad?" she demanded, lunging for him as soon as the door was closed again, pushing past him to stuff the rags back into place. A single shaft of light touched her bare arm, and she drew back as if from a burning brand, hiding the offended limb under her tunic while she blocked up the hole with her other hand.

"I'm sorry." Her pretty face was pale as milk with fear, and he touched her arm. "I didn't know." She was trembling. "Lady, what is it? Why should you fear the light?"

She looked up at him, eyes flashing with fury as if he were the dimmest idiot she had ever known. Then her expression softened, her eyes going blank. "I am not, of course," she said, turning away. "But I should think you might be more careful." Her voice was husky for a woman, at intriguing odds with her delicate appearance, with an accent he couldn't place. "I saw those men try to kill you," she went on, going back to kneel beside her couch. "I don't want their friends to find you here."

"You saw them?" he echoed, following her more slowly, the pain in his side getting worse. "What happened to them? How was I saved?"

"I . . . I couldn't say," she answered, folding her blankets. Then suddenly she stopped and turned on him with a frown, as if he were the one being evasive. "Who are you?"

"I am Gareth," he answered, bemused. "Knight of the house of Lord Emory of England." She seemed unimpressed. "Grandson of the laird of the Clan McKail." Still nothing. "Did you not know that?"

"How would I know that?" Roxanna was fighting the need for sleep and still badly shaken. The fool could have burned her to a cinder. On his feet, he seemed much taller, too big for the tiny room, and he was far more lucid than he had any business being in his condition. She had half expected to wake and find him dead. She certainly hadn't expected him to wake her and start asking questions. She had never imagined conversing with him at all, and now that she had to, she wasn't quite sure what to say. "I've never seen you before."

"What is your name?" He lowered himself gingerly to the floor beside her. In truth, his head was spinning, and his chest was beginning to feel heavy again. But he'd be damned if he'd lie down and die before he knew just who his savior was and what she wanted with him.

"Roxanna." He offered his hand in the knightly fashion. She stared at it for a moment as if she didn't understand, then she took it. "I am Roxanna," she finished.

"Well met, Roxanna." He lifted her hand to his lips as if she might have been a duchess and smiled.

He was smiling again, she thought, shivering and smiling back. Allah save us both. His kiss on her hand had sent a tremor through her, fool that she was. "You should lie down," she said, drawing her hand from his. If he was going to bumble about opening doors, she would do well to kill him and be done. "You are badly hurt—I didn't expect you to live."

"I didn't expect that either." She was even more lovely when she smiled, he thought. But she was still shaking all over. Was she afraid of him? "I don't mean you any harm, Roxanna," he promised. "I am grateful to you for your help."

"As well you might be," she answered. "You were no great joy to carry all this way."

"You carried me?" he said with a laugh. "You did not."

Damnation, she silently swore. He had her so flustered, she might as well just blurt out what she was now and have it over. "Of course I did," she said with all the hauteur of her royal birth. "Who else is here to have done it?"

"No one, it seems, at the moment." She had turned her face away, avoiding his eyes again, and he gently touched her cheek, making her face him. "That is my question, Roxanna. Who was here before?"

He said her name as if he had known her forever, she thought. Even before she became a vampire, no one save her parents and Orlando had ever dared to address her so familiarly, even her lovers. But strangely, she found she did not really mind it. She was more intrigued than offended. Of course, he had no idea who she was, but still . . . he was bold, this Gareth, no matter how wounded he might be. "No one was here before but you and I," she answered him. "Believe me or not as you will."

I don't, love, he thought but didn't say. She couldn't possibly have carried him any distance at all, and this house couldn't have been close to the clearing where he was attacked, or he and Marcus would have seen it. Not to mention the small matter of his escape from half a dozen brigands bent on his murder—had she managed that as well? Not likely, to say the least. But it was obvious he would accomplish little by pressing her, and he did owe her his life. "Then I thank you for your trouble," he said.

"Thank me by lying down again before you tear your stitches." He obviously didn't believe her, but he was apparently willing to let the matter drop. Perhaps she could let him live a little longer. She looked into the pot he had emptied and frowned. "You ate all of this?"

"All of that?" he echoed. "It was barely more than a mouthful." As soon as he said it, he cursed himself for a fool—he had likely exhausted all of her supplies. She had saved his life, and now because of him she would go hungry. "Not that I am not grateful—"

"Stop being so grateful and be wise instead," she cut him off. "Your fever has just broken; it could still come back. You should have eaten just a little to start." She broke off, softening again. "But you must have been starving," she relented. "Are you still?"

"No," he lied in the tone of a promise.

"Good." She draped another blanket around his bare shoulders. "As soon as it's dark again, I will go hunting." With an effort, she resisted the urge to run her fingers through the light brown hair that curled at the nape of his neck. In daylight, she had less control over her demon nature; he didn't realize how dearly she wanted to do a bit of hunting right now.

"Hunting in the dark?" he said, raising an eyebrow.

"It worked well enough last night." She rearranged the nest she had made for him earlier. "Now come, lie down before you hurt yourself."

"Roxanna?" He caught her hand as she moved to back away. "Why are you wearing my clothes?"

"I had to." She tried to pull her hand away, but this time he held her fast, something he most definitely should not have been able to do. She thought of the night before when he had held her down to the floor to make love to her. Why should this stranger have such power over her when no one, not even another vampire, had ever had it before? "I had to burn my gown because your blood was on it," she explained.

A vision of her kneeling naked by the fire flashed through his mind—another memory? "Don't you have another?"

"No." She smiled. "Sadly, my luggage train seems to have been lost." She tried again to pull away, and this time he allowed it. "I have been awake for two nights running nursing you, Gareth. I want to go to sleep."

"In a moment." She spoke of a luggage train like she might have been a noblewoman, and her accent, strange as it was, did not sound like that of a peasant, he thought. "Is this not your home?"

"This hovel?" she said with a laugh. "No, Gareth." She pulled the blankets up to his chin. "Go to sleep."

"I'm not sleepy." In truth, he felt more likely to die if he closed his eyes than sleep. His heart was thudding in his chest, and the wound through his middle burned as if he'd just been stabbed, this time with a sword of molten iron. "If you are my nurse, tell me a story."

"I don't know any stories." She brushed the hair back from his brow. He looked even paler than usual, and there was a tremor in his voice. He should never have tried to get up.

"Tell me who you are." His beautiful blue eyes were losing focus; she could tell. "Tell me where you come from."

"All right, if it will keep you still." He is dying after all, she thought. She had seen it before in wounded soldiers. They would rally so much that it seemed they were healed, then their souls would leave them. "I was born in a palace in a range of mountains very like these where we are now, but very far away."

"A palace?" He did feel better lying still, he thought, and her voice was very soothing.

"Yes." She took his hand between her own. "My father was a caliph—a kind of king."

"So you are a princess."

"Yes." He smiled. "You don't believe me?"

"I'd be a cad to say it if I didn't," he answered. "Go on, princess. Tell me of your palace."

"On the outside, it was ugly." Ever since she came out of Orlando's bottle, she had tried very hard not to think of her home or remember all the things that she had lost. But she found it strangely comforting to talk about it now. "More a fortress than a home, with lumpy gray towers that looked like some kind of fungus growing out of the cliff."

"It sounds lovely," he said with a wry grin. The lady had a vivid imagination, he thought, whoever she might be.

"Inside, it was magnificent. The walls of my father's main hall were covered all over with silk and cloth of gold. The floors were polished marble, white and black, and the columns and arches were pure gold, studded with jewels to look like an arbor of vines. My bed was made of gold as well, with cushions of pure silk." And when I left, the whole place stank of rotting flesh, she thought but did not say. "From my window, I could see the desert far below. In the morning when the sun would rise, the sand was painted scarlet and purple, a carpet of light." How long had it been since she had seen a sunrise? Orlando had sworn she would see one again, that she would be mortal again. But Orlando had abandoned her or died.

"A mountain castle above a desert?" The way she spoke of it, he could almost believe the place was real. Her face, always exquisite, was heartbreakingly beautiful as she described this sunrise. He and Marcus had met many returned Crusaders, fighting for their patron, and some of them had spoken of just such a desert. And her accent . . . but no. No woman from the Holy Land could have found her way to the Highlands. More likely she was the child of some other Crusader run mad, a religious fanatic who'd had what little brains he was born with burned out in the desert sun and come home to play the hermit in these woods. A mad Crusader could also have saved him from the brigands, he thought.

"Yes," she nodded. "I told you; it was very far away."

She met his eyes with hers and smiled. "In truth, Gareth, I don't really know where I am."

"You are in the Highlands." If her father was a madman, perhaps she was mad as well, or at least an innocent. For all he knew, she might believe her tale. There was a sadness in her eyes and a kind of calm in her manner that made her seem wise beyond her years. But perhaps that was madness as well, the serenity of one who knew naught of the world. "In Scotland, Roxanna."

"Scotland," she repeated. Caledonia . . . Orlando had spoken of this place, had shown it to her on his maps. It was important to him and to Kivar, but she had never known just why. Before she was cursed, she hadn't cared to learn, had thought the dwarfish wizard's tales no more than fancy. After, she had never had the freedom or the time. "The other side of the world." She touched his forehead and found it burning with fever. By tomorrow, she was likely to have lost him forever. All she would have was her quest. "But I am glad to be here now," she said, smiling down on him.

"Don't leave me." He tightened his grip on her hand. He had faced death in battle many times and never thought to fear it. Even before, when he had seen Sir John dead already and his cousin, Marcus, fall, he had not stopped to think of what death would mean for him. On the battlefield, death was a knight's constant companion, as near and necessary as his horse. But here he had too much time to think; the shadows crept too close. All that seemed to hold them back was his angel, this mad beauty beside him.

"I will not," she promised. She lifted his hand to her lips, their fingers laced as one. He closed his eyes, and she closed hers, tears of blood staining her cheeks. Who knew she still had tears? "I promise I will be here when you wake."

4

Gareth did not die, but it was another three days and nights before Roxanna stopped expecting that he would. His fever raged and broke and raged again, making him delirious and still as death in turns. When he was waking, he shouted at shadows, swearing vengeance on someone named Jamey, a murdering bastard, she surmised as she tried to soothe him by holding him close. When he was still, she listened jealously to every breath he took and every beat of his heart, willing the rhythm to continue, cold with terror thinking it would not. Once, his heartbeat slowed so much, she felt his flesh go cold.

"Forgive me, dear one," she whispered, her lips close to his bearded cheek. She had not left him for so long, her hunger was like a demon writhing inside of her. "I am so sorry, Gareth." If he were dying, he would be of use to her for only a little while longer. She could not afford to wait. She brushed her mouth over his, his breath nearly as cool and slight as her own. He sighed, turning his head on the pillow, and she bent her head to his shoulder, fighting back tears. How had he become so dear to her so quickly? Was she truly so afraid to be alone? Perhaps it was nothing more than the fact that he did not know what she was, that for the first time in so many years she could barely remember, someone had treated her as a woman, not a monster. But now she would prove he was wrong.

She kissed his throat, tasting his skin with her tongue. She was a talented demon. If she tried, she could make him barely feel the bite. In truth, she would likely be doing him a service, releasing him from pain. But shame made her feel sick as she bent over him, the taste of it bitter as gall. Steeling herself against it, she bared her fangs, preparing for the bite.

"No . . ." She would not have believed he could have spoken, and indeed, his voice sounded hollow, as if he were a ghost. But his hands clamped down hard on her arms. She drew back to find him looking up at her, his eyes somehow glassy and lucid at once. "No, Roxanna." Her tears spilled over, the last blood in her body falling on his skin, but he did not react. "No," he repeated, touching her cheek as if he were moving in a dream.

"No," she promised. Was he dreaming? she thought. Or in his fever, did he finally see her as she was after all, know her as the wolf had known her in the woods? "I will not." She kissed him softly on the lips, sweet and tender as a living maid. "You are safe from me."

When she drew back again, his eyes were closed.

Touching his cheek, she backed away, fleeing the warmth of their shelter for the cold of night.

She staggered out into the darkness, headed into the forest. After that first night, the wolves had learned to stay away from her, and the blood of the game she had managed to capture for Gareth was not enough to sustain her. But the cold of the night was reviving her somewhat, making her feel stronger. She still had time to hunt before she lost control.

She turned her face up to the wind and willed herself to change, her human form melting into the black velvet shape of a panther. Lucan Kivar had taught her this trick, one of the few things about being a vampire she had loved from the very first time she tried it. As the demon cat, she raced through the forest, the air around her now thick with the rich smell of life. In less than an hour, she had brought down a stag and fed until her hunger was bearable again.

But as she returned to the hillside shelter, she caught the scent of better prey—a human. Still in her feline shape, she crept closer to the hovel, crouching so low to the ground she would appear as no more than a shadow on the grass. Her ears picked up the heartbeat coming from the trees on the other side of the tiny clearing, slow but strong and healthy. As she moved closer, she heard a small gasp, then the sound of bare feet running through the brush. For a moment, she considered giving chase. But she was no longer starving, and she had left Gareth alone long enough. At least she knew now there were other humans nearby. Turning away, she went back into the hovel.

She found Gareth soaked with sweat again, but his color was better, and his breathing was easy and deep. Coaxing a bigger flame from the fire on the hearth, she peeled back the blankets and bathed him with warm water from the kettle. He stirred, mumbling something in his sleep. "Hush now, dear one," she soothed in her native language, covering him with a fresher blanket she'd put outside to air the night before. "Whoever he is, you can fight him tomorrow." She held the water cup against his lips and coaxed him to drink a few swallows, then tucked the covers tight around his shoulders. "You should be here to see me, Orlando," she muttered, getting up again. "I am a mother at last."

She took the first blanket outside and draped it over the rough thatched roof. Once as a child in the palace of her caliph father, she had ripped her silken sheets to ribbons out of temper. "They scratch me!" she had insisted. "I hate them!" When she was done, a servant had taken them away without a word and made her bed with new ones. Now she prized a pair of smelly woolen blankets as if they were cloth of gold.

Something prickled along her spine, and she turned, looking back at the spot where she had heard the other mortal earlier. But no . . . this was not a mortal presence. She felt another vampire, the same shiver she had felt with Kivar when others of their kind would come to call. "No," she said aloud, turning toward the cliffs above, her mind racing immediately to the man lying wounded inside. "Go away. He is mine."

As if in answer, she felt the presence leaving her, the tingle fading from her skin. It was not Kivar—she would have known him at once. But she was still afraid. Retrieving a sword from inside, she went into the forest and cut a jagged stake from a fallen tree. At dawn when she had finished blocking the light from the shelter, she lay down to sleep in front of the door, holding the stake in her fist.

5

Gareth awoke as Roxanna was opening the door for the night. "Hello," he managed, his voice coming out as a croak.

She turned and smiled. "Hello to you." He sat up as she brought him water. "I was afraid for a time I had lost you."

"Afraid?" he asked, arching a brow. "Or hoping?" He took the cup and drained it gratefully.

"You have been rather a bother." She had a very pretty smile, he thought. "How do you feel?"

"Dry to my toes." He felt much less dizzy than he had the last time he'd tried to get up, and the pain in his stomach and back was more a dull thud than a burning. "And hungry."

"Drink this more slowly," she ordered, handing him the cup again. "I will bring you something to eat."

The night breeze drifting through the open door was fresh and cool, a welcome change, but he gathered the blanket closer around him, fearful of his fever. He watched her use his own dagger to slice meat from a joint of venison roasting on a spit over the fire. "Who brought the meat?"

"I brought it, of course." Her movements were unskilled but delicate, as dainty as any noblewoman he had ever seen at court. "I just wish I had a better knife." She brought the wooden trencher back to him. "This one is better suited to killing than cooking."

"Thank you." She seemed capable, but unaccustomed to service—she put the trencher in his hands like another man might have done and sat down beside him without checking his cup. It seemed clear she was no servant, and from her speech, he was quite sure she was no country peasant, either. But what would a noble lady be doing alone in the Highlands? "Do you not mean to join me?"

"Of course," she said with a frown. "Am I not here?"

"No," he said, smiling in spite of himself. "I meant, are you not hungry?"

"Oh." She gave his trencher an unmistakably wary glance. "No. I am not."

He stopped eating, a slice of venison poised halfway to his mouth. "Have you poisoned me?"

She laughed, a surprisingly musical sound. "Yes, Gareth, I have." She shook her head as if he were the greatest fool she had ever heard tell of. "I nursed you through a fever for the joy of poisoning you after. Go on and eat, or my design will fail."

He had to admit, it seemed unlikely. But nothing about his present situation or his companion had made any sense so far. "I had terrible dreams," he said through a mouthful of meat, his hunger beating caution.

"I shouldn't wonder." She picked up a satchel that he recognized as Sir John's and unlaced the top. "Half a dozen men were trying to murder you." She took out a flagon of wine and handed it to him. "I think you may be well enough to risk something better than water."

"That isn't what I dreamed of." The last time he had tried to press her, she had told him wild tales of being a princess. He doubted he'd fare any better questioning her now.

"Very well, then." She folded her hands, neat and slender, with no calluses he could detect. "Tell me your dream."

"It doesn't matter." In truth, he could barely remember the details—a steep hillside of glassy ice, pure white stained scarlet with blood. Trying to remember the nightmare was like trying to remember the night he'd been wounded—flashes of pain like lightning in a fog.

"'Twas you who mentioned it," she pointed out. He heard no sarcasm in her tone, but there was no womanly sweetness, either.

"You should learn to speak your mind, Roxanna," he grumbled, taking a swallow of wine. "You try to spare my feelings overmuch." She must be the daughter of a penitent hermit indeed, he decided. She knew much of language and manners, but nothing of society.

"Forgive me, Gareth," she retorted. "I have been too busy sparing your life to give your feelings that much thought." She came and briskly snatched his blanket back and began examining the bandages on his chest.

"'Swounds, girl," he swore, feeling rather breathless. If his nakedness embarrassed her, she hid it well. "Bring me my clothes."

"I am wearing your clothes, as you can plainly see." She probed the gash in his stomach none too gently, making him gasp. "There's no more pus," she announced.

"May Christ be praised." She touched him as if his body was no more interesting to her than the joint she had roasting on the fire, but he found himself responding even so. "Roxanna, stop it."

"Be still," she ordered, tracing the line of stitches on his back more delicately. "You should lie on your stomach awhile." She reached past him to straighten his pillows, unconsciously crushing her breast against his arm as she did it.

"Roxanna!" He caught her firmly by both arms, and she turned her face to his, dark eyes flashing annoyance. Bless her, she truly was an innocent, no more aware than a newborn kitten of the effect her touch could have on him, he thought, suppressing a smile. "I can do it," he promised.

She opened her mouth to protest that she had been tending him quite well without instruction for nearly a week. Then she noticed the swelling of the blanket in his lap. "Do it, then," she answered, sitting back and biting the corner of her lip to keep from smiling. He must be better indeed.

He hunkered down to his side, keeping a firm hold on the blanket at his waist. "If you think I'm going back to sleep again, you're mad," he grumbled.

"Oh no, of course not." He rolled gingerly onto his stomach, giving her a tantalizing glimpse of his beautifully muscled behind. "You're ready to fight off the Hun."

"Keep my sword handy just in case." He let out a hiss of pain as he settled, and she clenched her fists against her thighs to stop herself from helping.

"I will, I promise." For the first time, she found herself wondering what she would do if the men who had attacked him had friends who would come for him again. Coming straight out of the bottle after Allah only knew how much time, she had been crazed with hunger, a ravenous demon able to tear his enemies apart without a moment's thought. But what if an army should turn up to avenge them?

"Whoreson bloody shite . . ." Before, when he was barely conscious, he had hardly seemed real to her. Their little world inside this hovel had felt like a dream. But awake, he was very much a living, breathing man. "Those bastards murdered me."

"Very nearly, yes." His face was pale and drawn with pain again from the effort of moving, and she let herself brush the hair back from his brow. "Who were they, Gareth? Why did they mean to kill you?"

"I had hoped you might tell me." Her hands were cool and soft, her touch too comforting to resist, but he felt foolish even so. A few days ago, he had been a powerful lord's second best knight; now he couldn't even roll himself over without breaking out in a sweat.

"I told you before, I don't know." She lay down beside him, her head pillowed on her arm, and again he marveled at her innocence. No woman with any notion of the world, peasant or princess either one, would be so easy with a man she barely knew. "Don't you have any idea?"

"Oh, aye." Even now, she seemed vaguely unreal to him—no living, mortal face could be so beautiful. He had called her an angel before, and even now, he halfway believed it. "I have an idea."

"I was born in the Highlands," he went on when she did not answer. Just saying these words gave him pain, she thought as she watched him. His blue eyes, usually so bright and full of life, had turned dark. "My mother's clan lives not far from here, or did when I was a child."

"And your father?" She didn't understand some of what he said—the Highlands, his mother's clan; these things meant nothing to her. But he spoke of them as if they should. He still believed this was her home.

"My father was an English knight—a Sassenach, they called him," he answered. His accent was changing, she realized. As he spoke of these Highlands and his mother's people there, his speech took on the broader, slightly lilting rhythm of the song she had first heard him sing, deep in her mystical sleep. "He came here as protector to a priest who would minister to the clans, bringing a party of his own soldiers, paid from his own purse." He seemed proud of this, and she smiled. "He never made war on any Scotsman for the English crown. In truth, he never intended to stay here at all."

"But he met your mother." It seemed strange to think of him having a family and a past before she found him. As silly as it seemed, she had become accustomed to thinking of him as hers alone, her prey and her charge, her reason for staying in this hovel.

He smiled, a spark of the life she so admired coming back into his eyes. "I suppose that was the reason," he admitted. "The priest had stopped over with the Clan McKail to give communion, and they were caught by the snows. My mother's father was laird." His eyes clouded over again. "As he is now, I hope."

"Laird of the Clan McKail," she repeated. She is learning the word, Gareth realized, surprised. Her tongue seemed to be testing the burr on the *r* in "laird," as if she had never heard the sound before.

"Their leader," he explained. Even if her mother were dead and her father a hermit, she would surely know about the clans. "He was none too pleased to think of his daughter marrying a foreigner, I suppose."

"Is England far?" she asked, apparently surprised.

"No," he said, bemused. "And yes—the other end of Christendom. Do you see what I mean?"

"Yes." He spoke of Christendom as if it were the world entire, she thought with an inward sigh. "I think I do. So your grandfather the laird refused to let them marry."

"He did at first," he answered. "Then my father swore fealty to my grandfather as lord, not only for himself but for his men. He fought for the clan for three years before he and my mother were wed, like Jacob fought for Laban to win Rachel." Actually, he wasn't sure if Jacob had been a soldier or a shepherd, but the reference was sound, he thought. She might not know the clans, but surely she knew the Bible.

Like who fought for whom? she thought but didn't say. "Who did he fight?" she asked instead. She liked listening to him tell this tale. It was soothing.

"Other clans," he answered. He had not spoken of his father to anyone since he was a boy, but she seemed genuinely interested. "They fight over the grazing lands in summer, and sometimes for power over one another. Sir John says . . ." His voice trailed off for a moment. "Sir John was accustomed to say they fought more for the fun of it than anything else," he finished.

He had looked away from her, and she reached out and touched his cheek. "Who is Sir John?"

"He was my tutor." Once again, she touched him as if she might be his, and a shiver raced through him. "One of my father's soldiers who went back to England with me and my mother after my father died." His eyes met hers. "He died in the same battle where I was wounded, the battle where you found me."

The old man she had found, she thought. "Did your father die in battle?" She clasped his hand in hers on the floor between their pallets.

"No." He liked the way her hand felt as if it belonged clasped in his. "They said he died by accident in a hunting party," he said. He had tupped his share of willing wenches in his time and even courted a few noble maidens—the handmaids of Marcus's conquests, for the most part. But he had never known any woman like Roxanna, who seemed neither wench nor lady, nor had he ever spoken to any woman but his mother at such length as he had already spoken to her. A hired knight with no future, he had been obliged to see women as either conveniently available for the nonce or out of his reach entirely. So opening his heart or even his mind to one had seemed a waste of time.

"But you don't believe it." She was watching his face, her dark eyes serious and sad.

"No," he said again. He wanted to trust her, to believe she was exactly as she seemed, impossible or not. "By the time he and my mother married, my grandfather had grown very fond of my father. Some said he favored him over his own son."

"That can't have made your uncle very happy." In her father, the caliph's, house, a foreigner who had found favor would have been in very grave danger indeed.

"To say the least," he said with a wry smile. "When I

was born, my grandfather declared that I was a full-blooded son of the clan, with full rights of inheritance. At the time, my mother said, most people thought very little about it. My uncle was young and newly married; it was assumed he would be laird after my grandfather and would have a son to have the title after him."

"That seems reasonable." The night had been half over when he woke. Now she could feel the first tingles in her flesh that signaled the coming of the dawn. She should leave him to feed before she lost her chance. But she wanted to hear how his story would end. "But I suppose the fates saw things differently."

"God's plan was something else," he agreed. "When I was five years old, my uncle was thrown from his horse and crippled, with only one daughter and no son. When it became clear he would have no more children, my grandfather declared I would be his heir when he died, with my father to guard my claim if I should not yet be of age."

"So God decided that your uncle must be disappointed and a five-year-old boy should become his enemy." Immortal demon she might be, but she would never live long enough to understand these Christians and their God.

"Apparently." He had never in his life heard any woman speak of God's will in such a tone, but he found he rather liked her for it. He would never have confessed it to a priest, but there had been many times when he had felt the same.

"So let me guess your uncle's name." She leaned toward him and kissed him lightly on the lips, shocking him to the marrow of his bones, then drew back again. "Jamey."

"What?" She was still looking at him with perfect innocence, as if she had no idea what she had just done or why she ought not to have done it. "Yes . . . how did you know?"

"You shouted at him when you were delirious." He was staring at her as if she had sprouted horns, and for a moment, she couldn't think why. Then she realized—she had never kissed him before when he was awake to know it. "You said you were going to kill him," she explained.

"I don't doubt it." He seemed to be waiting for her to explain, but that seemed unwise, so she said nothing, waiting for him to go on. "Jamey was always very kind to me," he finally said. "But my mother never trusted him again."

"Nor would I have done." Growing up in her father's palace, she had learned much of power and weakness, including the fact that a woman's mind captured their subtleties much more quickly than a man's. But she doubted he would agree. "So he arranged a hunting accident."

"My mother always thought so." He let go of her hand to caress the curve of her delicate wrist with his fingertips. Perhaps he was still dying, dreaming of a beautiful confidante to whom he could confess his heart. Or perhaps she was a more clever agent of his enemy, torturing him with sympathy and sweetness before the final kill. But what would be the point? "Jamey was not with the hunting party, but many of his best friends were, men who were never comfortable with my father's position in the clan. And my father was a great hunter; he would never have gone after a boar with a spear that could break."

"Any weapon can break, Gareth," she said gently.

"So my grandfather said," he answered. "But my mother never believed it. She openly accused my uncle, and he accused her in turn of treachery against her people for setting a Sassenach to rule them."

"Meaning your father."

His smile was grim, not at all his usual smile. "Meaning me," he answered. "After that, even my grandfather had to admit I was not safe in the clan. When my mother said she was taking me to England to my father's people, he did not try to stop her."

"But now you have come back to take your rightful place." No wonder he appealed to her, she thought. He was a kind of prince.

"No," he said, shaking his head. "My grandfather sent for me, but I will not stay. My place is in England now with my lord."

"Is your grandfather not your lord?" she countered, confused. "You said he was the leader of your clan—"

"My mother's clan," he corrected. "But my mother

will never come back here, and I have a place in England. My cousin, Marcus—" He stopped again, as he had when he had spoken of the old man who was dead. "There is nothing for me in the Highlands," he finished. "The clans are barbarians, fighting amongst themselves for nothing worth having, seeing a priest once a year if they're lucky, caring for nothing but their own."

"And yet your father thought it right to pledge himself to them." With every word he spoke, he was less the beautiful creature she had saved from death for the sake of his blood and more a living man who mattered—a luxury she could ill afford to keep.

"My father was a man in love." He made himself sit up again, restless under her ebony gaze. "Not only with my mother but with this place, the wildness of it, the beauty of the mountains." He looked back at her, searching those eyes for some hint of who she really was. "He died for it."

"And so you will avenge him." She sat up as well, reaching out to run a hand along his arm. He would heal; soon he would be strong. She would have to let him go to fight—just the thought of it made her long to touch him, to hold him to her while she could.

"Yes." He caught her hand and held it, seized with desire mixed with sudden anger. "Who are you?" he demanded. "Why have you stayed with me? Who put you here to care for me?"

"Let me go." She tried to pull free of him, gently at

first, then with real force, but once again, her demon's strength failed her against him. "Gareth—"

"I don't want to hurt you," he insisted. "I only want to know who you are, what you want—"

"I saved you!" she cried. "For days now I have stayed here in this pigsty, nursing you, feeding you—why is that not enough?" Why could she not break free? By all rights, she should be able to fling him through the nearest wall with barely a thought.

"You act as if you know me—"

"I do not," she cut him off. "I do not know you any better than you know me—less, in fact." She twisted her wrist in his grasp, and this time he let her go. "You know at least that I mean you no harm, that I care if you feel pain." She rubbed the marks his hand had left on her, fearful and awestruck at the sight. How long had it been since she had been bruised?

"Roxanna, of course I care." She seemed so fragile suddenly, so frightened. "You are my angel—"

"Then let me be that." In truth, she was anything but that, but she wanted the illusion even so. She wanted him to look at her as he had when he had made love to her, as if she were his and he loved her. "Do not question me, Gareth." The look in his eyes now was suddenly unbearable. She had to go out, to get away, even if the dawn was close. "I have told you who I am," she said, getting up.

"A princess." Gareth watched as she seemed to gather her dignity around her like a blanket as she moved away from him, the brittle hauteur she wore like a cloak to hide herself from him. Could a simple peasant girl adopt such a pose?

"Yes." All the warmth he had seen in her eyes only moments before was gone, replaced with a cold disdain. "If you cannot believe me, I will leave you." She paused, a tiny swallow giving her away. She was pretending, playing a part just as he had guessed; he could see it. But what was the truth? "If you think you can manage without me now, I will leave you in peace."

"And go where?" She arched a brow at him. "Or is that question offensive?"

"That you question me at all is offensive," she retorted briskly, her strange accent suddenly more pronounced. "Without me, you would be dead—if I leave you now, you will almost certainly die."

"I will," he admitted. If her intentions were completely good, why was she so frightened of his questions? But she was right; he had no hope of surviving without her.

"Then trust me." A tiny smile quirked at the corner of her mouth. "Or at least pretend." She picked up a bucket. "I will be right back."

Halfway to the well, she tripped over something in the path. Bending down, she found a bundle of something soft, something that had most definitely not been there the night before. Unfolding it, she found a woman's gown of softest linen wrapped in an overshift of wool. "Where in Allah's name . . . ?" she mused, stroking the fabric.

Gareth struggled to his feet, breathing only a little like a horse that has just run a race. His legs seemed almost willing to hold him. "Trust me, she says," he muttered, moving around the room, searching for some clue to his angel's true identity. "A princess . . ." But everything he found was either the rough furnishings he might expect in such a hovel or his own belongings—nothing that seemed connected to Roxanna at all. The pain in his stomach was a little worse for his efforts, but not unbearable. "I will find you out, Your Highness," he said, sinking down on his pallet again. She was right; he still needed her to survive, but not for very much longer. Soon he would not be an invalid. Then he would know the truth.

Roxanna slipped out of her borrowed clothes and into the gown, savoring the feel of fine cloth against her skin again. It wasn't silk, and it wasn't gorgeous, but it was still better than Gareth's tunic, she thought. "Thank you," she said aloud, turning in a circle to search the shadowy woods. For a moment, she thought she heard a human heartbeat among the whispers of the leaves. "Show yourself," she called out. "I won't hurt you." But the sound was gone, if it had ever been.

6

Gareth was sitting on his pallet, leaned against the wall, when Roxanna returned, dressed now in a maiden's gown with his own clothes in a bundle in her arms. "Do you like it?" she asked, holding out her skirt as she turned before him.

"Very nice." In truth, she would have been exquisite wrapped in a saddle blanket, but it seemed imprudent to say so. The memory of her kneeling naked by the fire to wash flashed through his mind, and he studiously pushed it away.

"I found it outside." She sat down across from him and smiled, the picture of ladylike compliance. "Someone left it for me, I think. It was right in the middle of the path."

"Someone," he repeated, bemused. "Who?"

"How should I know?" Indeed, her entire manner had changed, as if the girl who had left him a few minutes before had gone for good and sent a sweeter sister in her place. "Come, don't be cross." She yawned, stretching like a cat. "Sing me a song and make us both feel better."

Sweet or not, she was still giving orders, he thought. "What makes you think I can sing?" he asked as she made herself a nest of blankets.

"I heard you." She lay down and snuggled herself into her cocoon like a child, and he smiled, charmed in spite of himself. "Before you were attacked." She yawned again, covering her mouth with a delicate hand. "That's why I came to you, because I heard you sing."

"But you said . . ." He let the question trail off. She had said she had found him after the attack. But if she had been close enough to hear him singing, that must have been a lie. "What shall I sing, my lady?" he asked instead.

"You choose." Her eyes were closed, her dark lashes long against her pretty cheeks. Liar or not, he couldn't believe she truly meant him harm. Perhaps she was afraid of someone else. "Sing me something you like," she said with a drowsy smile.

"As you will," he said, smiling back even though her eyes were closed. That must be it, he thought, feeling a fool for not thinking it before. She wasn't meant to have cared for him at all—perhaps the men who had attacked him were her kin. She was hiding him and hiding herself from punishment. That was why she wouldn't tell him who she was or how she had found him, why she insisted on hiding inside through the day and only creeping out at night. Poor angel, she must be terrified. "Go to sleep," he said, resisting the urge to move closer. "I will sing you to sleep."

"Lovely . . ." 'Twas passing strange, Roxanna thought as her night-creature's need for sleep overwhelmed her. She had never felt so comfortable in her life, even in her silken bed at home. Gareth's voice was so soothing, warm and strong, masculine but sweet. She drifted off to the sound of his song, words she couldn't understand but that sounded beautiful. In her mind, she saw a hall of burnished wood and smiling faces gathered by the hearth, old and young alike, all warm and safe. "What a pretty dream," she murmured in her native tongue, lost to sleep at last.

Gareth heard her say something, but he couldn't make out the words. Singing more softly, he did move closer, bending over her. Her lips were slightly parted, rosy pink, and he let himself barely touch her cheek. She stirred slightly but did not wake. "Sleep well, princess," he murmured. Soon he would be strong again, he thought. Then it would be him protecting her.

He waited until he was certain she was sound asleep, then dressed himself in the dark. His clothes carried her spice-and-flowers scent, faint but unmistakable, and he smiled, burying his face for a moment in the crook of his elbow to breathe it in before buckling on his sword. He wrapped some of the meat she had roasted for him in a rag and stowed it in his pocket, then filled his waterskin and hung it over his shoulder. If there were more bandits or worse outside, he would no doubt regret not putting on his armor, but he doubted he could carry it more than a few steps out the door. Careful not to wake Roxanna, he moved slowly to the door and slipped out, closing it carefully behind him.

The tiny clearing where the hovel stood was unfamiliar, but he could see the road he and his friends had been traveling in the distance, winding its way out of the valley to the hills above. "Save me, Christ," he muttered. Just moving around the hovel had left him aching and out of breath; how was he to manage such a climb? For a moment, he considered giving up and going back inside, waiting until nightfall, when he might convince Roxanna to go with him. But the thought of leaning on her made up his mind for him. Even by his fever-addled reckoning, he had been helpless as a newborn babe for days now, maybe as long as a week. 'Twas nothing short of a miracle that his attackers hadn't come for him already, and his nurse as well. He had to find his feet.

The walk back to the clearing where they had been attacked was every bit as slow and painful as he might have predicted, but he made it just the same, leaning against a tree bare inches from the spot where he fallen just as the sun reached its peak. He took a long swallow of water and looked around, the sharp ache in his side making him breathe harder. He would have liked to have sat down for a moment, but he was fairly certain he couldn't have gotten back up.

A huge bonfire had burned itself to embers just across from where he stood, releasing foul-smelling wisps of smoke into the air. Moving closer, he saw it was in fact a pile of corpses, burned down to armor and bone. He poked at the edge with his sword, and a skeleton collapsed, sending up a plume of sparks. If there had been any mark or insignia to be found on his attackers' clothing, it was burned away.

At the far end of the clearing, he found two graves, each covered carefully with stones to keep the scavengers out. At the head of one he found Sir John's shield propped against a stone. At the head of the other, Marcus's sword had been planted in the ground to make a cross. He fell to his knees before it, his legs giving way beneath him, tears rising in his eyes. "Forgive me, Marcus." If not for him, his cousin would be safe in England with a rich, full life before him, not rotting underneath the rocky Highland turf. For love of a nameless, penniless wretch who didn't deserve it, a noble knight in the flower of manhood had died, stabbed in the back by a coward.

Sitting back on the ground, his sword dropped beside him, he thought back to that night. He had found Sir John's body; he had turned to shout to Marcus. He had seen Marcus fall. Three men had attacked him . . . For a moment, his mind's eye caught a glimpse of something else, a deadly flash of scarlet in the fog, the glow of green-gold eyes, and his heart beat faster. But just as he was about to catch hold of the image and make it come clear, it faded again, white fog into black.

"Someone buried you," he said aloud to his dead friend, barely knowing he had spoken. Someone had piled half a dozen or more corpses together in a heap and set them aflame like the carcasses of sheep killed by a flux, but had taken the time to dig careful graves for the two good men they had murdered. How could they have known the difference unless they were there to see the battle? *I heard you before you were attacked,* Roxanna had said as she drifted off to sleep. *That's why I came to you, because I heard you sing.* His mind snatched at the image of glowing green-gold eyes again, making him shudder. But whatever evil lurked in his memory could have nothing to do with Roxanna. She could have taken no part in the battle or the burning of the dead. She was a woman, a tiny, delicate thing, barely as tall as his shoulder. His gaze strayed to the graves again, to a handprint in the mud. Trembling slightly, he put his own hand over it, covering it completely.

"No," he said aloud, shaking his head as if someone else were arguing the point. Roxanna had saved him. He could not help but trust her. Taking up his sword again, he used it to climb to his feet, ready to start back.

Roxanna awoke with a scream, the tiny beam of sunlight piercing the bare flesh of her leg where she had flung it from under her blankets like a rod of molten steel. She scrambled back more by instinct than will, shielding herself with the blanket, ready to be burned up entirely. But it was only one beam that had found its way through a crack in the doorway. "Holy Allah," she muttered, letting the blanket fall. One of the rags she had used to block the cracks must have fallen out . . . but no. All of the rags were gone. "What . . . ?" She looked around the room, nonplussed and rather scared. Had someone come inside? "Gareth?"

But Gareth was gone.

"No . . ." She got up and moved to the doorway, careful to avoid the light. He couldn't possibly have gone out alone; he was still too weak. But how could someone have come into the hut and taken him without her knowing? "No . . . it can't be." She could tell from the way she felt that it was very late in the afternoon. The beam that had burned her was dark amber, one of the last rays of the setting sun. She paced the shadows like the cat she could become, chewing at her thumbnail, something she hadn't done since she was a little mortal girl. Where could he be? Who could have taken him? *Kivar*, a fearful voice whispered in her mind. *Kivar could have done it.*

"No," she said again, shaking her head. If Kivar had returned, he would have no reason to steal Gareth. At least not without making a great show of it—he would want her to know; otherwise there would be no point. Something else must have happened. He must have gone outside somehow—he had been walking before. Perhaps he was stronger than she had realized. "Gareth!" she shouted, withdrawing to the darkest shadows farthest away from the door. Surely he was right outside; surely he would come to her as soon as he heard her voice. "Gareth, answer me!" But he did not.

"Ungrateful wretch," she muttered aloud, but in truth, she was starting to panic. In her mind, she could see the handsome young knight lying unconscious in some forest glade just out of hearing, his wounds reopened, bleeding to death. And here she was, a helpless, cursed thing trapped by the sun, unable to go to him. "Why should I care?" But she did care; she cared horribly, more than she had thought she would ever care for anyone again. Somehow this man she had taken for convenient prey had become important to her, so important that the very idea of losing him now made her frantic. She paced the length of the hovel again, stealing a glance every few moments at the beam of light as it retreated, desperate for sunset. When it had finally disappeared, she ran for the door, throwing it open and running outside.

The sun had barely disappeared behind the hills, and for a moment she was blinded, her skin prickling with heat. Then she saw Gareth limping toward her, leaning on his crutch. "Gareth!" She started to run toward him, then stopped, remembering her dignity. Who was he that she should run to him? She waited, arms folded, as he made his way to her.

"Where have you been?" she demanded as soon as he seemed close enough to hear her. His face was pale, she noticed, and he stopped walking to gather his strength before he answered.

"I went back to the place where I fell." His shirt was soaked with sweat, and a spot of scarlet was spreading on his stomach where he had torn open at least one of her stitches.

"And why would you do that?" He took another few steps toward her, and she had to steel herself to keep her tone stern and cold as he deserved. "Did I not say it was dangerous to go out in the daylight?"

He stopped just out of her arm's reach, scowling down on her. "Am I a child and you my mother?" He sheathed his sword, taking obvious pains to pretend it didn't near kill him to do it.

"Not I," she retorted. "If you were mine, I should have beaten the stupidity out of you long before you got so old." In truth, the idea that he had made it all the way to the clearing where he had fallen and back on his own made her admire his courage and strength more than she could ever have told him. But he had frightened her, and she hated being frightened. He didn't even bother to answer her, trudging past her toward the hovel. "Here," she said, taking his arm. "Let me help you."

"Stop it," he ordered, flinging her off. In truth, he was exhausted; he could have lay down on the grass and slept for days, and he thought he had probably done dangerous harm to his stitches. But he'd die and be damned before he'd let her treat him like a naughty child. Who was this slip of a girl to scold him and order him about? He was a man full grown and a knight besides. But this stranger, this little Roxanna, treated him like he might be a half-wit, keeping him shut up in the dark and telling him tales no child of five would believe. All the long, painful way back from the clearing, he had turned her story over in his mind, the broken images of the battle mixed in with what he remembered of his illness and the madness she had said until he thought he might run mad himself. Now she had the gall to stand there with her little arms crossed and her little jaw set, calling him stupid. "I don't need your help," he said, refusing to acknowledge the sudden, stabbing pain he felt in his side as he pushed past her.

For a moment, Roxanna didn't know if she was furious or hurt. Suddenly, it was horrid past all bearing that this mortal idiot could make her feel either way. "Don't you?" She could tell from the way he was moving that he was in terrible pain, but for that wicked moment, she wasn't at all sorry. Without even bothering to answer her, he kept making his dogged way toward the hovel, looking as if he might fall down dead with every step. "Fine," she said, setting her heart against him. If he wanted to behave like a spoiled child, let him. Why should she care? "Take care of yourself, then. I'll waste no more time on you."

She's bluffing, Gareth thought, refusing to look back. Finally she was behaving like an ordinary woman. He had wounded her pride, and she was pouting. But in a moment, she would give in. She wouldn't have spent so much time and effort nursing him to let him die now. And perhaps the sting of his indifference would be enough to shake the truth out of her. He kept moving toward the hovel, certain at any moment he would feel her little hand on his arm again. He would let her help him now, he thought, his legs beginning to go numb, they ached so badly. He wouldn't bear any more scolding, mind, but he would let her help. The open door of the hovel was in reach now, and he grabbed it, a poor, shuddering crutch, and waited for her to catch up.

But she didn't come. When he'd stopped feeling quite so dizzy, he turned around, expecting to find her standing in the clearing, perhaps with her arms crossed again. But she was gone. "Roxanna!" he called before he could stop himself. She couldn't really mean to leave him. But she didn't answer.

"Fine." She was hiding, he thought, punishing him for not letting her berate him as she thought he deserved. But she would be back. "Fine," he repeated, heaving himself inside. The fire had almost burned itself out, and with his last burst of energy, he made it to the hearth. "I will take care of myself." The evening breeze was chilly, and he shivered, remembering the agony of the fever he had just escaped. "Princess my arse," he muttered, poking the coals back to life. "Demon is more like it." It was she who was the child, he thought, a spoiled brat who demanded absolute obedience. She didn't want a lover, she wanted a pet—

He stopped, appalled. What twisted corner of his brain had conjured up that thought? He was not Roxanna's lover; he barely even knew the chit. In truth, he didn't know her at all. For all he knew, every word she had ever told him was a lie or a delusion.

"I am losing my mind," he decided. 'Twas no great wonder—he had been nearly murdered. His best friends in the world were dead. He had no idea why he had been attacked or really by whom. He had no way of reaching either his lord in England or his grandfather here in the Highlands. And the only person to whom he had spoken for days was the most beautiful, most maddening creature he had ever seen or heard tell of in his life. He wrapped his blanket around his shoulders like a mantle and waited for her to come back.

Roxanna stood in the deepening dark of the forest on the other side of the clearing, watching him through the open door of the hovel. Close the door, she ordered in her mind. You'll catch a chill and be sick again. But he didn't obey—most likely he couldn't move from the spot where he had fallen, and it served him right if his fever did come back. For a long moment, she debated whether or not she should go to him and allow him to beg her forgiveness. She could be gracious; she was a princess, after all, and he was only an ignorant heathen. If he called to her again, she would go.

But he didn't call. "Stubborn fool," she muttered. Let him suffer, then, she thought. A few hours on his own and he would give her the thanks she deserved. Turning her back on the clearing, she transformed herself into the cat and prowled silently into the wood.

7

Gareth dreamed he was a child again, a small boy in the hills outside his grandfather's village. "Leave her alone!" he was shouting, raising the stick he was supposed to be using to herd a cow home against a gang of boys all twice his size. "She isn't hurting you!" The weird woman looked up from her conjure and smiled at him, her forehead bleeding from one of the rocks they had thrown. He saw her eyes, young amidst the wrinkles of her face, green with wide black pupils like a cat's eyes in the dark. . . .

Then he woke up.

The fire had died down again; the hut was dark and cold. He sat up, feeling surprisingly well. His head felt clearer than it had since he was wounded. His joints felt stiff and sore from his walk that afternoon, but the burning pain hadn't returned to his wounds, and he didn't feel the least bit feverish. In faith, he was finally healing.

Roxanna had not come back even to peek at him; the door was still standing open. "I won't waste any more time on you," she had said—could she have meant it? The night before, she had threatened to abandon him if he asked too many questions, and he had stopped asking. Wasn't that enough?

You told her you didn't need her, a voice reminded him inside his head. But he had meant he didn't need her to help him back to bed like a cripple, not that he didn't need her at all. And besides, even if he didn't need her to survive, he would still have wanted her to stay. He wanted to thank her for all she had done for him already. Surely she realized that. And he wanted to find out who she really was, which she apparently did not want, but still . . . to just disappear this way hardly seemed kind. And she was kind, for all her fussing. He smiled, remembering how she had ordered him to sing, like she might be a princess indeed and he her favored bard. He thought of the way she had almost run to him across the clearing, the look of relief on her face when she had seen he was safe, and the way she had drawn up and turned cold when he had refused to let her scold him without fighting back.

"Oh, no," he groaned, silently cursing himself for a fool. Marcus had always told him he had no more way with women than a pig in a wallow, and now he believed it. She had been afraid for him; that was why she had chided him so. He might not know where she came from, but he knew her well enough to know she would never cry or wring her hands or flutter like a pigeon to tell him she had worried about him. She would hate to be frightened; it would make her angry at herself and at him, too, for making her so. No wonder she had scolded him. And he, like the fool that he was, had snapped back instead of comforting her. He had made her think he didn't care that she was frightened, that he didn't need her at all. No wonder she had run away. Now she was alone in the dark somewhere, angry and probably hurt. . . .

As if in answer to his thoughts, a wolf howled in the forest. Another answered, then another, making his blood run cold. He remembered only too well what a pack of wolves could do to anyone foolish enough to wander abroad after dark. In his grandfather's village, the gates were barred at sundown and guards were set all night to watch the flocks. "She goes out alone every night," he muttered to himself, getting up and putting on his sword, barely feeling the ache in his joints. "She is perfectly safe." His heart beat faster as he rummaged through the packs she had brought to the shelter, finding his crossbow. The night before, he had barely been able to lift a bowl of broth, now he meant to arm a crossbow and face down a wolf pack . . . he could almost see Marcus rolling his eyes in his heavenly reward. But what choice did he have?

"Roxanna!" he called sharply when he reached the door. Perhaps she was just outside the clearing, still pouting, waiting for him to apologize. "Roxanna, I'm sorry!" The howling started up again, punctuated with eager, doglike barks. "I didn't mean a word of what I said." She was behaving horribly and deserved to be spanked, but she didn't deserve to be ripped to pieces, not if he could save her by swallowing his pride. "You're right—I need you!" The howls were getting closer, drawn by his voice, no doubt. "I need you right now!" He pulled back the string on the crossbow with his left arm, the stronger at the moment, and gritted his teeth as the muscles in his side flared in painful protest. "Stupid girl," he muttered under his breath as he fitted the bolt into place. "I ought to spank you, truly."

Be quiet, idiot, Roxanna thought, watching him from the wood. The wolf pack was between her and Gareth, pacing at the very edge of the trees, preparing to attack. She had come running as soon as she had heard his voice, but the wolves were faster. "Go back inside," she whispered through gritted teeth, trying to move the knight by sheer force of will. He had a crossbow, and if he had the strength to fire it, he could probably take down one of the wolves, and she could take down another. But there were half a dozen, all hungry and all of whom could smell his blood.

"Roxanna, come back now!" he called to her, and the largest of the wolves raised his head and yelped in ecstasy. The knight was coming closer, the crossbow raised to his shoulder, headed straight for the pack. "Please, love, it isn't safe."

Oh, holy Allah, she thought. He thinks he's saving me. It was a perfectly reasonable thought, she realized. For all he knew, she was every bit as delicate as she appeared. And he was a noble knight, sworn to protect the weak. "Gareth, please," she whispered urgently. "Go back to the shelter." Still so badly hurt he could barely walk, he still meant to face down a wolf pack to protect her—she felt rather dizzy just thinking about it.

But she had no time to think. The leader of the wolf pack was attacking, running straight for Gareth, a huge black shadow racing over the grass. He fired the crossbow with deadly accuracy in spite of his injuries and the darkness, piercing the beast straight through the heart and dropping it dead with a single shot. But the other five were close behind.

Gareth had no time to thank God for the accuracy of his shot—the others were all but upon him. He dropped the crossbow and drew his sword in a smooth motion so well practiced, he barely felt the pain. With far more luck than he had any reason to expect, he might kill one more and frighten the others. And even if he could not, at least they were attacking an armed knight, not an innocent maid.

Suddenly he heard a terrible, unearthly scream as another, smaller streak of black shot out of the forest, much faster than the wolves. It was a huge cat, blue-black in the moonlight but the size of a small lion. It circled the wolves and turned, putting itself between him and the pack. The wolves froze for a moment, confused and whining. Then the new leader advanced, snarling and baring its teeth. The black cat bared its fangs and hissed, crouched low to the ground, its long, sleek tail swishing restlessly in the grass. Gareth took a slow step backward, crouched himself with his sword held out before him, ready to strike. The cat was so close, he could have touched its tail with his sword point, but it seemed not to have noticed him at all, completely intent on the wolves.

The pack leader lunged, and the cat reared up, striking with razor-sharp claws and screaming again in fury. It swiped the wolf across the muzzle, sliding quickly to the side as the wolf moved to snatch it up by the neck, and struck again, this time at the larger animal's throat. The wolf let out a yelp of pain and fell back, scrambling in the grass, but still the cat went after it, nipping again at its leg. The pack turned and fled into the forest, and the cat screamed again, giving its prey one last bite on the heel as it fled.

Gareth held his breath as the creature turned, his grip tightening on his sword. It was beautiful, like nothing he had ever seen before, and the eyes were almost human, gazing at him with every appearance of intelligence. It moved like molten steel, the moonlight gleaming on its velvet fur as it came closer, and his mouth went dry. A wolf he might have hacked to pieces, but this creature was too fast, too graceful. If it came for him, he was a dead man.

"What are you?" he demanded, his voice barely louder than a whisper. Roxanna was still in the forest; the wolves could be catching her scent even now. Somehow he had to make it past the cat to find her first. "Stay back!" he ordered, waving his sword like an old woman frightening crows. "Begone!"

The cat stopped, one paw poised above the grass. "I said begone!" he repeated, roaring at the top of his lungs and taking a strong step forward. The cat tilted its head to one side, its ears pricked forward. Gareth frowned, waving the sword again, his heart pounding madly in his chest. The cat turned and trotted off into the forest.

As soon as she was safely hidden, Roxanna transformed into her usual shape and leaned against a tree, both hands clamped over her mouth to hold back helpless laughter. She had never seen or even imagined such foolish, magnificent courage as this mad mortal had—waving his arms and shouting at a panther to frighten it away? Madness—glorious! Her legs gave way beneath her as tension gave way to relief.

"Roxanna!" He was apparently still looking for her, half mad with worry.

"I am here." She stood up just as he appeared. "I am well."

"Thank God." He dropped his sword and gathered her into his arms. "Didn't you hear me calling you?" he demanded, crushing her close.

"Yes." She felt dizzy again, flushed with a kind of foolish joy she could never remember feeling before that moment. Had anyone ever dared to hold her so? "But . . ." He moved as if to let her go, and she wrapped her arms around him, pressing her cheek to his shoulder. "I was afraid." He felt so good, so warm and strong. "I was afraid of the wolves."

"Poor angel." He stroked her hair, pressing a kiss to the top of her head. "Of course you were afraid." In truth, she must have been terrified, he thought. All her thorny pride was gone; she was trembling all over, so much so that he couldn't enjoy the change for wanting to comfort her. "I am so sorry, sweeting," he went on, squeezing her closer for a moment before he let her go. "I didn't mean to hurt your feelings before." The beast he had seen could come back at any moment. They had to get inside.

"You . . ." She looked up at him, astounded all over again. What manner of country was this that could make such a man? The soldiers of her father's kingdom would sooner have torn out their tongues by the roots than beg a woman's pardon. It would never have occurred to any man she had ever known to wonder if her feelings might have been hurt, much less apologize. "You did hurt my feelings," she admitted, just as astonished at herself. When had she ever let on that she had feelings, much less that they could be hurt? "But I forgive you."

He smiled, the smile that always made his eyes twinkle and her heart feel light. "Thanks." He took her hand in both of his and raised it to his lips, and without thinking, she gasped, a sudden flash of desire making her feel weak.

Gareth heard her gasp and looked up, his eyes meeting hers, and his blood turned hot in a moment. The look on her face was enough to make him drunk, her lips slightly parted as if waiting for a kiss and her eyes wide with innocent longing. "All is well now," he said, his mouth going dry. He had thought her beautiful from the first moment he had seen her, but he had never expected to see her looking up at him so, as if . . .

"Come," he said, cutting off the thought before it formed. "We must go inside."

"Yes." She let him go and bent down to pick up his fallen sword as if it weren't nearly as heavy as she was herself.

"Here," he said, laughing, crouching down to pick it up himself. "Let me."

She looked up sharply, barely missing bashing the top of her head into his chin. "As you will." She put a hand on his arm as if to brace herself to stand up. Then she leaned forward and kissed his mouth.

He let the sword fall and dropped to one knee, framing her face in his hands to pull her closer. Her lips opened easily, welcoming his tongue, and for a long moment's madness, nothing else mattered. Then he felt her arms entwine around his neck, the luscious softness of her breasts pressed to his chest. "Roxanna, wait . . ." He drew back, dipping to brush her lips with his one last time, unable to resist. A tiny, demanding line appeared between her brows, making him smile, and the swollen pink of her freshly kissed mouth could undo him completely if he let it. "The wolves could come back," he pointed out gently. "We have to go back to our shelter."

He's so handsome, she thought, her body aching to be held again, the demon inside of her aching to possess him. So handsome and warm and alive. Before, when she had made love to him, believing he would die, he had been little more than an object to her, a beautiful thing to be used while he was useful. But now he was Gareth, the madman who refused to die, who confounded her at every turn and comforted her when he thought she was frightened. He was the brave and foolish knight who had faced down a panther and a pack of wolves to save her, the voice that sang her to sleep, the smile that made her heart feel whole. He was all of those things and more besides, a mystery she had only begun to unravel, and she longed for him with all her cursed soul.

She touched his mouth with her fingertips, taking a ragged breath. "Aye." She nodded. "As you will." He took her hand and helped her to her feet as if it were she who was crippled, moving with a masculine grace that belied his injuries. "You are much better."

He smiled. "'Tis an illusion. Come." He sheathed his sword and took her hand again. "Let's go inside."

She expected him to collapse to his pallet as soon as they reached the shelter, and would have thought no less of him if he had. He had done a labor of Hercules that day, considering his condition. But it was he who closed the door behind them and dragged a broken trunk in front of it. "You must be starving," she said, going to the fire. "We still have meat, and I found some apples." She straightened the blankets he had left in a muddle by the hearth. "Here, come and lie down."

"No." She turned to find him smiling. "Not just yet." He touched her cheek and kissed her, bold but tender, stealing her breath away. She raised her hands to his shoulders, feeling his heart beating under her palm, and he deepened the kiss. She swayed toward him, letting her head fall back, and his arms enfolded her.

He had thought she would protest at least a little, that now that the worst of her fright had passed, she would resist him on principle. But while she seemed surprised, she never once tried to hold him back or pull away. Again he wanted to ask her who she was, where she had come from, how she had come to be with him. Nothing in the life he had known before had prepared him for her; no one he had ever met was like her. "Are you real?" he whispered, twisting a strand of her ebony hair around his fingers as he looked down on her face.

"No," she answered, smiling. "You are dreaming."

"I believe it." He kissed her again, opening her mouth to his, thrilling to his bones to hear her sigh. She raised up on tiptoe to reach him, and he longed to scoop her off her feet completely. But he didn't quite trust his injuries to give him that much strength just yet. Soon, he thought, nuzzling her throat. Soon he would have her in a proper house with a proper bed, and he would be strong. But for now, he couldn't wait.

Once again, she was shocked at his strength as he drew her closer, the power she could feel in him that seemed to make her own strength melt away, vampire or not. She closed her eyes and pressed her cheek to his throat, the thrill of his pulse against her skin making her shiver. He leaned over her, lowering her to the blanket, and she let herself fall slowly, trusting him to hold her safe. His kisses turned more urgent, deep and wet, and she drew his tongue deeper still inside her mouth, daring the most gentle of bites. His heart was beating faster; she could hear it, and the sound made her own breath come short. He was braced above her on one arm, the other hand tugging up her skirt, and she let him, caressing his arms and rubbing a foot along his calf. "Gareth," she breathed through a sigh as his mouth moved to her cheek.

He kissed her ear, swirling his tongue for a moment inside, and she gasped, her hips rising a little off the blanket without her will. He raised his head to look at her, his eyes bright with desire. "You are beautiful," he told her solemnly, making her smile. Such a simple thing to say, but it warmed her heart.

"You are beautiful," she promised. She laid a hand against his cheek, rough with beard, then cradled his neck to draw him down to her again. His hands pushed her skirt up over her hips as he kissed her, and she wrapped her arms around him, caressing his back as he eased himself inside her. "So beautiful," she murmured in her native language, arching up to meet him.

He made love to her deliberately, kissing her face and moving slowly, holding her still to move faster. She cried out as the first waves of her climax began to break, and he stopped altogether, nuzzling her throat and murmuring soft words, caressing her hip with his hand. "Not yet," he whispered in her ear and kissed her cheek. She opened her mouth to protest, and he kissed her, moving inside her again.

He unlaced the ribbon at the neckline of her gown and pushed it from her shoulder, kissing her skin with the reverence of an idolater. "You should be naked," he murmured, his voice rough with desire. "Someday you will be naked."

"Yes," she promised, preening under his caress, release building inside her again, making her feel faint. "For you." She buried her hands in his hair, grasping, tugging his face back up to hers as she braced her heels against the floor, pushing up to make him move faster.

"Yes," he answered, an animal's growl as he pounded inside her. "Now, my angel . . ." His face above hers was flushed, his mouth slightly open for breath, and nothing she had ever seen before had been so beautiful as he was. "Let it go."

She let her eyes fall closed, her climax breaking over her, trusting him completely. Her curse was forgotten, the demon inside her, her enemy, everything . . . nothing was with her but him. She felt him reach release as well, heard him call her name, and the waves rose up again. She held him to her, enfolding him against her breast as he collapsed, a terrible joy like nothing she had ever felt making her want to weep.

"Roxanna," he mumbled, a scratchy kiss against her cheek before he rolled onto his side. "Come here." She turned her back to him to hide her tears of blood, and he drew her against him, wrapping his arms around her. "Tell me, darling," he pleaded, kissing her hair. "Please, tell me who you are."

"You mustn't ask me." She bent to kiss his hand, the words caught in her throat. "Please don't ask." She didn't want to tell him, didn't want to know herself. For just this moment, she wanted to be his.

"Forgive me." He squeezed her more tightly. "I'm sorry."

"Yes." Once again, he was asking her for pardon when she was the one who was wrong, the demon who had meant to take his life. "I forgive you."

"Good." He could tell she was crying, and he felt like a villain for causing her tears. But he could not say he was sorry for making love to her; that much he would never regret. "All will be well," he promised. "I will take you from this place." He kissed her shoulder, still bare from before. "I will keep you safe."

She smiled, his innocence breaking her heart. "I know." She kissed the back of his hand again, savoring the warmth of him around her. Sheltered safe in his embrace, she tried not to think of anything at all until she felt him fall asleep.

8

Isabel awoke to darkness, surprised she could even wake at all. Orlando had left her some time before—a day or a week, she couldn't be certain. She had heard him shouting her name, heard Kivar laughing, but she had not had the strength to answer the little wizard or even lift her head from the demon's shoulder. Now she had the sensation of flying and realized she was being passed from one pair of arms to another, from the back of a horse and down into a boat. Her eyes adjusting to the dark, she saw what looked like blue-white mountains rising all around them, and her breath came out of her mouth as a mist. "Where are we?" she mumbled, trying to catch hold of the sleeve of the man who was putting her down. "What is this place?" The peaks were ice, she realized, floating in the sea.

"Home." Kivar was sitting beside her, his hood drawn up and his arms crossed tightly over his chest. "We have come home." As always, the sound of his voice made her shiver; now with the cold, she thought she might never stop. The first time she had seen this monster from so close, he had been inside a rotted skeleton with living eyes. But now, he looked like any other man, was handsome, even, with straw-colored hair to his shoulders and a slightly darker beard. He looked down on her and smiled. "This is where we began, you and I," he explained.

"Not I," she said, fighting to find her voice. Their boat was low and broad, its prow marked with a serpent curving up as if rising from the sea, and was rowed by half a dozen men, three on each side. "I did not begin here."

He touched her cheek, making her cringe, and his eyes seemed sad, almost warm. "Your people began here," he answered. "And here is the place where you will end."

They rowed between two jagged peaks of ice into a natural harbor. Turning her gaze away from Kivar, she saw what looked like a statue on the shore, a woman reaching out toward the sea with what looked like bundles on the ice at her feet. Then she realized the shape was made of ice as well, a thick, translucent blue layer of ice over something darker. As the boat drew closer, she looked into the statue's face and saw a living woman's eyes peering out through the blue, her mouth open as if she were screaming.

"Holy Christ," Isabel breathed, crossing herself.

"And who is that, exactly?" Kivar asked, amused. He moved closer, draping the edge of his mantle around her shoulders and drawing her to him. She tried to squirm away, but she barely managed a flinch before she collapsed against his side, exhausted.

"You will hear of Him in hell," she muttered, barely louder than a whisper.

"That woman was alive," he said, giving her a mocking kiss on the top of her head. "As alive as you. But I am the villain." His voice had turned cold again, bitter as gall. "The gods who banished her to ice are blessed, but I must be hated." Even barely conscious, she could hear the madness in that voice, feel the evil in his flesh-warm touch. "What of the god who made me? Why is he atoned? His sin was love alone, they said." She knew a little of this creature's history, but she had never heard him speak of it before. In truth, she had never heard him speak so long at all. "Would my mother have said the same?" he mused. He put a hand under her chin and turned her face up to his. "Is it love to bewitch a creature lesser than yourself, to put a monster in her womb?" He smiled, making her flesh crawl. "Will you not answer, child?" he asked with silken sweetness. "You are the one to know."

She shuddered, feeling sick. "Liar." With all her strength, she pushed at him again, and his mantle dropped from her shoulder to let in the biting wind. "You cannot frighten me." She tried to turn her face away from him again, but he would not allow it, holding her with the lightest pressure of his fingertips along her jaw.

"I do not want to frighten you," he promised. "You

are my daughter, blood of my blood." She closed her eyes against him, willing herself away, back home or dead or anywhere but there. Simon, she thought, reaching out for the lost half of her soul, the vampire she loved. Help me, darling, please. . . .

"He will," Kivar said, answering her thoughts as easily as if she had spoken aloud. Her eyes snapped open, and he smiled. Had he guessed, or could he really see into her mind? "Soon we will all be home." Without further explanation, he let her go and rose to go to the bow of the boat. She tried to call after him, but she was too tired. In exhaustion, she let her eyes fall closed again and slept.

Gareth awoke to the sound of Roxanna weeping in his arms. "I cannot," she was saying, struggling in his grasp. "I never promised this. . . . You cannot make me. . . ."

"Hush, sweetheart," he murmured, loosening his hold to wake her. "'Tis only a bad dream." He kissed her shoulder. "Wake up now." In her struggles, she must have scratched herself, for tiny streams of blood streaked down her face. "Poor angel," he said, sitting up beside her to caress her cheek, and she moaned in anguish, a horrible sound that broke his heart. "You must wake up." He bent close to lightly kiss her mouth.

"No!" She shoved him back, her eyes wild with horror. "Leave me!"

"I will not." He had once had a squire who was given

to such terrors in the night; he knew she still would not know she was safe or even where she was. She was fighting against the tangle of blankets around her, and he helped her free herself, keeping a firm hold on her arm lest she fight her way into the fire. "You are safe, love."

"No." She stopped struggling, and this time when she looked at him, her eyes were lucid. "I am not."

"Of course you are." He smiled as he drew her close against his chest. "It was only a bad dream."

Roxanna clung to him, hiding her face against him, feeling his heartbeat against her cheek. "No," she repeated, barely louder than a whisper. In her dream, she had been back in her father's golden hall, being dragged to the dais to marry against her will under the eyes of Kivar. But this time instead of some English duke she had never seen, her groom was Gareth, her beautiful mortal love. His light brown hair glowed golden as the torchlight on the walls, and his blue eyes broke her heart. All around them, a hundred or more of her vampire kin awaited their master's command to attack, their demons' eyes glowing with hunger, but Gareth had smiled at her, innocent of all. "I will never hurt you," he had promised in the dream, just as the duke had promised in reality, offering his hand. "Do not be afraid." And all the time, Kivar was smiling, already tasting her beloved's mortal blood. Kivar wanted Gareth for his own. A sob racked her as she thought of it, the image refusing to fade.

"I must leave you," she said, weeping, clutching his

shirt to hide her tears of blood. "You do not need me anymore. You must go to your grandfather and forget you ever saw me."

"I cannot." She could hear him smiling in his voice, imagine the mischief that was dancing in his eyes, and her heart clenched like a fist. He was her perfect opposite—blithe while she was melancholy, light while she was dark. Good while she was evil. Mortal while she was undead. "I have ruined you." His fingertips trailed along her jaw in a lover's caress, and she stiffened, desperate not to want him, helpless to resist. His touch was like a drug to her; all the warmth and tenderness Kivar had stolen from her returned. But she could not have him. "You say you are no peasant wench," he said, teasing her. He still thought her terror was only a dream, that he could comfort her with kisses. "If that is so, then you must be my wife."

"Great Allah save us," she answered, weeping and laughing at once at the horror of the thought, remembering her dream. "Never." The image of Kivar rose up inside her mind, making her tremble all over. "Never that."

"And why not?" In truth, Gareth was shocked and rather insulted. He had expected her to protest on principle—heaven knew she had never given in willingly to any other suggestion he had ever made. But was the prospect of having him for a husband such a horror? She had taken him as lover readily enough. "Do you think me too common for you, princess?"

"No." She loosened her grip on his shirt, laying her palm over his heart instead. "I think that you are perfect."

"I am hardly that." He traced the shape of her jaw with his touch, his heart aching with tenderness for her, his mad, infuriating angel. "But I can protect you." A small sob escaped her, breaking his heart. "Just tell me why you are so afraid, love, please—"

"I am not," she answered.

"Of course you are." He wrapped his arms around her again, pressing her close. "Tell me what you dreamed that made you cry." He kissed her hair, stroking her back to soothe her. "Tell me why you must hide from the sunlight and pretend to be a princess. Tell me the truth, Roxanna, please."

"Gareth." She wept, wrapping her arms around his waist and holding on to him with all her might as if she feared some evil spirit meant to rip her from him.

"I beg you, darling, tell me," he pressed, her obvious distress making a lump rise in his own throat. "It cannot be so bad as you believe."

Her sob became a laugh, as bitter and despairing as her tears. "Think you not?" She pressed her cheek against his chest for one more moment, taking a long, shuddering breath. Then she drew back and looked up at him. Blood was smeared across her face, down either cheek—his shirt was red with it.

"Holy Christ, Roxanna!" He took her face between

his hands, raking his fingers through her hair, searching for the wound. "What have you done—?"

"Look at me, Gareth." Her expression was blank as a statue of an angel in a church, but her eyes were changing, the dark brown irises turning iridescent green, glowing like the windows of a lantern. The blood on her face was her tears, still falling from her eyes, scarlet liquid shining for a moment in the glowing green before spilling down her cheeks. "You must remember," she said, her voice going husky, seeming to echo in the air around them. "You must remember all that you have seen."

The scarlet mist that had clouded his memory since he had fallen in the grove was suddenly lifted, and he saw her, whirling like a dervish among his attackers, a lethal flash of scarlet gown and ebony hair that ripped grown men apart. Now before him, her shoulders still clutched in his hands, she drew her lips back in a snarl, exposing the long, curved fangs that had torn open their throats. She had drunk from them, drunk their blood, all but bathing in it. "The bottle," he said, his tongue thick in his mouth, his flesh gone cold. "You came out of the bottle."

"Yes." She did not try to touch him, nor did she try to pull away. "I am a vampire, Gareth. A demon that can only walk at night." Her voice was normal again, but her eyes still glowed. In his mind, he saw her kneeling naked by the fire the first night she had brought him to the hovel. She had thrown a bundle of scarlet into the fire—the gown she had worn, soaked with the brigands' blood. "When first you saw me, I was starving—I feed on living blood."

"You saved me." He still held her by the shoulders, and her flesh still felt the same. She was still his beloved, still his angel—surely she must be.

"Yes. I was afraid I would find no other prey in these mountains." Her tears had stopped at last, but her voice was sad. "I kept you alive to feed my thirst."

"But you didn't. . . ." He let her go abruptly to wipe the blood from her face, desperate to make her look like herself, the woman he knew, not some monster from a dream.

"I could not," she admitted, pliant as a doll under his efforts. The green fire had faded from her eyes, but he could not forget it, could not make himself not see the truth now that she had revealed it. "I wanted not to care for you, Gareth, but I did." She reached up to touch his cheek, and he flinched, drawing back. "I do," she said with a sad smile.

He caught her hand in his before it could fall, bending his face to her palm to kiss it. The sadness in her eyes was unbearable; he could not bear to hurt her, no matter what she was. "How did this happen?" he asked, his voice catching in his throat. He felt her other hand caress his hair, and tears rose in his eyes. "Who has done this to you?"

"It doesn't matter." She still sounded just the same;

the smell of her skin was just as he had come to love it, sweetness and spice.

"It matters to me." He raised his eyes to hers again in sudden fury at whatever had cursed her so. "We will fix this, find a priest—"

"Your priests are nothing to me, Gareth," she cut him off, putting a hand to his mouth. She could not believe he was still there, that he could still bear to look at her, much less touch her. How could he still act as if he cared for her, knowing what she was? "They cannot save me." When she went into the bottle, she had thought she knew despair, that the grief she had felt in that moment was beyond all human reckoning, more pain than she could bear. But somehow this was worse, this feeling she saw in his eyes. No one had ever looked at her this way, not even her mother, not even Orlando. "Gareth, I am lost." A black hole seemed to open in her heart, darkness engulfing all that she had lost. She should have been a mortal princess. She should be home, bringing her people peace, filling the golden hall with the laughter of children, heirs to a land of prosperity for all. If Gareth had come to her then, this beautiful knight who looked on her with love like nothing she had ever known, she would have given him her soul. "You must let me go." She tried to rise, but he caught her by the shoulders.

"I will not." She twisted in his grasp, but as always, her demon's strength failed her against him. "I saw you kill those men," he said. "I saw you save me—"

"It wasn't to save you," she protested. "I was starving. I needed to feed—"

"But we have been alone," he pointed out. "How have you—?"

"The same deer that fed you their meat fed me their blood," she answered before he could finish. "And the wolves." Again, he froze in shock, his handsome face stunned as if she had struck him. "I am a demon, a monster."

"Have you always been so?" He seemed to be determined to make sense of what she said, to push away his fear. He was so brave . . . how could she help but love him?

"No," she answered. "I was born a mortal, just like you. But a demon named Lucan Kivar attacked my father's fortress and made me what I am." The injustice of her fate had never seemed so terrible; she had never hated Kivar so much as she did at that moment. "I am sworn to destroy him."

"Then I will help you—"

"No!" The very idea that Gareth and Kivar could meet was too horrible to imagine.

"Why not?" he asked. "Did you not help me, save me from death? Why can I not save you?"

"Gareth—"

"You say you are lost—why must that be true?" He rose to his feet, drawing her up with him. "I may not be a demon, but I am no weakling, Roxanna. I would have killed those brigands myself in a fair fight."

"I know you would," she said, almost smiling in spite of her grief. Could he really think she doubted his valor? "You faced down a pack of wolves alone. I saw you."

"Then let me save you." He cradled her face between his hands. "At least let me try." Before she could answer, he kissed her, as tenderly as if she might have been the angel he had called her. She swayed on her feet, and his arms closed around her, enfolding her in an embrace. His kiss was sweet as honey, warm as blood, and her need for him was like a fever, burning to the marrow of her bones. How could she have let this happen? How could she have let them come to this? He should be frightened; seeing what she was, he should not want to kiss her. He should know she would hurt him.

"How can you do this?" she said softly as his kiss moved to her cheek. "You saw me kill." He nuzzled underneath the curtain of her hair, and she turned her head abruptly, scraping her fangs along the tender flesh of his throat to make him stop. "You see what I am," she finished when his eyes met hers.

"Yes," he answered, the blue eyes she adored still warm with love. "You are my angel."

She gasped, her heart twisting with grief. "Fool," she said softly, taking a step back. "You are blind." She had seen mortal women besotted by Kivar and his vampire sons, the demons' beauty blinding their prey even after they were bitten. The thought that Gareth could be the same was horrible; that she could be the cause was even worse. She had always taken her beauty for granted, had used it as a weapon more than once, even as a mortal. But she would not use it on him, would not let his desire lead him to destruction.

"Roxanna . . ." Gareth reached for her again, but she drew back, her lips drawn back over her fangs like the snarl of some wild beast. But still he would not give her up. "Darling, please . . ." Her form seemed to shiver in the firelight like a reflection in water. Then suddenly she was gone, replaced by the panther he had seen attack the wolves. The creature bared its fangs as well, crouched low as if ready to strike. "Roxanna," he repeated, breathless with shock. He held out a hand to her, more tentative this time, and she screamed, making the hair on the back of his neck stand on end. She struck out at him, and he recoiled, falling backward. With a single graceful spring, she leapt over his prone body and streaked into the night.

"Roxanna!" He scrambled to his feet and ran after her, but it was hopeless. She was gone. "Roxanna!" The weight of all that he had seen seemed to fall on him at once. The attack in the clearing; Roxanna rising from the bottle, slaughtering the brigands—the images once forgotten now captured him completely, drowning every other thought. All that she had told him echoed in his head. . . . She was a demon, a vampire . . . made by Lucan Kivar. His legs buckled under him, dropping him to his knees in the grass. His beloved was a demon, a shape-shifting creature from a nightmare. But she was still herself, still the angel who had saved him, who had loved him. And he loved her. May Christ save him. . . . The ground seemed to rise up to meet him as he felt himself fall into the dark.

9

The sun was high enough to light the clearing by the time Gareth opened his eyes. He heard horses, at least half a dozen, coming from the direction of the road. He leapt to his feet with surprising grace, considering his condition, and went back into the hovel, slamming the door behind him. Roxanna had not returned. He drew his sword and positioned himself just inside the door, pushing all thought of her out of his mind as he prepared to make a defense. If he were to find her and help her, he had to survive the next few moments.

He heard men's voices as the horses entered the clearing, footsteps drawing closer, swords being drawn from their scabbards, and he tensed. "Someone is here," he heard someone say in the lilting Gaelic he remembered from his childhood.

"Aye," another man answered. "But who?"

Before Gareth could try to identify the voices, the door was kicked open. He took a strong step forward, sword raised, and his blade made jarring contact with another held by a tall, broad-shouldered man with long red hair and beard. "Gareth!" the man said as he knocked him back with a parry that nearly sent him off his feet. "God's breath, boy, do you not know your own kin?"

Gareth froze, blinking, struggling to focus on the hulking shadow outlined in blazing daylight before him. "Brian?" The man took another step inside, dropping his sword, and Gareth smiled, elated with relief. His mother's cousin had changed very little since the last time he had seen him, fifteen years before. "It is you."

"Who else?" Brian said, embracing him. "Come out into the light so we can have a look at you." He looked around the tiny room as he put a beefy arm around Gareth's shoulders and led him outside. "He is alive," he announced to the others gathered there. "But only just, from the look of him."

"You should have seen me a week or so ago," Gareth answered. All of the men, nine by his count, seemed vaguely familiar to him, but they were clustered so closely together, it was hard to tell one from the other.

"I would have known him anywhere," another older man said with a grin. "He is the very picture of his mother."

"Aye, that he is," Brian agreed. "Excepting the beard, of course." His sharp eyes took in the bandages around Gareth's waist and the stitched gash visible through the opening of his blood-stained shirt. "What happened to you, lad?"

"I was attacked." Not all of the men were smiling, he noticed. But all of them were watching him with interest. "My companions were both murdered—Sir John of Leeds you know, and another knight, my cousin, Marcus."

"Did you see who attacked you?" Brian asked.

"No," Gareth answered. "But I can guess." One of the men hanging back unsmiling looked to be near Gareth's own age, slight of build with jet black hair and eyes. "Duncan?" he said, taking a step toward him. "Is it you?"

"Aye," the man answered as Gareth embraced him. As boys, he and Duncan had been inseparable, so close that Duncan's father had offered at the boys' insistence to keep Gareth as his foster son when his mother insisted on going to England. But now Duncan barely returned his hug before he moved away. "Well met, sir knight," he said, speaking the title like it tasted rotten in his mouth.

"When you didn't turn up as planned, the laird thought something wicked must have found you," Brian said, giving Duncan an unmistakably sour look. "He'll be pleased to have you safe home now."

"My home is in England," Gareth said, almost a reflex. Now that he didn't feel in peril of imminent attack, his mind wandered back to Roxanna and all that she had told him the night before. Where could she have gone? She had said she could not move about in the daylight, and he had seen himself how frightened she was at the prospect. Where would she have hidden herself now? "What of my uncle, Brian?" he asked. "Will he be glad to see me?"

"Jamey can't be glad nor sorry neither one," his elder cousin answered. "He's been dead these ten years past." Gareth looked at him, surprised.

"How is it you are still alive?" Duncan interrupted. "You said both of your companions were killed—who stitched that wound you carry?"

Gareth felt as if his head were spinning; there was too much to think about. His uncle was dead. Duncan apparently hated him for some reason he could not begin to guess. Roxanna was a demon called a vampire and meant to abandon him forever. "I don't know," he answered, deciding on caution until he sorted matters out. Roxanna had come out of a bottle dropped in the woods; chances were good his kin knew nothing of her. Chances were fair they should not. He loved Brian, and he respected his grandfather; 'twas why he had come. But he did not trust the clan. He indicated the bloodstains his love's tears had left on his shirt. "I came to myself as you see me."

"We saw the graves by the roadside," Brian said. "And the pyre." He paused, waiting for Gareth to comment, but Gareth said nothing.

"Perhaps he was saved by the Wee Folk," offered the man who'd said he looked like his mother. Several of the men laughed, but neither Brian nor Duncan joined them. Duncan muttered something under his breath and turned away. But Brian looked genuinely troubled.

"The laird sent us to find his grandson, and found him we have, may God be praised," he said. "However it is he has been spared, we must be grateful."

"Kyna might have nursed him," another man offered. "She has been seen in this valley."

"Aye," Duncan said, his eyes meeting Gareth's. "She would want to save you."

"Why should Kyna be here?" Gareth asked. He remembered Kyna well, the weird woman and midwife of the clan. She and his mother had been close. "Why is she not with the laird?"

"Your cousin Tess cast her out of the clan," the man who had mentioned Kyna said, giving Duncan a wary look.

"Cast her out?" Gareth echoed. Tess was his Uncle Jamey's daughter. She had been a child of eight when he and his mother had left the clan.

"She was conjuring black spirits in the laird's own hall," Duncan said angrily. "You all heard the priest when he was here. The creature was a witch."

"Duncan and Tess are betrothed," Brian explained. "As for Kyna, there'll be time enough to speak of her when we are safe at home." He put a hand on Gareth's shoulder. "The laird has had no peace in more than a week, fretting over you," he said. "If you truly mean to honor your promise to him, you must come." His grip tightened. "Now."

Gareth thought of Roxanna, his angel who called

herself a demon . . . kneeling naked in front of the fire, water pouring down her back . . . lying beside him on her pallet, talking, her head pillowed on her arm, the sweetness of her laugh . . . the rose-colored flush of her lips as she arched beneath him, calling out his name. He knew her as he had never known anyone else, woman or man, trusted her in spite of her terrible secret. Angel or demon, she was his heart's desire. Somehow he would find her. Somehow, once his grandfather was settled, he would save her from this Lucan Kivar and make her his forever.

He bent down and picked up the blanket that had covered her before she fled, her scent still clinging to its folds. "Come then," he said, straightening up with the blanket over his arm. "My grandfather is waiting."

Roxanna sat alone in the pitch-black darkness of a tiny cave, her back against the wall, her arms wrapped around her knees. A knot of aching grief was choking her, making her gasp for breath as if she needed it. But her eyes were dry.

When her mother had died, she had not wept. With a pride that befitted her title as princess, she had stood with her infant brother in her arms and watched the beautiful woman who had borne them wrapped in her own sort of swaddling. She was carried from the castle through a servant's passage to be buried like a slave, a concubine with status in neither her home nor her religion, and her daughter had not cried.

When her father was slaughtered by Lucan Kivar with all his knights and nobles, she had railed and shrieked in fury, bound to a column of jewels and gold where she could see it all. But she had not cried. Even when her own mortality was lost to save the life of the baby prince, she had faced the demon without flinching, swallowing her terror with her tears.

When her darling brother, her precious little Alexi, had died at last, she had wept for him, but only for a moment. There was no time; Kivar had been banished from his body, his vampire kingdom scattered. All she had wanted was rest, to escape the sadness once and for all. When Orlando had denied her that, she had gone into a bottle, a vapor without form, incapable of grief.

But for Gareth, she had wept. Wrapped in the arms of this mortal man who barely knew her, she had cried as if her heart would truly break. Every pain she had ever suppressed had seemed to rise up inside her at once, blinding her with sadness, tearing her cursed soul apart. And Gareth had held her. Even when she had told him the truth, even when he had seen the monster she was and remembered the evil he had seen her do, he had still wanted to hold her, still wanted to comfort her and keep her safe. But all she had to offer him was death. She could not cry to him anymore.

"What now, Orlando?" she said, speaking to the wizard who had taught her all that she knew of the world, the teacher who had abandoned her, willing or not. "What must I do now?" In all her mortal life, she had never known a purpose. She was a beautiful, useless thing with nothing to do but amuse the caliph and herself. As a vampire, she had found it much the same; all that had changed was her ruler and her appetites. It had pleased her to learn things because learning was diverting, but what good was her knowledge to her now? What good had it ever been? If she had been a man, she would have held power, been responsible for the safety of her people, and she would have failed—Kivar would have slaughtered her as well. But as a pretty princess, she could amuse him as she had once amused her father, decorate the palace he had stolen just as she had always done. Possession by pure evil had done little to damage her character; she had little character to damage.

Finding Gareth had given her purpose, though she hadn't known it at the time. Caring for him had distracted her from the wicked cycle of her endless, immortal life, and in his eyes she had seen a strange reflection, a new Roxanna like no one she had ever been before. To Gareth, she was not a demon but an angel. She was not a princess; the very idea had made him laugh. She was his savior and his love. Even when he knew the truth, he had still reached for her, still called her name as she left him. He had seen her as a woman, a creature like himself with a heart that could love and a will to go on. With him, she had wanted things, wanted them desperately—his life, his safety. His love. With him gone, there was nothing left to want.

She felt the daylight stupor leave her and knew it was night. The time had come to leave this valley, leave Gareth and continue on her quest. Her love was lost, but Kivar still lived. Taking a long, rattling breath, she made herself get up and leave the cave.

As soon as she stepped outside, she heard a heartbeat close by. For a moment, she thought Gareth had found her, and her own foolish heart flipped over. Then she saw the old woman standing in the shadow of the trees. She smiled as the vampire turned to her and bowed her head a moment in respectful greeting. "Fair evening, my lady," she said. "I am Kyna."

"Kyna." The woman was so stooped, for a moment she thought she was like Orlando, a dwarf. "And who is that?"

"I serve the young laird, your lover, and have done since he was a child." She drew closer, leaning on a twisted stick. "Though he knows it not." She smiled. Her face was wrinkled as old leather, her mouth pursed over toothless gums, but her eyes sparkled with life. She has eyes like Gareth, Roxanna thought, relaxing in spite of herself. "He has gone, my lady. His clan has come for him."

"His clan? Is he—?"

"He is well, my lady," the old woman hastened to assure her, holding up a hand. "They still serve the old laird for now and will not harm him. But he will have need of you soon."

"No, Kyna," Roxanna said, shaking her head. "Not me." It was strange; she felt as if the two of them were picking up an old acquaintance, returning to a conversation begun long ago. "If he is with his kin, he is safe now." Kyna surprised her with a bitter laugh. "Safer than he could ever be with me," she insisted. "I never should have wanted him at all."

"If you had not, he would be dead." The crone spoke to her with reverence, like a servant, but her familiar air was still rather disconcerting. "You could not let him die."

"Of course I could have." This must be the living creature she had sensed in the woods for days, the one who had left her clothes. "I have let others die." She fixed Kyna with a piercing gaze, letting her eyes go demonic for a moment. "Many others."

"But you will save so many more," the woman answered without so much as a blink. "You and the young laird. I have seen it."

"You sound like someone I knew once," Roxanna said, turning away. In truth, the creature reminded her very much of Orlando.

"You will find the Chalice." Roxanna turned back to her, shocked speechless. "But you must let young Gareth help you."

Roxanna resisted the urge to snatch the wizened little creature off her feet and merely circled her instead.

"You act as if you know me," she said, demonic persuasion creeping into her voice, subtle as the hissing of a snake. "Do you know what I am?"

Kyna trembled, but her voice was steady. "You are a child of the wolf, Kivar. He has given you his thirst for blood."

"Yes." How could this creature know aught of Kivar? She felt as if she had fallen into a dream.

"But you are a child of the Highlands as well," Kyna insisted.

"No, I am not." What was this place? She thought of Gareth saying he would save her, that he would fight Kivar on her behalf, and she shivered, feeling sick. By no means could she ever let that happen. Yet this strange, witchy creature seemed to be saying the same thing. "The wolf, as you call him, traveled far from your Highlands to make me."

Kyna smiled an enigmatic smile that reminded Roxanna even more of the dwarfish wizard she had lost. "And yet you have returned."

"Not by choice, Kyna." Orlando had brought her here, but why? And why had he abandoned her?

"And yet the young laird found you." Kyna reached out and touched Roxanna's arm as if she could not help herself, a tender, loving touch. "He has the mark, my lady. His mother knew it, just as the old laird knows. She should never have taken him away."

"You speak in riddles, old woman." She turned away

from her again, moving away from her touch. "I think you must be mad."

"You are not the first to think it." She laughed, a birdlike cackle. "I am mad, my lady. But I know the truth. I have the sight."

"What do you know of Lucan Kivar?" Fresh tears of blood had risen to her eyes without her realizing, and she dashed them away. "What is he to you?"

"All that is evil, just as he is to you. Just as he is to all." She moved closer again, reaching out as if she meant to touch Roxanna again, then letting her hand fall. "What is your name, my lady?"

"Roxanna." The crone looked filthy, but she smelled like the forest, fresh and sweet. "How have you heard of him?"

"He was born here in the Highlands. His father banished him, flung him across the sky." This time she took hold of the edge of Roxanna's sleeve with two fingers like a child who was afraid of the dark. "But now he has returned," she said, her voice trembling with fear. "He has come for the Chalice."

"How do you know this?" Roxanna said, making her voice gentle. "Have you seen him—not in your visions, but in truth?"

"No, my lady," Kyna said, shaking her head. "I hid when I knew he was near, hid in my cave where he could not smell my blood. But I felt him pass." Roxanna opened her hand, and Kyna put her own into it gratefully, clasping hard. "His stench lingers in the forest even now."

"Yes," Roxanna agreed. "I can smell it, too." The woman was mortal. She could hear her heartbeat, smell her blood. But she did not lie; she had a demon's sight. Roxanna had asked for a purpose; here it was. If this creature could tell her where to find Kivar, she must try to destroy him, try to finish Orlando's quest. He had told the same tale as this woman, of Kivar's birth in mountains far from Roxanna's home in the Urals, of his father, a pagan god, flinging him across the sky. "Can you tell me where he has gone?"

"Yes," Kyna answered eagerly. "I can take you there." She tightened her grip on Roxanna's hand. "But you must not go alone, Roxanna. We must go to the clan and tell them who you are."

"You are mad," Roxanna laughed.

"They are your people," the old woman insisted. "You must help your Gareth take his place as laird before you face Kivar. You must face the wolf together."

"No." She put her hands on Kyna's wrinkled cheeks as if the old woman was a child and she the elder. "Listen to me, Kyna. Gareth must never, never face Kivar. I will never let that happen."

"You are strong, my lady." Kyna smiled Orlando's rueful smile. "But you have not power over all that is."

"No, in truth, I do not," Roxanna agreed, letting her go. "But I still have power over myself." For the first time, she realized this was true. She was alone, subject to no other's will but hers for the first time in her life. As lonely and frightened as she was, she took a certain comfort in the thought. "I will not go to Gareth." Kyna frowned. "Not until Lucan Kivar is destroyed." For a single, dizzy moment, she let herself imagine this was true, that she could be free of Kivar and his curse, that she could return to Gareth the woman he had thought she was. That blissful thought alone was worth any danger she could imagine. "You call me your lady, Kyna." She offered her hand to the woman again. "Am I truly so? Will you help me?"

The weird woman seemed to debate with herself for a long moment. "Aye, my lady, Roxanna," she said at last. She took the vampire's hand. "I swear I will show you the way."

10

The fortress of the Clan McKail was not a castle by the Norman standard, but it was impressive nonetheless, its three stone towers rising from the craggy cliffs, black against the purple twilight. Tired and racked with pain from his long day in the saddle, Gareth still felt his heart lighten as he saw it. "My mother should be here," he said to Brian, who rode at his side.

"Aye, lad," his cousin agreed. "That she should." They should have arrived long since, but Gareth had been forced to stop and rest twice on the way, his wounds still too fresh for such a journey. As darkness fell, he noticed Brian and some of the other men drawing their mounts closer to his. "Not much farther now," Brian said with a cheerful smile, but Gareth could tell he was worried. Did he know who had attacked Gareth and his friends before? Did he fear them still?

He would have expected the village to have grown in his absence, but in fact it was smaller, the scattered sprawl he remembered now a single rough circle of cottages surrounded by a wooden stockade fence. The green was crowded with people as they rode in, some smiling, some with faces pale and drawn in the torchlight. "He lives!" he heard someone shout as the gates shut behind them, and there was a smattering of applause. But it was obvious not everyone was pleased.

They passed through another, stronger gate into a circle of stone to reach the laird's castle, a series of thatch-roofed wooden outbuildings arranged in a square courtyard with the oldest tower rising behind them, set slightly above on a cliff. Behind this, he knew, the cliffs dropped off sharply to the sea. He could hear the roar of the waves even now and smell the sharp salt in the air.

"Your grandfather will be wanting to see you first thing," Brian said. "Do you think you can manage?"

"Of course." He climbed down from his horse with gritted teeth, refusing to show just how much the effort hurt him. Roxanna would be horrified to see the damage he had done to her neat stitches on this ride.

Where was she now? he thought, following Brian and the others across the courtyard to his grandfather's house. She would think he had abandoned her, that all his talk of saving her had been a lie. She would think he was frightened of her, horrified of what she was. But soon he would be well again, well enough to go after her and this creature who had done her this wrong. He would save her from this evil curse, beg her forgiveness, and convince her he had never wanted to leave her at all. *But what if you cannot?* a voice that sounded suspiciously like Marcus whispered in his head. *What if she cannot be saved? Will you still love a demon?*

So lost was he in these thoughts, he passed through the doorway into the house almost without seeing it. "We've brought him, my laird," Brian said from close beside him, bringing him back to the present with a start. "He is safe."

When he was a boy, his grandfather had been a giant, his great presence looming over all in his keeping like the cliffs on which they lived. He was shocked now to see him rise slowly from his chair, a stooped old man, barely as tall as Gareth's own shoulder. "Grandfather," he said, bending knee to him with the slightest grimace of pain. "I have come as you commanded."

"And glad I am to know I can still command you," the laird answered, but the stern words were softened by the twinkle in his eyes. "Rise, my son." He offered his hand for assistance, and Gareth took it more for courtesy than any hope this old man could help him up. But Colm of McKain's grip was still strong, and he gave his grandson a tug that all but yanked him to his feet. "We're no English royals here," he scolded, drawing Gareth into his arms.

"No," Gareth agreed, shocked and appalled to feel tears rise in his eyes as he hugged him back. "But that is no bad thing." He drew back as his grandfather let him go and smiled. "I am glad to see you."

"As am I." The laird patted Gareth's cheek as if he

were a child, for all he had to reach up to do it. "Are you well?"

"I will be." The atmosphere in the room had relaxed the moment they embraced. The men who had ridden in with him had broken off and wandered to their own seats in the hall, and women moved forward quickly to serve them. Gareth saw Duncan cross the room to the archway that led to the laird's private quarters to meet a strikingly pretty young woman with shining red hair worn loose on her shoulders.

"Sit down, lad," his grandfather said. "Tell me how you were wounded."

"We were ambushed in our camp," Gareth answered, taking the chair opposite the laird.

"We?" the laird answered. "You did not come alone, then?"

"My cousin came with me." The old man's expression did not change, but his blue eyes darkened. "Marcus. And Sir John, my old tutor. They were both murdered, Sir John while he slept." He raised his tunic to show the wound in his stomach. "I was attacked from behind."

"Jesu." His grandfather whistled. " 'Tis a miracle you live, lad."

"He was saved by the Wee Folk," Brian said, coming to join them. He handed Gareth a bowl of stew that smelled delicious.

"I woke up in a hovel in the valley," Gareth corrected. "I do not know how I was brought there or who attended me." His grandfather's eyes were watching him sharply, and he turned his own gaze on his bowl. As a child, he had never been able to lie; his grandfather could dig the truth out of him with but one such look. But he wasn't a child any longer.

"The old shepherd's hut," Brian said.

"Did you see aught of anyone else when you found him?" the laird asked Brian, patting Gareth's knee.

"Not at the hut," Brian answered. "But someone had buried the dead English in proper graves and burned the brigands on a pyre." The memory Gareth had so recently regained of Roxanna slaughtering his attackers took the edge off his appetite. A vampire, he thought for what must have been the ten thousandth time since he woke that morning. She is a vampire. "Duncan believes 'twas Kyna who nursed Gareth," Brian went on, leaning closer and lowering his voice. "But she would have no more cause to bury the English than we—" He broke off, glancing at Gareth's face.

"Whoever buried young Marcus and good Sir John did us all a service," the laird said sternly, the tone of authority Gareth remembered still well intact in spite of his age. "Have no fear, laddie," he said to Gareth. "You will see your kin avenged."

For the second time, Gareth was embarrassed to feel his eyes filling with tears. He had convinced himself that he did not miss the Highlands, that he was as much an Englishman as any knight in his master's service. He could sneer at the rustic appointments of the hall; he could resent the chill of the welcome he got from Duncan and the others like him. But in his heart he knew no English lord would ever welcome him with the warmth he felt from his grandfather now. Even with half the clan stealing fish-eyed glances at him over their cups, he knew he would always belong here in a way he never had in France or even England. This was the home of his mother's blood and his father's heart. He might run from it; he might deny it. But it would always be his home as well.

"Why was Kyna banished?" he said aloud, changing the subject. "Duncan said she was conjuring spirits here in the hall."

"And so she was," his grandfather agreed with a wry smile. "She frightened your poor cousin half out of her wits with her talk." He looked past Gareth to the red-haired maiden. "Tess!" he called. "Come and greet your cousin."

"That is Tess?" Gareth asked Brian in an undertone, amazed. His cousin had been barely walking when he left, a cantankerous little creature with wispy hair whose face had always seemed to be sticky. The disappointment, he had always privately called her. If she had been born a boy the way she was supposed to be, his uncle would have had an heir, and Gareth's own father would have been safe.

The woman she had become turned toward them with a sweet smile on her face that looked rehearsed. She was pouring wine for Duncan, and he half rose from his seat as if to come with her. But she put a hand on his shoulder to press him down again, a small gesture Gareth would barely have noticed if he hadn't been watching her so closely. "Well met, cousin," she said, filling another cup from the flagon she carried as she came. She pressed it into his hand, then bent and pressed a dry, fleeting kiss to his cheek.

"Gareth has been sorely wounded," the laird told her. "He will need tending."

"Then we will tend him." Her eyes met Gareth's, and he saw a challenge there. "I hear tell you were taken by the fairies," she said. "Why did they give you back?"

"I wasn't taken by anyone," he answered. He was no master of intrigue, but even he could see she was no more happy to see him than her father would have been. And Duncan was in love with her. "Are you disappointed, Cousin Tess?"

"Only for you," she answered without so much as a blink. "I should like to see the fairies. They say they live in halls of gold and jewels." He sputtered over a sip of his wine, remembering Roxanna's description of her father's hall. Tess raised an eyebrow. "Is that not so, Grandfather?"

"You should not speak so lightly of the Good Folk, lass," their grandfather scolded, but he was smiling and reached for her hand. "Is Gareth's room prepared?"

"Of course." She held the laird's hand and smiled at Gareth, that same sweet, deadly smile.

"Take him there, then," the laird said.

"I will send a maid with him to put him right," she said, moving to obey.

"No," the laird said, catching her arm. "Tend him yourself."

She looked to Gareth as if he should know why she must, her green eyes narrowing in suspicion. "Aye, Grandfather," she answered. She leaned down and kissed the old man's cheek much more warmly than she had kissed Gareth. "As you will."

"I don't need tending," Gareth protested.

"Take some rest," his grandfather said. He took Tess's hand and put it into Gareth's. "We will speak more in the morning." He clasped both their hands together, and Tess bristled slightly, but she smiled.

"Good night, Grandfather," she said. "Come, cousin. I will tuck you in."

She led him to the rooms he remembered as the laird's private apartments when his grandmother was alive, a round room at the foot of the tower with a private stairway leading up and a trapdoor in the floor leading down. "We were afraid you might have been wounded," she said, closing the door behind them. "So I thought it best if you didn't have to climb the stairs."

"That was very kind." He sat down on the edge of the bed, feeling dizzy. In truth, he was exhausted and in pain. "But why should you think I was wounded?"

"Because you didn't come, of course." She dragged a small table over to the bed and put a basin and a basket on it. "And you are wounded, are you not?"

"Yes." She filled the basin from a pitcher on the hearth. "But I have been well tended."

"By whom?" She got down on her knees before him and began to unlace his boots, making him even more uncomfortable.

"I know not. I woke up alone." She pulled off one boot and started on the other. "Tess, you needn't bother."

"Did you not hear the laird command me to attend you?" she countered. "We have no fancy squires here." She straightened up and smiled, a more genuine but much less sweet smile than the one she had shown their grandfather. "Besides, your bandages need changing—you've bled through your shirt already." She took a roll of bandages from the basket. "If you die, I would rather not be blamed for it."

"From what I've seen, you might be praised." She reached for his shirt, and he quickly pulled it off himself, wincing as the drying blood pulled away from his wounds.

"Not by the laird, I would not be," she answered. She wet a rag in the basin and soaked the bandage on his stomach gently before peeling it away. "You look like your father."

"No, I do not." His father had been dark, with dark brown eyes. He had his mother's reddish blond hair and blue eyes. In truth, he looked more like this girl than he did his father.

"You are tall like he was," she said with a shrug. "I remember he was very strong."

"He was." His father had towered head and shoulders above most of the men in the clan. "I'm surprised you remember him. You were very young when he died."

"I remember him, though." She apparently knew her business. She cleaned the wound with a compress of sweet herbs and bound it up again in clean rags before moving to his back. "Kyna stitched you very well."

"What makes you think it was Kyna?" She was kneeling behind him on the bed, an intimate posture that made him suddenly aware they were alone in the room with the door latched.

"Who else?" she said with a laugh. "Unless it really was the fairies." This time when she pressed her compress to his wound, a burning pain shot through him, making him draw in his breath. "You will likely have a fever, cousin," she said. "The wound in your back is quite deep."

"That's because some coward ran me through from behind," he retorted. "But I've had a fever already." Not that this really made a difference, he thought. "Does our grandfather truly believe in the Good Folk, as he calls them?" he went on, changing the subject.

"You heard him," she answered. "He believes very many things that can't be true." She wrapped a wider swathe of bandages all the way around him, and the pain in his ribs lessened a bit, his breath coming easier. "He thinks he can give you the ruling of the clan, and you will keep us free of the English." She climbed down from the bed and moved where he could see her bitter smile. "For one example."

"I will not rule anyone." All he wanted was to lie down and sleep, to be back in the hovel with Roxanna where he could rest. But Roxanna was not what he had thought she was, and she had left him. And he had the feeling that this conversation with his cousin was important, that he would have but this one chance to make himself known to the clan. "I do not know what our grandfather intended when he sent for me," he said. "But I am sworn to service to an English lord." Her green eyes were guarded, as if she weren't quite certain she believed him. "You may trust me, cousin. I am going home."

"The laird believes you are home." She opened the shutters to let in a cool night breeze. "He will have his way in the end." She turned back to him and smiled, a sad smile that reminded him shockingly of his mother. "He always does." She lit a small lamp and set it beside the bed. "Do you need help with your hose?"

"No." She didn't sound quite so openly hostile, but he was not much encouraged. He had seen enough feminine intrigues at his English uncle's manor to know how deadly they could be. His cousin Tess was no lady of refinement, but she was obviously intelligent, and her pretty face would be enough to buy her influence with most any man she chose. If she truly bore him a grudge, he did not doubt she could hurt him just as well as any man. "Tess," he said, stopping her at the door. "How did your father die?"

"An accident." She opened the door. "The same as your own father did." Outside, he could hear singing from the hall. "Sleep well, cousin. Call if you need someone." Before he could answer, she was gone.

He lay back against the pillows, letting his body relax. Outside the window, he could see the moon rising through the branches of the trees at the foot of the hill, a perfect orb of gold. A month ago, he had been in England, standing guard duty under the full moon, a knight with neither property nor cares beyond staying awake for his watch. How had he found himself here?

He thought of Marcus, dead and buried with no marker but his own sword. Marcus had died for him. If he had been there, he could have sorted out the clan's fears in an hour and charmed Tess out of her shift in the bargain. But Gareth had never had the mind for diplomacy or politics. He was a plain soldier, nothing more. And Marcus was dead.

I buried him, of course, Roxanna had said. *Who else could have done it?* She had called herself a demon, had sworn she must leave him for his own good, that she could bring him nothing but evil and pain. Yet she had saved him from those who would have murdered him—to feed, she had insisted. She had kept him alive, tending his every need like the basest of slaves, she who had been born a princess. To drink his blood, she said. But she had never done it. And what part of her own survival did she ensure by giving Marcus and Sir John a proper burial? What evil purpose did that mercy serve?

He turned his face into the pillow, remembering the smell of her skin, the way she had clung to him and called his name as he made love to her. She might be this cursed, demonic thing she called a vampire. But she was not evil. "I will save you, sweetheart," he whispered to the darkness. "I will find you and keep you safe, just as I promised." Remembering her tears, he felt his heart clench in his chest. "I will find you," he repeated, drifting into sleep.

11

Three vampires on horseback stopped at the crest of a hill, looking down on a vast, black Scottish loch. "Holy mother," their leader, a massive lion of a knight, said softly. "What have they done?"

"What is it?" said the second, a fine-boned female with glossy black hair and huge blue eyes, as she drew up beside her husband. Then she saw. "Oh, no."

The third said nothing, his beautiful face blank with shock. "Simon?" the woman, Siobhan, said as she reached out to touch his arm. He spurred his own horse hard without answering, galloping down the hill.

Simon, Tristan, and Siobhan had tracked Lucan Kivar and his minions for weeks, and in truth, it had hardly been a challenge. The ancient demon, safe inside the living body of Siobhan's brother, Sean, had moved openly in daylight, provisioning his cursed legion from the villages they passed like any conquering lord. Most of the people the vampires questioned believed him to be an English noble with new Scottish lands to tame—they didn't rejoice to see him, but they were not surprised. One old dame had spoken to Siobhan of "his lady wife," a beautiful woman with long red hair. "Dying, she was," the peasant woman had confided. "Any fool could see it." But Siobhan had chosen to keep this particular clue to herself. And many spoke of the dwarf who traveled with them, tied to his pony like a captured beast.

At first, their trail had led steadily northward, across Scotland into the Highlands. Once in the mountains, they had come upon a pile of burning corpses, marked with a skull pinned to a tree with a sword, and two neater graves, one marked with an English broadsword. But none of the corpses had been familiar to Siobhan as brigands she had led once with her brother, now as possessed as their captain but by lesser demons, minions of Kivar. They had all sensed Kivar's lingering presence at the site, and Simon thought he felt the presence of another vampire. But they had seen no further sign of one, and the trail of their quarry had clearly led on.

Two nights later, it had turned sharply west, away from roads and villages, straight down the mountainside. Every hour they expected to overtake their quarry—surely such a large force must slow down on such terrain, and the trail always looked fresh. And now, at moonrise on the second night, it seemed at last they had found them. The trail ended in this lake, but the force they pursued had not sailed across it. They had ridden straight into the water.

"Simon!" Siobhan called, plunging down the hillside

with Tristan in pursuit. Her first thought was to stop her friend before he saw something he shouldn't. But when she reached the water's edge, she realized her own loss might be worse. "Sean," she said softly, a despairing moan. The corpses of men and horses littered the shoreline, washed back by the gentle tide. Barely aware of what she was doing, she slid down from her mount and waded into the water, a vampire's tears of blood pouring down her cheeks.

The flanks of the horses were bloody, as if their riders had beaten them to force them into the lake. One poor beast's throat had been slashed. But the men seemed utterly serene, their eyes wide and staring in death but without so much as a grimace on their faces to show pain or even fear. "How could they?" she said, falling to her knees beside a man she had known since childhood, a huntsman who had taught her how to shoot her bow. "Why would they do such a thing?"

"They were possessed by Kivar and his demons," Simon said. Unlike the others, he had tracked Kivar for more than ten years. No horror the monster could devise could shock him anymore. "They could not stop themselves."

"But why?" She closed the dead man's eyes. "Why should Kivar want to drown them? Why take them if he meant them all to die?"

"To put us off his trail," her husband, Tristan, answered. Wading out to the tops of his boots, he could see other bodies under the crystal clear water, carried to the bottom by their armor. Bloated corpses of other horses floated like islands on the surface of the center of the lake. "He made them ride west," he said, turning back to his love, his face the mask of stone she knew hid deep grief. "Straight west until they drowned."

She closed her eyes, but she could not shut out the image from her mind. "Do you think they knew what was happening?" She had known these men all her life, had fought beside them since she was twelve years old. "Do you think they were afraid?"

Tristan came back to her and raised her to her feet. "I couldn't say, love," he answered, drawing her into his arms. "I don't know."

Simon took a long, shuddering breath. "I am sorry, Siobhan." Sometimes he thought all he ever did was beg forgiveness, never expecting to receive it. Nothing he could do or say could ever make his evil right again. Both of these vampires were of his making—he had made Tristan by accident, and Tristan had made Siobhan. "I led Kivar to you and to your brother."

"No." She pressed a kiss to Tristan's throat before she left his embrace. "I don't believe you did." She wiped away her tears and drew a short but lethal sword from the scabbard on her belt. "I have had this sword since I was a child, remember? The sword that can wound a vampire—the sword from the same drawing you have of the Chalice. I found it years before you ever came back to Britain. Who knows how long it was buried under the druid's tower on my father's lands, the ancestral lands of my family? Kivar was meant to find us, just as he was meant to find you and your Isabel." The lady the peasants took for Kivar's wife was actually Simon's, his mortal beloved. Like Siobhan, she had grown up on a castle built over ancient ruins that held signs and records of Kivar's evil from centuries ago. Siobhan turned and took her own husband's hand. "Just as you were meant to find my Tristan and stop him from dying. None of this is an accident."

"I've never been much of a believer in prophecy," Tristan said. When Simon had first told him of the Chalice that could restore them to humanity and somehow destroy Kivar, he had been hard pressed not to laugh at him, and Simon knew it. "But I know that sword of hers is real." He looked back out at the lake and the men who were drowned in it. "Sean isn't here, love," he finished, squeezing Siobhan's hand. "Kivar is still inside him, and Kivar is not here."

For a moment, Simon looked as if he would argue, then he nodded, understanding dawning in his eyes. "A diversion."

"And he would keep Isabel with him." He looked back in the direction they had come, scowling. "Of course, we have no way of knowing where they went."

Siobhan let go of Tristan's hand and took a few wandering steps along the shoreline. "Do you hear that?" The bank had been churned to slippery mud under her feet, making her walk daintily to keep her balance, the sword she still held poised before her.

"Hear what?" Tristan said, following her with a bit less grace.

"A voice." She waded a step out into the water "I hear a man's voice in the water."

Simon paused, listening as well. "Orlando." He sprinted past his companions, stripping out of his chain mail shirt as he went, and dove into the water.

The wizard was still tied to his pony, the poor little beast tied to the horse that had walked before him, both now drowned at the bottom of the lake a few scant feet from shore. Immortal as the vampires, Orlando couldn't drown, but he couldn't break free of his bonds, either. Simon broke the leather straps that held him with his bare hands and dragged him sputtering to the surface.

"It is Orlando," Siobhan said, astonished, as Tristan waded out to help.

"Where is she?" Simon was already demanding, all but shaking the dwarf as he set him on his feet.

"Northeast," Orlando managed to say between hacking coughs that brought up what looked like buckets full of water.

"Give him a moment, Simon," Tristan urged, knocking the little wizard gently on the back.

"No," Orlando said, shaking his head. "No time . . ." Leaning on Tristan's arm for support, he brought up another racking cough. "The creature means to take her to the source." He straightened up, looking at Simon. "She is not well, my friend. But she is alive."

"The source?" Siobhan said, bringing a blanket from her saddle to wrap around Orlando's shoulders. "The source of what?"

"The place Kivar was born." The dwarf smiled briefly at her, patting her hand in gratitude, but his manner was still grave. "The source of his power." His eyes met Simon's. "The first gateway to the Chalice."

Tristan was still looking out at the lake. "How long were you—" he began, then stopped, shaking his head. "Never mind." Typically unmindful of the wizard's dignity, he scooped him up under his arm as he would have his own little daughter and headed for his horse.

"Tristan, what are you doing?" Siobhan said, but Simon was smiling.

"The wizard said northeast." He set Orlando on the saddle and swung up behind him. "Let us go."

Roxanna stood upon a frozen plain, staring up at a pair of massive obelisks of stone. Together they formed a kind of gateway into what was once a circular grove of oak trees. But now the trees were dead, nothing but mottled black trunks with branches like the bony fingers of a witch. Each tree was covered completely with a layer of crystal-clear ice. It had taken them three days to reach this place. They had passed through a seaside village that had been frozen over as well, houses and people and fences and even livestock encased in glassy ice. "What has done this?" she asked Kyna.

"The ancient gods," the weird woman had answered, crossing herself as they passed close to a man and his dog, both of them frozen in an attitude of terror, the man kneeling with his hands upraised, the dog crouched snarling on his belly. "The same as flung Kivar away."

A winding path had led from the village up a hillside of jagged ice, and she had seen fresh footprints in the snow. But here at the gateway and beyond, the wind had swept the ice as clean as freshly polished marble. "You are sure Kivar came here?" Roxanna asked. She could smell blood on the air, but the roar of the wind made it impossible to hear anything beyond the gateway, and the swirl of snow in the darkness was blinding, even to her demon's eyes.

"This is the gateway to the Old Ones," Kyna answered. The old woman must have been freezing, but she did not betray so much as a shiver. "This is the way to the Chalice." Roxanna reached for a burning torch that was mounted on one of the obelisks, and the old woman caught her arm. "You must not go alone, my lady." Her grip was like the talons of an eagle. "You must go back for your love."

"No love of mine will come to such a place." She met Kyna's gaze until the mortal woman looked away.

"As you will, my lady." She let her go.

"Wait for me here." She took down the torch, a shiver racing up her arm as soon as she touched it. She had expected it to be made of wood, but in fact it was metal, so cold it burned her skin. But the tip was burning. "Demon magic, no doubt," she said, trying to laugh. But in truth, the longer she stood in this gateway, the more uneasy she felt. It felt familiar somehow, like a recurring nightmare.

She stepped through the space between the obelisks, and the ground rumbled beneath her feet. A crack opened up in the ice before her, and she struggled not to fall, praying this plain was not really a lake, waiting to swallow her up. As a vampire, she didn't think she could drown, but the idea of being trapped under ice for all eternity was more than she cared to imagine. But after a moment, the rumbling stopped, and the ground seemed stable again. She swung the torch before her, turning in a circle, but now that she was inside the frozen grove, she could see no more than a few feet before her in any direction. The trees and even the gateway had disappeared in swirling white. She thought she remembered which way she had come, but she couldn't even be certain of that.

"Lovely," she muttered, moving in what she hoped was a forward direction. If Lucan Kivar really was here, she hoped he was as blind as she; otherwise, she was done for. Not for the first time, she wished she had thought to steal one of Gareth's weapons when she left him. She had stopped along the way and made a fairly lethal-looking stake, and she drew this from her belt with the hand not holding the torch. But how she would see to wield it was more than she could guess.

A dozen or so steps farther, she tripped over the first

corpse. The man's throat had been torn open, his flesh drawn and wrinkled as if every drop of blood had been drained from his body. Among the hundreds of vampires she had seen since she was cursed, only Kivar could have fed so thoroughly. Suppressing a shudder, she crouched beside the dead man and touched his face. He was cold, but his skin was still supple. Whatever had killed him had not been gone for long. She picked up her stake again and made herself go on.

Moving forward against the wind, she found another body, then another and another until she seemed to be following a trail of the dead. She counted six corpses, stopping to examine each. The sixth was still warm. "Where are you, Kivar?" she whispered, the words snatched from her lips by the wind. If her vampire maker were close, he could hear her thoughts; there was no use to be silent. The smell of blood was stronger, she realized, though it could not have come from any of these men. She closed her eyes for a moment, reaching out with her vampire's senses, trying to shut out the sound of the wind. Dropping the torch but opening her eyes again, she took another step forward, reaching out before her. Just ahead of her, she saw a dark shape, a long, flat surface rising like an altar from the ground.

Suddenly she heard movement from close beside her. Whirling fast as lightning, she caught hold of what felt like a man, driving him to the ground with her stake held high almost before her eyes opened. "Wait!" he shouted, prone beneath her, but she barely heard his voice. Only when the stake was poised a scant inch over his breast did she hear his heartbeat. "Mercy," he begged. "Please . . ." His words trailed off into a fit of violent coughing, but there was no mistaking that he was alive.

His hair and beard were blond, she saw, still crouched above him, and his eyes were blue. "Who are you?" she demanded, the point of the stake still touching his chest. His clothes were soaked with blood—this was what she smelled. She could hear his heartbeat like thunder now, racing with fear. "Answer me!"

"Sean," he said, shaking so much from either cold or fear she could barely understand him. "My name is Sean Lebuin."

"How did you come here?" For one long, strange moment, she had the nearly irresistible urge to drive the stake into his heart, mortal man or not. But that was madness—if he was mortal, he must be Kivar's victim, not a demon.

"I know not." She withdrew the stake slowly, and he let out a long, slow breath. "But please, my lady," he said, sitting up as she backed away. "Please help us." One of his wrists was clumsily bandaged with rags; the other still bled.

"Where is Lucan Kivar?" she asked. The snow was not falling so thickly, she realized; the clouds above them were opening, letting in the moonlight. A bluish beam fell on his face, and again, she felt the urge to strike out at him. But there was no reason; he seemed frightened and confused, barely coherent. Hardly dangerous.

"Was that the creature's name?" he said, his eyes meeting hers. "I barely saw him before . . . it is like a dream." He rose to his feet, and she followed, still keeping the stake at the ready. "I can hardly remember." He looked around as if trying to find his bearings. "I saw it for just a moment before it disappeared in the snow—it had the shape of a man." He suddenly turned and grabbed her arm, making her tense. "My sister," he said, clutching her, desperation plain in his eyes. "We must help her." He staggered as if about to swoon, and she caught him, dropping the stake. "Please," he said, still holding her fast. "She is sorely wounded, but she lives. I lost her in the snow." He looked around wildly. "I have to find her."

"Hush." The wind was dying down. She could hear another heart, much more weak than this Sean's, but still beating. "Come," she said, leading him with her as she went toward it. She could see the trees again, making a circle around them. At the center was the altar she had barely made out before, a table of black stone, and lying on the ground before it was a woman, curled on her side with her long red hair spread around her.

"The creature who brought us here did this to her," Sean explained. "Not a man—I don't know what it was."

"I know." Roxanna bent down beside the woman

and turned her face gently toward her. She was pale as the snow; even her lips looked blue.

"Her name is Siobhan," Sean said. "Please, my lady . . . she is all I have."

Roxanna thought he would not have her much longer, but she had the grace not to say so aloud. The woman's wrists had been opened, soaking the ground all around her with blood.

"Where is this place, my lady?" Sean asked. "Who are you?"

She looked up at him, feeling pity she didn't want to feel. "My name is Roxanna," she said. "But I have never been to this place before either." She raised the woman's head and propped her against her own shoulder, slapping her gently but getting no response. "Kyna!" she called. "Can you hear me?"

The old woman was already hurrying toward her. "I am here."

"Come and help." Still cradling the woman's head in her lap, she turned to Sean. "Did Kivar attack you?"

"No," he answered, then looked down at the blood on his clothes. "At least, I don't remember if he did. There's so much I can't remember."

"Bind his other wrist, Kyna," Roxanna ordered. "He seems able to walk."

"I am fine, my lady," he promised. He reached out and touched his sister's cheek, and she moaned, turning her head and muttering something Roxanna couldn't understand. "Only Siobhan matters." A strange, haunted light had come into his eyes that did not seem entirely brotherly to Roxanna. "She must live."

"We must take them back to the clan," Kyna said. "The laird will take them in."

"The clan?" Sean echoed, his head snapping up.

The clan was where Gareth had gone. Kyna had shown her the turning in the road that led to their fortress, the castle ruled by Gareth's grandfather. "Is it far?" she asked.

"No, my lady," Kyna answered. "The Clan McKail lives in the shadow of this mountain."

"The Clan McKail?" Sean said. "The clan still lives." His face broke out into a smile for a moment, fading so quickly Roxanna could not interpret what it meant. "God's light," he swore, meeting the vampire's eyes with his. "They are kin to us." Kyna had finished binding his wrist, and he flexed his fingers. "Our mother's people traced their line back to the Highlands." He looked around again in wonder. "How can we have come so far?"

"You would know better than I," Roxanna said with an edge in her tone. "Take them back, Kyna." She shifted the dying woman from her arms to her brother's, and she moaned, a soft word that could have been a name. "Take them to your clan," the vampire said, standing up.

"My lady, no," Kyna protested, following her as she walked away. "You must come with us—"

"I can do nothing for that woman." The snow had

stopped falling altogether, and the wind had died down, leaving them at the center of an eerie hall of ice. She could see now that the trail of corpses she had followed led in a straight path from the obelisks to the altar. "Where are you, Kivar?" she said, burning with rage in spite of the cold.

"The woman can tell you," Kyna insisted. "Save her, and she will lead you to the wolf."

"You told me he would be here," Roxanna said, turning to her. "Why should I believe you?"

"He was here, my lady." The crone faced her with no sign of fear, the absolute faith of a seer burning in her eyes. "Do you doubt it?" Once again, Roxanna was reminded sharply of Orlando.

"Please," Sean called to them from the altar. "She is dying." He broke off, his words lost in another racking cough.

"Do you think we will make it back to the clan without your help?" Kyna said. "The woman will surely die, perhaps her brother, too."

"I don't care," Roxanna insisted, but that was a lie. The very idea that Kivar would snatch two more lives away from her, even these strangers, was more than she could stand. Her father and his court, her precious Alexi . . . all dead, no matter how she fought to save them.

"The man says he does not remember, but his sister will," Kyna pressed on. "If she lives, she will know where he has gone."

"She will know if he has found the Chalice," Roxanna said, more to herself than to Kyna. Surely that was what this carnage meant; surely Kivar had used these mortals somehow to find the relic.

"He has not," Kyna said, cutting into her thoughts. She smiled. "I promise you, my lady. The Chalice is still safe." She put a hand on the vampire's arm. "Come with me to the Clan McKail. We can save this woman. We can destroy the wolf."

"No," Roxanna said, shaking her head, but in truth, she was weakening. She had expected to destroy Kivar or be destroyed in the attempt, not end up nursemaid to more mortals. Now to save them, she would have to follow Gareth, the one thing she had sworn she would not do. But what choice did she have? She walked back to the dying girl and looked down at her face, so innocent and pale, freckles sprinkled on her cheeks. No doubt Kivar had found rare sport with her before he left her to bleed to death in the snow.

"She can still be saved, my lady," Kyna said as if she heard Roxanna's thoughts. "She can lead you to Kivar."

The man was looking up at her, his face impossible to read. "Come, Sean Lebuin," she said, kneeling beside them to pull one of the girl's arms over her own shoulder and putting her other arm around her waist. "You will have to help me carry her."

12

For two days and nights, Gareth had slept almost without waking, his broken body finding rest to heal at last. His dreams were broken by visions of the brigand attack, Marcus lying dead at his feet, and of Roxanna in the hovel, her beautiful face gazing up at him in love. Most of all, he dreamed of a vast, white field of snow and a circular grove of dead, black trees. In his dream, he was standing at the center of the grove before an altar of silver stone. Sometimes he was alone; sometimes he was surrounded by others. Once he looked down to find the sleek black panther that was his demon lover standing at his heel like a familiar, her long, white fangs exposed as she snarled at something he could not see. He woke from that dream to find his cousin, Tess, standing by the open window in a flood of golden sunlight with her back to the bed where he lay, but when he tried to speak to her, he fell asleep again.

The third morning, he woke with the sun. His joints were stiff, but when he sat up and swung his legs over the side of the bed, his head felt clear. He stood up slowly, scratching an itch on his chest where his wounds were healing, and walked to the window. He opened the shutter, a brisk, cold wind sweeping the last of the dreamy cobwebs from his mind. A spattering of snowflakes swirled around him—the first snow of winter. A cow stood just outside the window, gazing back at him in perfect serenity, and a flock of geese were quarreling their way around the corner. It seemed he would live after all.

He dressed himself in the clothes that had been left for him, the long tunic and breeches of his Scottish kin. His beard was long and rough like a Scotsman's, too—he would have to ask for a razor. His sword had been left propped by the door, and he buckled that on as well.

When he opened the door, he was nearly crushed by Brian; the massive warrior was snoring in a chair propped precariously against it, his arms crossed on his chest. Between Gareth's quick catch and his own flailing, he managed to stay upright, but it was a near thing for a moment. "Good morning, cousin," Gareth said with a grin as he levered him onto his feet.

"Ah, so you're awake, then," Brian answered as if nothing were amiss. "I'd begun to think you'd died in there, and young Tess feared to tell it." Before Gareth could answer, he clapped him on the shoulder hard enough to have made him stagger even if he'd been completely healed. "Come. You'll need your breakfast."

The household was just beginning to gather in the hall, some of the men obviously just coming in from a night guarding the walls. Brian commandeered two loaves of bread and a jug of milk from one of the trestle tables before it was properly set. "Fresh air is what you're needing," he said, motioning for Gareth to follow him into the courtyard.

Gareth took the jug as soon as they had settled on a bench near the kitchen garden, draining it halfway in his first long drink. "I'm starving," he admitted, handing it back to Brian and wiping his mouth.

"I doubt it not." His cousin tore off one end of a loaf and handed over the rest. "By my reckoning, you starved for more than a week if you were just waking when we found you."

"I had been awake." As a mischief-prone squire, he had faced this kind of questioning enough to know it when he heard it. "Someone had left me food."

"Someone," Brian echoed.

"Kyna, I suppose," Gareth offered.

"Kyna would never have left you." He took his own swallow of milk before handing the jug back as well. "And she would have done a neater job of bandaging your wounds."

Gareth shrugged, taking a deliberately oversized bite from the loaf. "Then perhaps it wasn't Kyna after all."

"Aye," Brian nodded. "Mayhap it was not." He sat in companionable silence and watched as Gareth devoured the rest of the first loaf and started on the second. "I do wonder where this angel of mercy might be now."

Gareth choked a bit on his milk. "Aye, Brian," he answered. "So do I." The worst of his hunger sated, he set the jug aside. "Tess doesn't seem so glad to see me," he said, changing the subject.

Brian grinned. "Tess is a good girl." He reached into his pocket and took out a lump of cheese wrapped in cloth and pared off a slice with his dagger. "The laird requires much of her, I think." He offered a slice to Gareth.

"She keeps his house?" Gareth said, taking it.

"Aye, and has done since she was a girl," Brian said with a nod. "Her mother ran off when her father died, back to her own kin. 'Twas right glad she was to be free of the burden of him, I think."

"But now Tess is betrothed to marry Duncan." Gareth's mother had often said that Brian could tell the history of the world, given a lifetime to do it.

"So they say," he nodded. "But they are not married yet."

"The laird does not approve the match?" Gareth asked, surprised. Duncan's father had always been one of his grandfather's most trusted retainers.

"The laird keeps his own counsel," Brian said. "But no, he has not given his consent." He offered the cheese again, but Gareth shook his head. "Many in the clan would be glad to see them married. The laird is old; people worry who will take his place when he dies. And Duncan is a good man, no question." He wrapped the cheese and put it away, sheathing the dagger as well. "But some would rather not be ruled by Tess."

"The succession is not necessarily tied to blood," Gareth pointed out. "Another man could step up, if the clan should approve."

"Aye, lad, but who?" Gareth raised an eyebrow, and he laughed. "Nay, not me," he said, shaking his head. "I've no stomach to rule. And besides . . ." His voice trailed off for a moment as his expression turned serious again. "What did your mother tell you of the line, Gareth?"

"Nothing," Gareth answered. "She knew I meant to stay in England." In truth, she had all but made him promise that he would, but he would not tell Brian as much, particularly when he seemed ready to say Gareth should inherit his grandfather's seat. "Brian, no one in the clan would ever accept me as laird—nor should they. I don't know why my grandfather ever said it when I was a boy." It was a testament to the trust he felt for Brian that he went on. "If he had not, my father might still be alive."

"He might indeed," Brian said with a nod. He reached out and gave Gareth's knee a squeeze, a gesture inherited from his uncle, the laird. "But the laird had no choice." Without warning, he caught hold of Gareth's wrist and pushed up his sleeve. "'Twas you who had the mark."

"What are you saying?" He looked down at his bare forearm, the underside turned up in Brian's grip. "What mark?" He had borne two irregular clusters of brownish purple freckles there since birth, but they weren't particularly remarkable—his mother had similar spots on her throat. "You don't mean this."

"Aye." Brian bent down and picked up a scrap of the charcoal that had been dumped in the garden to fertilize the cabbages and began to draw lines on Gareth's skin, connecting the spots into a rough design. The cluster near the bend of his elbow became a cross, thicker at two ends. The cluster just below his wrist looked like a cup when Brian's drawing was done. "I do mean that."

Gareth met his cousin's eyes, waiting for him to laugh. "You can't be serious. What is that meant to be, Brian?"

"Do you not see it?" his cousin said with a frown. "You bear the mark of the Chalice."

"Aye," Gareth nodded. "And the stars make dragons in the sky. But no sensible person expects them to breathe fire." He couldn't believe this wasn't some elaborate joke, that Brian wasn't teasing him somehow.

"A sensible person can sometimes be a fool," Brian answered, not returning Gareth's grin. "Did your mother tell you nothing of your people?"

"My mother told me my father was murdered by my people," Gareth answered, standing up. "So I chose not to have them as my people anymore."

"Your father was killed by a boar, lad," Brian said, standing up as well. "I was there beside him. I saw the spear he carried break."

"And why should it have done?" Gareth demanded.

"Because God willed it so. Because wood breaks, lad." He put a hand on Gareth's arm. "I love your mother dearly, and your father was my friend. If anyone had murdered him, do you think I would have let it pass?"

"If the murderer was your kinsman?" Gareth countered.

"You are my kinsman, Gareth, the same as Jamey was," Brian said, his bushy eyebrows drawn together in an angry frown. "More than that, you were the laird's choice to succeed him, and you were your father's son. I would have given my own life to let you keep him, would have risked more than the wrath of a discontented cripple to avenge his death." His grip on Gareth's arm had tightened painfully, but now he let him go. "If you don't know that much at least, I cannot help you."

"Gareth!" Tess was calling from the causeway to the tower. "The laird would have you come to him." Her voice sounded rough, as if she might have been crying, and she made no move to come closer.

"Aye, lady," Gareth called back. "I will come." This time it was he who caught hold of Brian's arm as he moved to turn away. "Forgive me," he said, meeting the other man's gaze. "I have never doubted your love, Brian; no more do I now."

Brian smiled. "Aye, lad. I know you do not." He gave Gareth's shoulder another bone-shuddering pat. "But come. We must not keep McKail waiting."

Once they reached the hall, Brian left him to follow Tess up the winding stairs alone. "You are better, I see," she said without looking back at him.

"I am." He expected her to stop on the second floor or at least the third, but she continued up the smaller, tighter wooden stairs that led to the watch room. "Tess, where are we going?"

"Our grandfather makes his room here now," she answered. " 'Tis a feature of his madness." Stopping at the closed door at the top of the stair, she had no choice but to face him, and he saw that her eyes were red and swollen. "But we must all pretend we don't notice he is mad."

"Tess, what is it?" He put a hand on her arm, and she flinched, looking down at it as if it were a snake that had fallen on her. ""Why do you hate me?" He remembered pulling her hair a time or two when they were children, but Duncan had put frogs down her dress as a regular entertainment, and she meant to marry him. "How do you think I have wronged you?"

"Stop lurking out there and come inside," the laird's voice called sharply through the door. Giving him a wry half smile, Tess pushed it open and led the way into the room.

When Tess had said the laird was mad, he had thought she was angry with him, not that he was actually insane. But one look around the watch room was enough to make it perfectly clear what she had meant. All of the heavy shutters had been bolted back, opening the room on all four sides to the gusting winter wind and flurries of snow. Any wall space remaining was covered with bits of rotting tapestry and ragged scraps of parchment, all pinned haphazardly to the finer tapestries someone had hung in an obvious effort to make the room habitable. The laird's huge, carved bed had somehow made it up the stairs and was made up in its usual splendor, the rough wooden floor had been covered with a carpet, and a comfortable-looking armchair was set in the least windy corner, a rich wool blanket thrown over its back and a cushion on its seat. But McKail sat on a three-legged stool at a crooked plank table, so cracked and dented it looked as if it belonged in the armory. This was covered with books and scrolls and strange metal instruments Gareth couldn't begin to identify. A set of mystic's bones had been thrown at the center, and these held the laird's attention. Indeed, he was bent over them so closely, his nose was nearly touching the table.

"Build up the fire, Tess," he ordered without looking up. "We don't want Gareth taking a chill."

"I can do it," Gareth offered, glad for something to do with his hands while his mind worked through what he was seeing. He had never known his grandfather to be a scholar or a mystic either one. He was a warrior, a plainspoken, pragmatic leader of men. A man could change with time, he supposed, particularly in his later years. But he began to think his cousin might be right.

"As you will, lad," the laird said as Gareth poked the

fire back into a blaze and threw on another log. "Tess, you may go."

"No, I will not," she protested.

"The matter is settled," the laird said, looking up at last to glare at her. "Go and do what must be done."

She was obviously trembling with the need to say more, but she kept her lips pressed shut. Bobbing Gareth an unmistakably mocking curtsy, she turned and fled the room, her running footsteps pounding away down the wooden stairs. "What must be done?" Gareth asked, keeping his tone mild.

"She must speak to Duncan," his grandfather answered, pushing back his stool. "He will be unhappy, too, I imagine." He gave the bones a final glance. "But it can't be helped." He scooped them up in his fist and stuffed them into a rotting velvet bag.

"Why will Duncan be unhappy?" He didn't want to take the armchair while his grandfather sat on a stool, so he dragged an empty chest closer to the table and sat on that instead. "For that matter, why is Tess? She acts as if I poisoned her cat."

"Tess is afraid of cats," the laird said with a smile—informative, no question, but hardly to the point. "But she'll get used to you in time." Gareth's thoughts must have shown on his face, because his grandfather suddenly sobered. "I know," he said in a tone of confession. "I know, lad." He filled a cup with wine and drained it. "Forgive me—time is running short." He looked down at the cup for a moment as if it held the secrets of the spheres. "Show me the mark," he ordered, setting it aside.

"Do you mean this?" Gareth held out his arm, Brian's rough drawings now smeared but still clear enough to see. "Grandfather, this is nothing. You could draw anything between these spots."

"You think so?" the laird said, now bending over Gareth's forearm the way he had bent over the bones. He traced the lines Brian had made, nodding in satisfaction. "Then why is it I have the same?" He bared his own arm to show the same natural markings. On his, the spots had been joined with paint forced under the skin to make a pagan tattoo. The shape of the cup was much clearer, and Gareth could see the cross was made from a sword and a rough stake of wood. But underneath, the natural markings looked as random and benign to Gareth as his own.

"Because you are my grandfather," he said. "I have your nose as well." This earned him a smile, and he returned it, feeling a bit less like he'd wandered into someone else's dream. "Is this the reason I was summoned?" he asked. "This mark?"

"This mark is the reason your mother never should have taken you from the clan in the first place," his grandfather answered, standing up. "But after what happened to your father, I thought perhaps she was right, that you would be safer far from here until your time had come." He went to the southward window.

"Grandfather, I cannot stay here," Gareth said, joining him. "Not if I have a map of the Highlands on my arm and the Holy Land on my arse. I am sworn to serve an English knight—"

"Then you will be forsworn." This was the tone he had used with Tess, and Gareth didn't like it any better than she did. "Where is your mother now?"

"In a convent." Looking down, he saw the rocky beach, the height of the tower tripled by the height of the cliffs below, and he closed his eyes, feeling dizzy. "She took the veil when I was made a knight."

"Hiding," his grandfather scoffed. His pale blue eyes seemed to search the distant horizon, sharp as starlight even now. "Though I shouldn't blame her." He turned his gaze on Gareth. "She explained nothing to you, I suppose."

"No." Arguing with so little information was pointless, Gareth thought. Better to let the old man have it out, lunacy or not. "Brian seemed to think that was bad."

"Not bad. And perfectly understandable under the circumstances." His manner had softened again, making him seem more like the man Gareth remembered from his childhood. But the light in his eyes was still there. "Your grandmother was the same. I loved her as I love your mother and as I love Tess. And I love you as well." He smiled, the charming smile that never failed to melt the heart of anyone who saw it, man or woman, and the strange sense of belonging Gareth had felt in his presence the night he arrived warmed him in spite of the wind. "But our line is charged with a terrible duty," he said. "Much has been forgotten." He went back to the table, his hand grazing over the pile of scrolls as if he wondered which to open first. "I have tried to find the truth, to make sense of Kyna's visions so I could explain them to you. But I have no talent for it."

"I thought Kyna was gone." The snow flurries had stopped, and a weak, wintry sunlight was shining in the windows, gleaming on the strange instruments on the table and the burnished carvings on his grandfather's cup.

"We thought it best to leave your cousin in peace while we could. She has not had an easy time of it, our Tess." He took a deep breath as if steeling himself to go on, and once again, Gareth was struck by how very old he seemed. "Do you know how long this tower has stood on this cliff?"

Once again, the sudden shift in the conversation made Gareth feel rather dizzy. "No." He looked around at the watch room, the irregular stones showing where the tapestries blew in the wind. "It seems very old."

"It is," his grandfather said with a smile. "Older than the Romans. Older than Christ." He crossed the room to touch a scrap of parchment pinned to the wall. "Our clan has lived here so long, even I know but the tiniest sliver of our history. I know that we were left behind . . ." His fingertips traced the strange writings as if to decipher them by touch. "But I do not know by whom. We were meant to guard the gateway."

"The gateway to what?" For some reason, his words reminded Gareth of Roxanna, her tales of a golden hall and a demon called "vampire."

"I know not. A gateway in the ice. The cursed places—you remember hearing of them, surely."

"Of course." When he was a child, people had spoken in whispers of a village to the north. Parents whose children were bad would threaten to send them there to live, and the bravest of the older boys would boast they would go there when they were grown. But no one to his knowledge ever had.

"The old ones were warned to stay away from there, to guard the gateway but never to go near it," his grandfather said. "Every laird from the first to myself was told this, and no one ever questioned why. Why should we want to go to such a frozen place? We prospered here. Of all the clans in the Highlands, the Clan McKail has known the least misfortune. We have never starved, never had to leave our lands. No enemy who has ever come against us in this place has ever beaten us in battle. Before your father, no foreigner but Christian priests had ever come inside our gates. But we were told something else as well, we lairds of the clan. That someday the wolf would return."

"The wolf?" As insane as it all sounded, Gareth found himself believing his grandfather's tale. Perhaps the fact that he had just recently lost his heart to a shape-shifting demon had softened his mind to such horrors. "An actual wolf?"

"I don't think so," the laird answered, shaking his head. "But I don't know. When my uncle, the last laird, was dying, he told me just what I have just told you. The clan must guard the gateway in the ice but never go near it, and someday the wolf would return. I gathered all of this myself." He gestured to the books and scrolls on the table and the papers pinned to the walls. "Some of it was hidden here in the castle. Some of it came from distant lands, bought from peddlers and scholars who heard of my interest. The prophecy was not enough for me. I needed to know the truth."

This sounded exactly like the laird Gareth had known. "And what have you discovered?"

"Very little, if anything at all," his grandfather said grimly. "Nothing fits together; none of it makes any sense. Most of the material found here is written in a language no scholar I can find can read. Much of it seems to be tied up with fairy tales, the druid stories of the ancients. But I can't be sure." He settled heavily into his armchair as if he were suddenly exhausted.

"But what real difference does it make, Grandfather?" Gareth said, drawing the stool close to his chair.

"Because the wolf is coming now." He leaned his head back against the chair and closed his eyes. "Kyna has foreseen it for years, since long before you were born. She was already a woman when I was born, and she says she has always known it was so. Before this year is over, I will die, and the wolf will return." He opened his eyes and smiled. "Now you know why you had to come home."

Gareth started shaking his head before the words were out. "No . . . Grandfather, even if everything you say is true, it can have nothing to do with me. You said it yourself, my father was a foreigner."

"Your mother was a daughter of the clan," the laird answered. "You bear the mark of the laird. It is your destiny to lead your people, to guard the gateway and vanquish the Wolf, whatever he may be."

"I am a stranger here," Gareth protested. "Someone tried to murder me to keep me away, remember? Even if I were not sworn to the English, even if I wanted to stay, the clan would never accept me as laird."

"That is why you will marry your cousin." Gareth was certain he must be jesting, but he didn't smile. "Those in the clan who disbelieve the prophecy and only want peace will still accept you as her husband."

"And what of Duncan?"

"Duncan will accept you, or he will leave the clan." Gareth started to move away, and the laird clamped a hand down on his arm with shocking strength. "It is your destiny, Gareth. You say you are a knight. Then you know what duty means, what it is to swear yourself to something beyond your own desires. This place has been yours since the day these stones were laid into a tower." He turned up the marks on Gareth's forearm. "Your blood has marked you, lad, and I am dying. I fear you have no choice."

Tess is right, Gareth wanted to say, you are mad. But in his heart, he still knew the laird was not, that this destiny was real. The mark might be a fairy tale, but his ties to the Clan McKail were not. The gateway was not. The wolf was not. All of these things he believed in as if he had known about them all his life. "I won't marry Tess," he said aloud. "She is promised to Duncan, and he loves her. And she loves him."

"Tess loved her father," the laird replied, his voice more sad than stern as he let go of Gareth's arm. "She has loved no other since."

"Then she will twice fail to love me." Now more than ever he wanted to find Roxanna, to make her stay with him and let him help her. He could not help but believe that somehow her quest was tied to his grandfather's tale—it could not be a coincidence that a foreign princess under a demon's curse had come to the Highlands now, the same time as this wolf that menaced the clan was expected. The wonder was that he, an ordinary knight, wholly unremarkable, should be caught in the thick of it all. He briefly considered telling his grandfather about Roxanna, but he dismissed the thought as soon as it was born. The laird was ill and worried; the knowledge that his grandson, the reluctant villain he wanted as successor, was in fact entangled with a demon would do nothing to steady his nerves. "I am here, Grandfather," he said, taking the old man's hand. "I will stay at least until this business you speak of is done."

"Not good enough," the laird said, tightening his grip. "Look at me, lad. Do you think I can live until you make up your mind?"

"You seem able to live until Judgment," Gareth retorted. "I am a knight, my laird, but I am not a child. I will not be ruled entirely, even by you."

His grandfather smiled. "You are your father's son." He let go of Gareth's hand and patted it instead. "Go, then. I will wait for you."

13

When he made it back downstairs, Gareth saw no sign of his cousin. But it was obvious from the looks he was getting from the other women of the household that they knew exactly what had passed. All talk ceased as soon as he crossed the threshold of the hall. Two young girls who had been wringing out laundry on one of the trestle tables took one look at him and burst out in giggles, burying their faces in either end of a still-damp tablecloth to hide their mirth. One older woman with the shape of a cabbage and a face to match gave him a long, sour look up and down, let out a meaningful "humph," and slapped a sopping wet shirt back into the washtub with a punctuating splash.

"Where is my cousin?" he asked the room in general. "Where is Tess?" As a knight in his English lord's hall, he could have commanded an answer; any woman doing laundry would have been of peasant stock. But this was not England. Even the ones who had been staring straight at him a moment before turned hastily away as soon as he spoke and acted as if they had never seen or even heard tell of him before.

He recognized the woman standing over the other tub—Duncan's mother, Grace. She wasn't so much ignoring him as purposely avoiding his gaze, her head bent so low over her work that she splashed a few droplets of soapy water on her face with every douse of the wash. He drew closer, and she stopped, closing her eyes. He saw that some of the droplets were tears. "Mistress Grace," he said gently, touching her arm. As a boy, he had thought of this woman as a second mother—he distinctly remembered her punishment for his poking a beehive once, spanking him silly for being a fool, then hugging him breathless for fear of the hurt he might have taken. "Where is Duncan?" he asked her now.

Her hands tightened on the washing until her knuckles turned white. "Not with Tess," she answered, still refusing to look at him.

"I don't care if he is or he isn't, I swear." He spoke softly for her ears alone, but the other washwoman caught her breath. "Where is he?"

Grace looked up into his face as if trying to be sure he was really the boy she remembered. "Can't you guess?" she answered with the palest ghost of a smile.

He smiled back, knowing where she must mean in an instant. "Aye." He brushed a kiss to her cheek. "Thank you."

The pathway down to the beach was just as steep and slippery as he remembered it, worse now with its spattering of snow. But somehow he made it to the bottom without breaking his neck and walked along the sandy stretch before him, a sudden flood of memory stealing his breath. As children, he and Duncan had fought a thousand battles among these tall black rocks, lying in wait for hours if need be to ambush Duncan's older brothers, dauntless in spite of a thousand defeats. When his father had died, Duncan had found him here, huddled in the cold shelter of one of these rocks, crying his heart out. Neither of them had spoken. Duncan had simply sat down beside him, thrown a boyish arm over his shoulders, and let him cry.

Duncan the man was leaning now against the selfsame rock, his black hair blown wild by the wind. He looked around as Gareth approached him and straightened up, his dark brows drawn together in a scowl. "I needs must talk to you," Gareth called when he was close enough to be heard.

Duncan's scowl deepened, but he didn't speak. He charged. Head lowered like a bull, he crashed straight into Gareth's chest, knocking him backward in the sand. Swearing an oath at the flare of pain in his still-healing wounds, Gareth punched him hard, aiming for his jaw and finding his shoulder instead. The two of them rolled like snarling puppies for a good ten minutes, neither able to win the advantage, neither willing to surrender. Duncan didn't seem to want to kill him, only hurt him, and Gareth's own temper, simmering hot since Marcus's death, had finally found an outlet.

He was still less than fit by knightly standards, but this was a brawl, not a battle, and he was by far the bigger and more practiced brawler. When Duncan finally tired, he was able to pin him to the sand.

"Do you think I would marry my cousin?" he demanded. "Do you think I would marry your true love?"

"You're an Englishman now," Duncan said sullenly. "Who can say what you might do?"

"Idiot." He let him go, rolling off him to sit up. "I am no more an Englishman now than I was when I left you," he muttered, wiping his bloody nose with the back of his hand. Saying the words aloud, he realized they were true. Hell, he even sounded like a Highlander again, his hard-won English diction all but lost.

Duncan still lay flat on his back, his eyes turned on the sky. "Christ, Gareth, why did you come back?"

"I missed you, too." But there was no bitterness in either of their voices now; the anger had drained out of them somewhere in the fight. "He's my grandfather, Duncan. He said he needed me."

"He's mad." When Gareth didn't answer, he sat up. "You know that, don't you?"

"Aye." He didn't know how much Duncan might have been told of what the laird had told him, and he didn't particularly care to find out. "I told him as much."

Duncan grinned. "That must have made him happy." He pulled a rag from his belt and handed it to Gareth for his bleeding nose. "Tess knew all along what he meant to do when he sent for you—'twas why she was so keen to be betrothed, I think. She never doubted you would come."

"She hates me."

"Aye, she does." Gareth started to say something, and Duncan held up his hand. "I know it makes no sense. She thinks if you had never been born, her father would never have died."

"So that's my fault?" Gareth grumbled.

"Did I not just say it makes no sense?" Duncan retorted. "After you and your mother had gone, Jamey went queer in the head. There were many who thought he had something to do with your father's death."

"Nay, you don't mean it," Gareth said sarcastically.

"My own father thought it, too," Duncan admitted. "But if Jamey did plot the murder, he took no comfort from it. He started telling anyone who would listen that the clan was done for, that the stain of McKail would be wiped clean from the earth as we deserved. People who knew of the prophecy and your mark feared he might be right, and everyone else just felt a chill whenever he started talking. Eventually there was no one left to listen to him."

"Except Tess." Even before his own father had died, Jamey had doted on his daughter, treating her more like a lap dog than a child.

Duncan smiled bitterly. "But Tess." He leaned back against the rock. "She has a sweet heart, Gareth, under it all. When Jamey finally died, may God assoil him, 'twas the best thing for her, but she couldn't see it. She grieves for him yet. She thinks he is the only living soul who ever loved her."

"But you do." A month ago, he would have thought his friend a fool, could never have understood his pain. Now, after Roxanna, he knew too well just how he must have felt.

He snorted half a laugh. "Aye, I do. Would that I could ever make her believe it." He turned to Gareth, his dark eyes grave. "If you say you will not marry her, she will be dishonored in the clan. I fear her mind won't bear it."

"You want me to marry her?" Gareth said in shock.

"Nay, of course not." He climbed to his feet. "'Tis a pretty tangle your grandfather has tied."

"It is." He got up himself. "He said he thinks he will die before the year is out."

"Aye, 'tis near certain that he will," Duncan said with a nod. "He has been sick enough for all to see it for two winters now. He won't survive another." He gave Gareth's shoulder a squeeze. "Do not think I begrudge you the title of laird—by all the saints, I swear that I do not."

"You just want Tess." He grinned. "You always were perverse."

"Oh, aye," Duncan retorted. "I want a beauty in my bed over the ruling of a bunch of stubborn, complaining wretches who wouldn't know gratitude if it chomped them on the arse. You're right; that is perversity indeed."

"So you shall have her."

"Gareth—"

"Just because I say we are betrothed doesn't mean we will ever marry," he said, cutting him off. "I will say I have to write my mother to come for my wedding—no one, not even my grandfather, can fault me for that."

"Then we wait him out." He sounded doubtful, but there was hope in his eyes.

"If he dies, you will support my claim until a better laird is found," Gareth went on. He was still not ready to surrender his old life completely, and he had no faith in his ability to be laird of his own life, much less the clan. But he could not shake the feeling that at least some of the prophecy his grandfather laid out for him was true. "And Tess . . . what will she say?"

"I will explain things to Tess."

"Good." The things Duncan had told him about his cousin had done nothing to put his heart at ease. He now knew Duncan for the friend he had always known. But Tess was something else entirely. "Duncan, someone tried to murder me," he said. "They murdered Sir John and my cousin, Marcus, who loved me, who I loved."

"We will find them, whoever it was," Duncan said, clasping his hand. "I promise, you will be avenged."

They spent the rest of the afternoon watching the tide come in, filling the void that had grown between them with talk. By the time they climbed back to the top of the cliff, the sun had long since disappeared.

"There you are," Brian said, meeting them as they passed into the candlelit tower from the darkness of the courtyard. "Come. We have visitors."

He led them through a hall that was once again buzzing with speculation and out the other side. In the hallway, they encountered Tess just coming down the stairs. Her eyes widened a bit at the sight of Gareth and Duncan together, but she recovered quickly, taking in their torn and sandy clothes and Gareth's bloody nose in a single pointed glance.

"In here," Brian said, passing by her with barely a nod. He opened the door to the room that led to the downstairs bedroom that Gareth had used these three nights past. He was unusually grave, Gareth noticed, his forehead drawn in an uncharacteristic frown. But he smiled a little as Gareth passed him to go into the room.

The first person he saw was Kyna, looking just the same as she had the day he had left the Highlands with his mother, bending over a cauldron of some foul-smelling brew at the hearth. Tess went up to her as if there had never been a quarrel between them and held out a small sealed cask. "Is this what you wanted?" his cousin asked.

"Yes," the weird woman answered, barely looking up. "His wound isn't deep; that should serve."

The laird was sitting at the table across from a man with golden hair who looked to be around Gareth's own age. He was stripped to the waist, and he bore ugly black and purple bruises down one side of his rib cage and a bloody scrape on his shoulder. "This is Sean Lebuin," Gareth's grandfather said as Tess began to treat the blond man's wound with whatever salve was in the cask. "He is our kinsman from the borderlands." The man offered his free hand, and Gareth took it without thinking. "The lady is his sister, Siobhan," his grandfather went on, but Gareth barely heard him. A weird shiver had passed from the stranger's hand to his own, making his breath come short. Lebuin's eyes narrowed for a moment, as if he had felt it, too.

"What ails her?" Duncan asked, breaking the sudden trance. Looking back, he saw a woman with beautiful red hair lying on the bed, her skin pale as milk, her closed eyelids so dark they looked bruised. Siobhan, his grandfather had called her. But that was wrong . . . he suddenly realized he was still holding Lebuin's hand, was gripping it as if he meant to break his bones, in fact. He looked back to see Lebuin looking down at the mark on Gareth's arm, still smeared with charcoal from the morning, a strange, chilly smile on his face.

"She has been ravaged by a demon," said a familiar voice from behind. He let go of Lebuin's hand to turn around, and there was Roxanna, standing in the shadows, swathed from her shoulders to her feet in a man's dark mantle.

"You," he said, everyone else forgotten. "You have come."

"Yes," she answered. "But not by choice."

"You know this lady?" his grandfather asked.

"I had an opportunity to offer him assistance," she said, looking away from Gareth to answer the laird as if he might have been a child eavesdropping on their conversation. "I am surprised that he remembers me."

"Her name is Roxanna," the laird explained. "She is a scholar from the east."

"I know her name," Gareth said. The last time he had seen her, she had shown him her true self, but she had also said she cared for him. How could she treat him so coldly now? "But I would not have called her a scholar."

Roxanna smiled, the arch, ironic smile he remembered from the first days of their meeting, but it was Kyna who spoke. "'Twas Lady Roxanna who first found Gareth when he was wounded, McKail, not me," the weird woman explained, bringing her steaming cauldron to the table. "She had stitched his wounds and made him comfortable before I knew aught of his coming."

Comfortable? Gareth thought, a sudden urge to laugh making him bite his tongue. He thought of the first time his vampire love had come to him, the joining he had first thought was a dream. His eyes met hers, and for a moment, he thought she meant to laugh as well. Then her gaze darted away. "'Twas she who saved his life," Kyna was saying.

"Then in faith, she is an angel," Lebuin said. Gareth snapped his head around to look at him, surprised. Why had he chosen that word? Swathed in black, Roxanna was still beautiful, but she no longer looked like an angel. Why should this stranger have chosen the same word that had come to him? The weird mistrust he had felt when Lebuin shook his hand deepened in spite of his supposed kinsman's fragile smile and the warmth of his words. "If she had not found me and Siobhan when she did, we would surely have perished."

"Where did she find you?" Duncan said, obviously confused. He had moved to stand beside Tess as she bandaged Lebuin's shoulder. "And what is this demon you spoke of?"

Kyna looked up from filling a small wooden bowl with her brew. "Lucan Kivar." Both Brian and the laird made a hissing sound of horror, but Duncan and Tess still looked confused. "He had taken these two to the forbidden gates. Lady Roxanna found them there." She looked up at Gareth and smiled. "Come and help me, lad." Without waiting for his answer, she took her bowl to the bed.

"Why should you have gone to the gates, my lady?" the laird asked Roxanna. "Where do you come from?"

"A very distant kingdom in the Ural mountains," she answered. "My master there had dedicated his life to Kivar's destruction. He taught me to do the same."

"Lift her up," Kyna instructed Gareth, indicating the woman on the bed. He sat down gingerly beside her and lifted her as gently as he could. She moaned, turning her head on his shoulder, but he could not make out her words. "Open her mouth." He cupped the woman's chin in his palm and urged her mouth open with his thumb. "Good," Kyna said, spooning the foul-smelling mixture into the woman's mouth. "Very good." He expected the poor lady to struggle, but she seemed to relax against him. "You will prevail, Gareth," the weird woman said softly for his ears alone. "I have seen it." He opened his mouth to answer, but she shook her head, glancing toward the others. "You need not tell every truth that you know."

"Where is your master now?" the laird was asking Roxanna. "I would like to speak with him."

"I fear he must be dead, my laird," she answered, her tongue stumbling a bit over the title. "We were separated some time past."

"So you truly believe this thing you are following is a demon?" Tess said as if she could not keep her peace a moment longer.

"Yes," Roxanna answered her. "I know he is." She looked back at Gareth for barely a moment, but it was long enough for him to see the sadness in her eyes, the same pain he had seen when she had told him she cared for him. "I have seen him." She had come to the clan, but not for him. A slow-burning anger he had barely realized he felt flared up inside him, fury at her for not trusting him. She would not even look at him for more than a moment.

"Then I would seek your counsel, my lady," the laird said. "You must be wiser than your years would make you seem." Kyna suppressed a smile, and Gareth had to admit, the obvious shock on Duncan and Brian's faces was something to smile at. The laird seeking the counsel of a woman was a thing unheard of.

"I have more years than you might see in my face, my lord," Roxanna answered with a gracious nod. "But I fear I must leave you as soon as I can question the lady Siobhan." Her gaze moved to Gareth again. "The creature has apparently moved on, and I would overtake him."

"Then I will go with you," Gareth said, standing up. He would make her tell him everything, make her listen to reason. He would not just give her up. She might be ready to surrender to fate, but he was not.

"No," the laird said, standing as well. "Your place is here."

"He is right," Kyna said, putting a restraining hand on Gareth's arm.

"I am old enough to know my place," Gareth said. "If you fear for me, Grandfather, send some of my kinsmen with me."

"I would go," Duncan said at once.

"The hell you would," Tess said, all pretense of maidenly prudence abandoned, and Lebuin laughed aloud, making them all look at him in shock. "No more will you, my love," she continued, ignoring him to turn to Gareth. "We have just today become betrothed, remember? Would you leave me on such a quest so soon?"

Gareth saw Roxanna start at this—at least she

seemed to care if he married another. But she said nothing.

"Forgive me," Lebuin said, his eyes still merry with amusement as he looked at Tess. "I have seen but a glimpse of this demon, for all he apparently forced me to ride across the length of Scotland." He sobered as he looked back at the laird. "But I have seen what he has done to my Siobhan." He turned to Roxanna, and Gareth felt his own prickle of jealousy at the warmth he saw in his eyes. "You may well be wise, my lady," he said. "But you should leave this creature be."

"Would that I could," she answered. To everyone else, she must have sounded perfectly calm and unconcerned. But Gareth knew that tone, knew it for the practiced mask that hid her deepest heart. She turned to the laird and made a formal curtsy with the grace of the princess she had always claimed to be. "As soon as Siobhan is well enough to tell me where the creature has gone, I will leave you, my lord." She looked back at Gareth, her eyes darkening with what he alone would know were tears of blood. "And I will go alone." She raised the hood of her mantle and hurried from the room.

"We can't just let that woman go after a demon alone," Brian protested as Gareth started after her.

"Don't worry, cousin," he said, giving his grandfather a swift, apologetic glance. "I will not." He left before anyone else could speak, the door slamming shut behind him.

14

Roxanna blundered through the crowded tower hall, head lowered, not daring for a moment to look up and meet a single mortal's eyes. It had been so long since she had entered a village of the living, she had lost the knack of blending in. Every heartbeat seemed to thunder in her ears, shutting out all other sound and making her vampire's hunger writhe inside her like an evil snake. *We have just today become betrothed. . . .* Of all that she had heard in that cramped, overheated little room, these were the words that kept repeating in her head, chanting to the rhythm of a hundred different beating hearts. She pulled the hood of the mantle some mortal had given her down farther over her face, certain that her eyes must have changed to the demon's, that tears of blood must surely be streaming down her face. *My love . . . we are betrothed.*

In truth, she had no clear idea where she was going or what she was meant to do next, would not have had any idea even if her head had been clear. She had left Gareth to go after Kivar, and every instinct she possessed, human and demon alike, told her that he had done just as Kyna had promised, that he had gone to the frozen grove to find the Chalice. The story Sean Lebuin had told had only confirmed this belief. But where had he gone? Kyna seemed certain he had not found the Chalice, but how could she know? In truth, Roxanna had never believed in the Chalice at all; did she believe now? What was she meant to do? She passed out of the tower into the courtyard, nodding to the mortal man who spoke to her in the doorway as if she had heard what he said. She wiped at her face and found blood on her hand. Stop it, she commanded herself, wiping it on the black mantle. Stop this foolishness at once. But she could feel the demon inside her growing stronger, feel herself losing control.

"Roxanna!" Gareth's voice cut through the chaos in her head like a beacon in a fog. She hurried faster, the mantle tangling around her ankles. "Roxanna, stop!" He caught hold of her just as she tripped, catching her as she fell.

"Let go of me," she snarled, turning to him in full demonic fury.

"I will not." His arm still locked around her, he guided her across the courtyard, away from curious eyes. The heartbeats of the others faded, gathered into one as she huddled against him, and she closed her eyes, letting him lead her blindly, helpless to resist. He was too strong for her; she wanted him too much. He was betrothed to another, a beautiful mortal with red hair and green eyes. Like Kivar, she thought, her insides twisting with jealous rage. She is colored like Kivar.

He led her into a dark little outbuilding and flung the door shut behind them. "We should be left alone in here," he said, bolting the door as she opened her eyes. A lamp was burning on a table just before them, and he lit a torch from it, illuminating the room.

"The chapel," she said, almost laughing. "Of course."

"No one ever comes here." He turned back to her. "Roxanna, why—"

"Why not?" She cut him off. He moved as if to catch her arm, but she sidestepped to avoid him, moving past him to the altar. "Is your clan not Christian?"

"They are." She could hear his heart beating faster; he was angry. "But so far, no priest has been willing to come so far north to stay."

"I cannot say I blame them." She faced the tall wooden cross mounted behind the altar, gazing up at it, bemused. She had seen vampires flinch before such symbols, bleed from their eyes if they looked too long. But she felt nothing. She reached up and touched the wood, all but willing it to burn her. If she could be turned by Gareth's God, perhaps she could be saved by Him. But the cross felt as cool and as dead to her fingertips as a stick of kindling.

"You told my grandfather you were from the east," Gareth said. He put his hands on her shoulders, making her take a sharp breath. "Are you not a Christian then?"

"No." It was his touch that burned her, even through the heavy woolen mantle, his love that made her grieve for the soul she had lost. She turned to him, her arms slack at her sides. "I believe in nothing."

A thousand different questions echoed in his mind as he looked down into her face. She was a vampire, a demon who could kill without a thought. He had seen it, seen the blood on her fangs, seen her change into a panther, a predator with no humanity at all. But she was his angel as well. She had saved him, cared for him as tenderly as if he were her heart's most precious love. But she had left him, trusting her curse more than his love. Looking down at the full, plump blossom of her mouth, he did not think of her fangs but of her kisses, the taste of her tongue, the softness of her body in his arms. Remembering, he could not help but kiss her, vampire or not.

She clenched her teeth, refusing to respond, but he would not be put off. He had seen her tears, had felt her arms around him. However she might try to hide it now, he knew she cared for him. He drew her closer, holding her arms through the mantle, brushing tiny kisses across her tightly closed mouth. "Kiss me," he whispered. He cradled her cheek in his palm, brushing the pad of his thumb across her lower lip to draw it down, bending close to trace the same path with the tip of his tongue. "Kiss me, Roxanna." Eyes closed, she tried to shake her head to tell him no, and he tangled his hand in her hair, slanting her face close to his, his other arm entwined around her waist under the mantle as he pressed his lips to hers. She sighed against his mouth, a soft, despairing sound that made his heart ache as dearly as he wanted her, and he drew her closer still, the mantle falling to the floor behind her.

"I can't." As soon as her mouth opened to speak, he kissed her, his tongue sliding inside, still gentle but insistent, capturing her breath. She put her hands on his arms as if to push him back, little fists clutching the fabric of his shirt, but her head fell back in surrender, her mouth opening to his assault. Nothing else mattered but this, the sweetness of holding her, having her. He pressed her back against the altar, his hands moving over her back and down her sides. She moved her mouth away from his, turning her cheek to his kiss, still trying to escape him, and he crushed her closer, refusing to let go. "You belong to someone else," she said, breathless from his kisses. "I heard her say you were betrothed—"

"A lie," he promised as he kissed her lips. She put her arms between them, clenched her fists against his chest, but her body was pliant even so, swayed against him. "She knows it is a lie for my grandfather. He wants us to marry, but we will not." He looked down into her eyes, his mouth curled in the smile she loved so much. "I am already promised to you."

"Don't say that." Cursed heathen that she was, she

still felt a shiver as he spoke of marriage before the altar, holding her fast in his arms. "Gareth, let me go."

"I won't." His mouth came down on hers again, a brutal kiss that made her melt against him. "I swear I won't." She twined her arms around his neck this time, rising up to meet his kiss, helpless to fight another moment. He swept her off her feet, lowering her to the cold stone floor, but he was warm above her, warm in her arms. She touched his face as he lifted his head, tracing the shape of his features, and he smiled. How could he still smile at her that way, knowing what she was?

"You will hate me," she said softly, her voice rough with tears. "You will curse me for the demon that I am."

"You won't be a demon," he promised. "I will save you." He bent and kissed her, drawing her lower lip into his mouth for a long moment before he moved away. "You are my angel, and I will save you." He kissed her again before she could answer, one hand sliding up her thigh, raising her skirt.

"Gareth, I am not." She wanted to give in as she had rarely wanted anything before. It would be so simple to believe him and let herself be taken, to let his passion rule them both, if only for an hour. But they weren't alone in an empty wilderness anymore, and she could no longer pretend. "Gareth!" She put her hand on his and pushed it back, clasping it but holding it away. "What will you do, make love to me inside your church?"

His beautiful blue eyes were dreamy with desire, and

his smile melted her heart. "Aye," he answered, still holding her hand. He drew her up until she was sitting before him where he knelt.

"And what then?" she said before he could kiss her again. "Will you tell your grandfather the laird that you will have me? Will you tell him what I am?" A lock of his hair had fallen over his brow, and she longed to brush it back, to press her mouth to his forehead and draw him back down to the floor. It had never been her nature to be wise; even as a mortal she had followed every impulse as it sparked without a moment's pause. But now she could not help but imagine what might happen if she didn't stop and think, not to herself but to him. As dearly as she wanted him, she loved him more. A risk she would take for herself without thinking she could not take for him.

"I will tell him you are mine," Gareth answered, hating the despair he could hear in her voice. If he was indeed chosen by fate to defeat this monster, who better to save her from her curse? In the space of a month, his tedious, well-ordered life had fallen completely to chaos, yet somehow, he felt stronger for it. For the first time, he was not just someone's son or someone's cousin or some lord's knight, following the whim and will of another with no purpose of his own. For all his life, he had never dared to want anything for himself beyond survival. Finding a place where he could serve and be no bother had been his only goal. But that inoffensive knight was not his true self. Being with Roxanna in that miserable hovel, he had learned to want, and now he could not stop. He wanted to be the man his grandfather believed he was fated to be. He wanted to save his clan, to defeat this demon wolf. Most of all, he wanted Roxanna, wanted to save her, to wipe away the fear and despair to which she clung like holy relics. "It doesn't matter what you are now," he said, putting his hands on her shoulders again.

"You say that because you don't understand," she said, putting a hand to his mouth.

"How can you say that?" he demanded, taking the little hand in his, refusing to be treated like a child a moment longer. "I saw you—"

"If you understood, you would not want me," she insisted. "I'm sorry I came back here; it was wrong of me—"

"No, it was not," he said. "Roxanna, listen to me." For a moment's madness, he felt a nearly irresistible urge to prove to her just how strong he was, to prove he could overpower her to make her believe she was safe. But she trusted him, and he could not betray her. "I saw you kill," he said, keeping his voice even as he held her gaze. "I saw you change. I know what you are."

"But you will tell me you don't care," she said with a laugh that was half scorn and half despair.

"Of course I care." He stood up with her hand clasped in his, drawing her up with him. If she decided to change her shape and slip away again, at least he would keep hold of a paw. "But not so much that I will give you up."

"Gareth . . ." She looked down at their joined hands and froze. "What is this?" She touched the rough charcoal design still smeared on his forearm. "I have seen this. . . ."

"My grandfather says it means I am meant to lead the clan," he answered. "He says it marks me as their guardian against the wolf." She looked up to meet his eyes, her mouth falling open in horror. "Worse yet, he says Kyna has seen a vision of this creature's return."

"No," she began, shaking her head. "I won't have it."

"I don't believe your rule will stand here, princess," he said, softening his words with a smile. "You said the woman inside, Siobhan, was attacked by a demon, by Lucan Kivar."

"Kyna took me to a place that was covered with ice," she said, her grip tightening on his hand. "She said she had seen a vision of me and of Kivar, here in the Highlands, and I knew it was true. I had sensed him here the first night I found you. I found the body of one of his kills. She said she could show me the way to find him." She looked up at him again, the fear in her eyes breaking his heart. "But we didn't find him. We found Sean and Siobhan—Kivar was gone. I have to find him—"

"We have to find him," he corrected.

"Stop it," she ordered, the princess again. "I won't let you face Kivar, I don't care what marks you carry or what your grandfather might say."

"And how will you stop me?" He put a gentle hand to her mouth, this time to stop her answer. "I will have you, princess," he said, cradling her cheek. "If that means I must vanquish a demon, so be it." She tried to turn away, but he would not allow it. "You are a vampire born half a world away who just happened to turn up here, in the Highlands, inside a bottle I just happened to pick up like a pebble from the ground," he went on, bending closer. "How can you doubt that we were meant to meet?"

"I do not," she admitted with tears in her eyes. "I thought you would die." She ran a hand down the muscles of his arm with a shiver, remembering the first night she had watched over him. "But I wanted so much for you to live, even then, when I did not even know you." She looked up into his eyes and knew that nothing else she ever saw would be so beautiful, no matter how long she might live. "Your life is worth everything to me, more than . . ." Again, she tried to pull away from him, and again, he would not allow it. "I have seen Lucan Kivar destroy whole cities, Gareth. My father was a mighty ruler; he had hundreds of soldiers in his personal guard, trained assassins, every one. Kivar slaughtered them like cattle." She kept her eyes fixed on the floor. "He fears nothing, cares for no one. He will think nothing of your death, less than nothing." In her mind, she saw Alexi, a beautiful child transformed into a demon with the hunger of a beast. She had destroyed him herself, cleaved his little head from his shoulders to save him from her fate. If Kivar should take Gareth, could she do the same? "That cannot be," she finished, setting her jaw. "I will not allow it."

Again, he could not doubt her. Indeed, the resolve in her voice was so cold, it made him shiver. But though she be princess and vampire, too, this decision was not hers to make. "And what of Kyna's vision?" he said gently. "What of my destiny?"

"I don't give a damn for Kyna's visions or your clan, either one—"

"But I do." As much as he had tried to escape it, the Clan McKail were his people; this fortress was his home. If some ancient design had made him their champion, he had no choice but to try. "The McKail says we are charged to keep this Wolf from the gateway in the ice, and knowing you and all you have told me, I know now it is true." He made her face him. "Do you not want me, angel?"

She stared at him in shock. "How can you ask me such a thing?"

"Then fight for me." He framed her face in his hands. "Let me fight for you." He pressed a kiss to her forehead.

For a moment, he thought she would give in; she turned her face up to his as if to kiss his mouth. Then she broke away from him, pushing him away. "Do you think I do not want to fight?" she demanded. "You speak of destiny and visions and what is meant—I have never known for a single moment what I was meant to do! Every impulse I have ever had has been wrong from the moment I was born. I was not supposed to read books or care about politics or worry about my father's people, but I did—I couldn't help it! I certainly was not supposed to become a vampire, I know. I should have died first, should have let Alexi die. But I could not." She turned back to him, fresh tears in her eyes. "I was not supposed to stay with you." He hurt for her, her pain like a wound in his own heart. "Once I knew you were safe, I was meant to leave you. But I didn't want to leave."

"Then don't." He wanted to comfort her, but he knew she wouldn't allow it, and in truth, it wouldn't help. He had to make her understand, make her see him as a man, not a child. "You're right, Roxanna. You cannot stay with me as a vampire, at least not forever. But if Kivar is defeated, if your curse can be broken, how can we not try?"

"I will try," she promised. "But alone—"

"No," he cut her off. "You cannot defeat the wolf alone—if you could have, you would have done it long ago." He saw a flash of anger in her eyes, but he would not stop. "And neither can I." He held out a hand to her, waiting for her to take it. "We must face this evil together." He would not plead with her anymore, or cling to her or try to hold her fast. As long as he begged, she would fight him without thinking. She must hear him and decide. "That is what is meant," he finished.

For a moment, he thought she would turn away. Then she took his hand. "And if we fail?" she said, a tremor in her voice.

"We will not." This time it was she who reached for him, wrapping her arms around his waist, her cheek pressed to his chest. "Trust me, angel," he said, kissing the top of her head. "I am stronger than you know."

"You are as strong as any warrior I have ever known," she answered. "You are my champion." What will I do when you are lost? she thought but did not say. She could not fight him anymore. He was right; they were meant to be together, for good or ill. But she was still so afraid.

"Then say that you will stay with me," he said, not willing to leave the words unsaid.

"And what will we tell this clan of yours?" she said, drawing back to look at him. "How will we explain my hiding from the sunlight?"

"We won't explain anything," he answered. "I am the chosen heir of the McKail, and you are my guest. There is a room under the tower that should be at least as comfortable as that hovel. The only entrance is through a trapdoor in the bedroom where the woman you say Kivar attacked is sleeping." She still hadn't said she would stay, he noticed. "You told my grandfather that you were a scholar. We will say you are caring for the girl and cannot be disturbed." He took her chin in his hand. "Promise you won't try to leave me," he ordered. "Swear it, Roxanna."

"I will stay," she answered. She arched a brow. "And you will pretend to be betrothed to this Tess."

"Pretend," he said. "Only pretend." He did kiss her then, and she allowed it, returning it in kind. "My grandfather will wonder what's become of us," he said when the kiss was broken, his voice low as a growl.

"As well he might." She leaned her head for a moment against his chest, listening to his heartbeat. She would have to find a way to feed—his plan for secreting her under the tower didn't allow for that. But somehow she would manage. "Come, then."

Outside, the snow was falling again, thicker now than the morning. By sunrise, the world would be covered in white. They met Brian halfway across the courtyard, swathed in a mantle of thick fur as if for a trudge in the wilderness. "There you are," he said when he saw them. "My lady, are you staying?"

"For now," Roxanna answered.

"Then the laird would speak with you." He looked pointedly at Gareth. "Alone."

"Why?" Gareth began, nonplussed.

"Of course," Roxanna interrupted. She had been clinging to Gareth's arm, huddled against him as much for warmth as love, but now she let him go. "I am his to command." Giving Gareth a final smile, she followed the older man back into the tower.

15

Tess straightened up from tucking in the blankets on the bed she was making for the foreign wench her grandfather believed was a scholar. "A pack of English tricksters turns up on our doorstep with a pack of lies a child in swaddling would not believe, and there sits McKail, taking every word as gospel," she said to Duncan, who was looking on. "If that golden-haired Sassenach bastard is our kin, I'm the fairy queen." She punched a pillow into shape with grim efficiency. "And if this devil, Lucan Kivar, truly does turn up as all of you seem to think he will, I'll kiss him on the lips." Duncan looked so shocked at this, he made her tired. One day spent with Gareth, and all the promises he'd made to her were forgotten. She did care for him, truly would marry him, given the chance. But she couldn't trust him with anything of real importance, and in truth, she had always known it. 'Twas why she had hired those brigands on her own. She just wished she knew who had turned up in the nick of time to kill them and save her cousin. She'd have a bit of vengeance to pay them, too. "A lot of foolishness that old bat Kyna made up out of her own stupid head."

"You don't truly believe that," he said. Lie to me, he added with his eyes. Tell me you are not what I see in you now. It was the same look she had received from someone every day of her life since her father died; indeed, it was the only way the laird had ever looked at her at all. She ought to be accustomed to it. But she wasn't. She wanted Duncan to trust her, to believe her and do as she asked, not because he had thought it through himself but because she asked it. But he was nothing but a man. She could only expect so much.

"I believe I am tired," she said, resting her head on his chest so she didn't have to look at him anymore. "You should go upstairs," she said, looking up at him with the smile she had learned to reserve just for him. "We aren't meant to be alone together anymore, remember?"

"I will risk the gossip." He touched her cheek and kissed her lips, the same as always, and the familiar knot of anger twisted in her stomach. Why did his kisses always make her angry? She raised up on her tiptoes to deepen the kiss for a moment, then pushed him gently away.

"I have to make up another room." She pulled a droll face at him, making him smile again. "My other English cousin needs a place to sleep."

"Then I will see you in the hall." He bent to kiss her again, and she offered him her cheek, playing the innocent maid. She kept her smile firmly in place until he was gone up the stairs.

When this Lady Roxanna creature's room was comfortable enough to keep her from being blamed, she climbed the stairs herself, opening the trapdoor on the tower bedroom, expecting to find Kyna still chanting her gibberish over her pot. But the weird woman was gone. Only the woman on the bed remained, with her brother, Sean, sitting beside her.

"How is she?" she asked.

"Very ill," he answered. He was sitting in a chair beside the bed but bent close as if to listen for his sister's every breath. But, she noticed, he did not touch her.

"I am sorry," she said. The lamp that had been on the table was out, leaving the room too dim to clearly see his face.

"Are you?" he said with a sound that she was almost certain was a laugh. But why would he be laughing? "I am surprised." He turned toward her, away from the bed, and she saw he was smiling. "I could hear you through the floor," he explained. "You need not trouble yourself, little one." He turned back to his sister. "I can make up my own bed."

Her cheeks flushed hot, and her heart beat faster. "Are you angry?"

"Of course not." The woman on the bed tossed her head on the pillow, and he touched her hair, brushing it back from her brow and murmuring something so softly Tess could not make out the words.

"I beg your pardon, my lord," she said, making her tone as contrite as she could manage. "My grandfather would not like to think I made you feel unwelcome."

"Then 'tis good I will not tell him." He got up from his chair so suddenly, she took a step back. "Are you afraid?"

"No," she lied by habit. There was something in his eyes, a sort of secret knowledge, as if instead of overhearing her words to Duncan through the floor he had read the deepest thoughts of her heart. But she would not let him know he frightened her, or she would be at his mercy indeed. "Tell him if you like," she said, turning her back on him. "It matters not to me."

"Perhaps he knows already. You don't hide your heart so well as you think, little one." She whirled around, cheeks flushed again, to find him still smiling. "But I don't fault you for it," he promised.

"You are very kind, in faith." Her heart was still racing in her breast, and she felt too warm all over. She had been baiting love traps for Duncan for more than a year now and never felt such heat.

"Oh, no," he said with a laugh. "I promise I am not." He touched her cheek, his smile fading to something else, mockery turning to desire. "You should not promise to kiss devils on the lips, little one." How could he have known what her father had called her? she thought. How could he have guessed? "The devils might like it." He bent as if he would kiss her, and she ducked away, slapping his face.

"Tell the laird what you like, Cousin Sean," she said with bitter emphasis. "Your silence is not worth that much to me." He was smiling again as if he knew just how near she had come to allowing the kiss and more. "Good night." Turning on her heel, she snatched up her basket and left.

Kivar caught sight of his face in a wavering copper mirror as soon as she was gone, and for a moment, he was shocked. Was that how he looked? He had barely caught a glimpse of this body before he had taken it over. In truth, he had meant to take the girl, Siobhan. But this one, this Sean, had stopped him. At least he was handsome.

He touched his cheek, meeting the eyes of his reflection. A living form at last . . . he should have been glad for it. It made his movements easier than animating the dead. But this body still possessed a soul. He had almost mastered it, almost silenced the true Sean forever. Then he had failed in the grove. His eyes narrowed, the face in the mirror looking more familiar, wearing an expression that was his alone. How could he have failed?

He looked back at the woman on the bed, sweet Isabel. He had bled her almost dry to open the gate, spilling her blood on the altar until the ice began to melt away, the trees began to flower into green. He had seen the other side, the world of the ancient ones, his birthright. The golden altar stood in the center of the grove, covered in its cloth of snow. He had felt the sunlight on his face, the light of eternity from which he had been banished. But the Chalice was gone. He had reached into the other world in fury, grasping at nothing as the woman of the ancient blood screamed out in agony.

"They took it," he said now, standing over her. "Merlin and his little beasts." This woman was a descendant of those mortal monsters, so beloved of the gods. All the time he had been certain the Chalice was still protected by the ancients, and they had given it to mindless animals, mortals who could never wield its power. His own son, Merlin, half mortal himself, had led them from the mountains, fleeing before the ice. In that moment, Kivar had believed Merlin had taken the precious Chalice with him. Perhaps it was hidden in this very woman's castle, the place he had left behind when its gateway was destroyed. He had seen a vision of it there, had he not?

Then Roxanna had come, his Roxanna, his favorite. He smiled, remembering the pleasure of seeing her face. He had always known she would be with him at the end. Then she had called the witch, this Kyna, and he knew his own village still existed. Even now, he could not help but smile in disbelief. The same barbarians who had made him an outcast as a mortal child still lived in these mountains, still farmed on this hill, still kept the ancient ways. Merlin and his tribe were no more than a distraction. The guardians of the true gateway were the Clan McKail.

He picked up Isabel's hand, and she shuddered, still repulsed by his touch even now. The soul that shared his body felt pain at this, pain he could not push away. Sean pitied her, would save her if he could. At the moment Lucan realized the Chalice was gone, Sean had tried to fight him, tried to take control of his body again to pull her back through the veil. In truth, it was likely that the sight of their struggle as they held her had broken her mind more than the loss of blood or the journey between worlds. And since that moment, living Sean had been growing stronger, so strong Kivar had begun to feel something that was almost like fear. He had never felt so closely enmeshed in another body before this one. Sean, like Isabel and these peasants of the clan, was of his blood. If somehow he should manage to overpower Kivar, the demon might be cast free forever, unable to possess another form.

But now, little Tess had given him the key. He smiled, remembering the smell of her, the vicious fury in her wide, seemingly innocent eyes. Sean was able to fight him because they wanted different things, a problem he had never known from the dead. Sean wanted to save his sister; he wanted justice; he wanted to lead his people as he believed was his right, and he was alive. Even with the spirit of the demon inside of him, his mind could still spark independent thought. He knew Kivar for evil, and he fought him, recoiling in horror as he drank Isabel's blood, refusing to let him rest. Sometimes he had gazed out of the shell of his body and made tears come to his eyes, a thing Kivar had never done, even as a mortal. And in Kivar's moment of weakness when he thought his quest had failed, Sean had seized his chance and nearly vanquished him.

But Sean wanted Tess. In his natural state, he might have felt no more than a momentary, innocent desire—he would have thought she was pretty, would have imagined what it might have been like to have her for no more than a moment. But the demon could exploit this moment's thought, could make it his obsession. For Kivar wanted her, too. She was a pure descendant of his enemies, a perfect creature of the mortal world he so despised. The hate and discontent in her eyes mirrored him much better than any reflection of Sean Lebuin's face. They would have her, and Kivar would be strong.

For the Chalice was still within reach. As soon as he had seen Roxanna in the grove, he had known his quest was not lost. He felt something near to love, remembering her making. She had been his most beautiful child, his most perfect protégée. A heathen princess, born to kill. And she was loved by the scion of the clan. He laughed, unable to stop himself. Nothing could have been more perfect. They would lead him to the Chalice. Their blood would open the gates again, and this time he would have the power to break down the barrier for good. At last, he would be free. The gods would be destroyed as they deserved, the mortal world remade as his domain alone.

He bent and pressed a kiss to Isabel's brow, smiling at her shiver. She would almost certainly die now, and that was a pity. He would have liked to have kept her, to torture Simon, if for nothing else. But he didn't need her anymore. He had an entire clan to bleed.

The door opened, and the old woman, Kyna, came in. "Has she stirred, my lord?" she asked him.

"No." This crone had spent her whole long life making ready to oppose him, he thought, struggling not to smile. Now he stood beside her, but she never knew he was there. "Is there any hope for her?" he asked.

"Oh, aye," she said, but he could see from her eyes she was lying, seeking to comfort him. "You go and take your rest. I will watch over her."

"Thank you, Kyna." He kissed the woman's wrinkled cheek, amused to hear the way her old heart skipped a beat. "Call me if she wakes."

16

Looking around the laird's high tower room, Roxanna half expected to see Orlando sitting in one of the chairs, his legs stuck out before him, a cup of wine in his hand as he pored over a scroll. It could easily have been the wizard's own nest in the caliph's palace, so much was the same.

"It is early for the snow," the laird said from the window when the door closed behind her, though his back was turned. "The shadow has fallen upon us." He turned back to her and smiled, the same charming smile he had passed on to his grandson. "Is there snow in your mountains, my lady?"

"Of course." She dropped him a curtsy, giving him the respect he deserved as a king.

"Of course." He was studying her, the mind that showed in his sharp blue eyes thinking her through like a cipher. "So Gareth convinced you to stay."

"For now." She felt no evil from this man, but there was power and a ruthless will. He was no doddering old fool to be swayed by her beauty or thwarted by lies. "He seems to believe I can help you and your clan."

"Kyna believes the same." He poured wine into a tarnished silver cup and drank from it without offering her any. "You must love my grandson very much."

Was this the trap? she thought. "I do," she answered, not bothering to lie. "I would protect him if I could."

"But you fear you cannot." Her answer seemed to please him; she felt him relax. But he sounded sadder now. "How long have you been a child of Kivar?"

"You are asking me my age?" she said with a coquettish smile. Again, she could see little use in lying when he knew the truth. "In truth, Laird McKail, I do not know. I had been a vampire for three years when I went into a bottle as a vapor. I have no way of knowing how long I was there." His eyes barely widened, but she heard his heart beat faster. He knew something of vampires, but not all. "One of the men who attacked your grandson released me by accident. I was ravenous for blood, so I imagine I was inside the bottle for some time."

"Kyna said you would awaken from a sleep." He sat down in his cushioned chair as if he were suddenly exhausted. "For three years, she has foretold your coming."

"She has told me of her visions, too." She found herself wanting to comfort him and trust him. Like Gareth, he had a strange energy about him that felt familiar, as if she should belong to him. She felt a kinship with him she had never felt with her caliph father. In truth, the only creatures besides her lover and this man who had made her feel so were Orlando and Lucan Kivar. "I did not want to believe her," she went on. "I wanted to destroy Kivar myself, to protect Gareth from him. I would see your people safe."

"Why?" He did not seem to mock her; he sounded genuinely curious.

"Because they are innocent," she answered. "Not as children—there is wickedness here as there must be in any city. But it is human, mortal wickedness. I feel responsible for them—do not ask me why."

"Because you are a princess," the laird said. His smile was broader now, warming her demon's heart. "Because you know your power."

"I fear my power," she answered. "I have done such harm, Laird McKail." She stopped, choking on the memory of the evil she had done beside Kivar. All the lives she had taken without thinking, human lives devoured like sweets, even vampires tortured and burned by the sun for her amusement. Orlando had spoken of the Chalice as salvation, a way to be forgiven, but she had never believed it, did not believe it now. How could such evil be forgiven?

"But you regret your fault." She was so lost in her own dark thoughts, she had almost forgotten he was there.

"Of course I regret it," she said, surprised by the

anger she heard in her own voice. "But what is that? Will my regret return the dead to life?" All her long life, she had been a child, first taking whatever caught her fancy, destroying anything that did not please her. Even when she had seen the wrong in what she had become, she had not faced it as a woman; she had tried to run away, to escape into oblivion. Neither her life nor her death had mattered, ever, not even to herself. What was she? An empty, pretty thing . . .

"You must speak to a priest to learn that," the laird said. "But do not expect to be satisfied with his answer." He drained his cup of wine. "I have never been."

"I did not lie when I spoke of my teacher, Orlando," she said, returning to the business at hand. The remedy for her own wicked nature had eluded her for years; 'twas hardly likely she would stumble on it now. "He was a great scholar, and he knew much of Kivar, had devoted his life to the demon's destruction."

"Yes, I know. Look at the scroll on the table behind you." His face revealed nothing, so she obeyed. There were two columns of writing on the scroll, one in a language she recognized from Orlando's library but could not read, the other in Latin she could. "The translation is hardly perfect," the laird said as she read. "It identifies the Chalice as the Cup of Christ, which I know it is not. But it speaks of your Orlando."

"Yes," she answered, barely hearing him, she was so shocked by what she read. Orlando was immortal, the natural son of Kivar from the time before he was cursed. How old are you really? she had often teased him as a child. How long have you lived? A hundred thousand years and more, he had always retorted, tweaking her nose. "I raised the first beams of the heavens and dug out the cellar of the earth," he had promised. Even then, he had seemed so wise, she had almost believed him. "He never told me," she said now, looking up from the scroll, her hands shaking. "Even when Kivar came and murdered my father and his people, he never said a word of being the creature's son."

"Perhaps he thought it would make little difference," the laird said, his voice warm and soothing. "Or perhaps he loved you too well to confess it." He smiled. "So you see why I must trust you."

"Must you?" she countered. "Orlando is real, and Kyna had visions, but you do not know me."

"No," he answered. "I do not. But Gareth does." She was shaking her head, and he laughed. "He does, Lady Roxanna, whether you will it or not."

"He knows the best of me," she answered. "When I am with him, I am someone else."

"So might any of us say of the ones that we love." He got up from his chair and took her hands in his. "How old were you when the demon took you, lady? Sixteen? Seventeen?"

"Nearly twenty." Touching him, she could feel the weakness of his heart, not his spirit but the body that contained it. He was dying, for all his will was strong.

"As old as that?" he teased. "I am eighty-four years old, and I have loved with all my heart for all that time. You must trust me."

"Gareth thinks you want him to marry his cousin, Tess," she said, her hands tightening on his. I want to be mortal, she longed to cry. I want to belong to your grandson, to be worthy of his love. I want to stay here and grow old.

"I want the clan to believe that he will," he answered. "They will never accept him otherwise." He brushed a fatherly kiss to her brow and let her go. "They must accept him, Roxanna." He went back to the open window, the snow now drifting on the sill. "When Lucan Kivar comes, they must believe Gareth will save them." He turned back to her and offered her his hand. "Will you help him, Roxanna?"

She went to him and took it. "Aye, my lord." She leaned against his side as she had done with Gareth in the courtyard. "As you say, I love him, so I must."

He pressed a kiss to the top of her head. "I think I will go down to the hall tonight." He let her go, a sad light in his eyes in contrast to his smile as he looked around the room. "This room is too cold."

"I will come with you." Somehow she would do as she had promised. Somehow Gareth must prevail over Kivar; she would give her immortal life and damned soul to make it happen.

"Aye, you must." He touched her cheek with the backs of his fingers. "What a beauty you are."

"Am I not?" she said sardonically. "But it has served me ill."

"Not always, my lady," he said with a smile. "You have my grandson's heart."

"I will not let the clan see it, my laird," she promised.

"You cannot stop them," he said, shaking his head. "Don't try." He touched her chin and turned her face up to his. "You must stop trying to be so wise in love." Before she could answer, he had let her go. "But come. Let us go to the hall."

The atmosphere in the hall that night was as jubilant as Christmas, as if the clan were determined to take the strange events of the day as cause for celebration. Or so Gareth thought, sitting in a corner near the hearth. Kyna was back, cause enough for joy. In truth, from the snatches of softer conversation he had caught in passing, Gareth thought this fact alone was the source of most of this giddy relief. Fear and despise her they might in calmer days, but in times of trouble, the clan wanted their witch.

For what must have been the hundredth time since he had taken his seat, he looked over at the archway that led to the stairs. What could the laird want with Roxanna? What had Kyna told him of her? What did he expect? He saw a shadow coming closer from the hall outside and half rose from his chair. But it was only Duncan, come back from helping Tess.

"To Gareth," he said as a song was ended and

applause broke out. He lifted a fresh cup of ale as he turned to his newfound friend. "Welcome home at last." The toast was repeated by everyone, some more boisterously than others. But every cup was raised. Some might question the laird's choice of a half-English knight as his heir, blood or not, and a few were still bold enough to say so. Duncan's obvious support had only helped the cause.

"I thank you," Gareth said, rising from his seat. "But let us drink to the clan." A few scattered cries of approval rang out with a smattering of applause. "The Clan McKail," he said, raising his cup. "We will not be moved!"

"Never!" Brian roared, and several of the other men joined him with fierce cries of their own, cups raised high. This time the applause was thunderous. Drinking deeply from his own cup, Gareth felt several people thumping him on the back, and as he set it aside, Duncan's mother, Grace, embraced him, tears on her cheeks. Duncan was right. He was home at last.

As he drew back from Grace's arms, he saw Roxanna standing in the archway, arm in arm with the laird. Both of them were smiling. An aching fist of love clenched in his chest, and he raised his cup again to them.

"Another song!" someone called out. "Who shall sing it?" Several people turned to catch hold of Duncan's father, Caleb, urging him to give them a war song in his fine tenor. Others called for Tess to sing of love as she came through the archway and tried to slip unnoticed into the hall, but she quickly demurred, taking a place in the corner.

"Gareth should sing," Roxanna said. She did not raise her voice in the slightest, but suddenly the room was silent. She took a lute from the last singer and walked across the hall to offer it to Gareth, a sweet, teasing smile on her face.

"Is Gareth a singer, then?" Duncan asked, breaking the silence into friendly laughter again.

"Oh, aye." Gareth was looking at her as if he didn't know if he should kiss her or throttle her, and that made her smile even more. "I have only heard him once," she said as he took the lute from her hands. "But I was much impressed."

"Sing for us, Gareth," the woman who had hugged him urged, and others took up the plea.

"Aye, princess," Gareth answered. "I will sing for you." He ushered her into his chair, mindless of the sudden murmurs of the crowd gathered around them. He was meant to be marrying Tess, they were whispering. Why should he look on this other lady so? But he didn't care. "You say you remember my singing," he said to Roxanna. "Do you remember my song?"

"I do," she answered.

"My kin will know it in another tongue," he said, winking at Grace. "But I will sing it in English as you heard it before." Testing the strings for a moment, he began the ballad Marcus had so loved, the Gaelic tale of the fairy princess. Grace gasped, putting a hand to her mouth. After what he had called Roxanna, his intention in his choice of song could not be misunderstood. But Grace was still smiling, he noticed as he turned around in his place to include the others in his performance. All of them were, smiling at him and on his beautiful love. They might be shocked to see him favor her so boldly, but it did not make them like him less. In truth, they probably trusted him more, seeing him act such a rogue. The only one who looked displeased was Tess. He caught her eye for a moment as she stood in the shadows, her arms crossed on her chest. He took a step toward her, still singing, and she turned away, leaving the hall.

Roxanna saw Tess go as well, and listening to Gareth's song, she could understand why. The first time she had heard this song, she had been in no proper state to understand it, but now she heard its tale, a red-haired princess of these lands losing her heart to a wolf. Did all of these people know their legend of Lucan Kivar and the name he was called? Did Gareth mean to insult his red-haired cousin? Surely not. He could be thoughtless as any man could, but he was never cruel. Then he turned back to her to sing the final chorus, and every thought of any other but him was forgotten. The princess was leaving her home to follow her love into darkness, and he sang, "I cannot live without my heart. I must follow it even to death." The last note died away into silence, the hall waiting with bated breath. Then wild applause broke out.

Gareth cared nothing for the applause, only the look he could see in his true love's eyes. "Beautiful," she whispered, her hand on her heart.

Tess stood in the shadows of the corridor, pressed against the cold stone wall. Sean Lebuin seemed to just appear behind her to put his hands on her shoulders. " 'Tis passing strange," he said, leaning close enough to whisper in her ear. "I thought he was your love."

"No." She should have been startled at his presence, should have been offended he should come so close. But somehow, it felt right. "Never mine." She watched the clan congratulate Gareth on his song as if he were the one who had lived among them all his life, not she. The foreign wench, Roxanna, was excusing herself, headed this way. "Good night," she said to the stranger behind her, pulling free of his grasp to hurry up the stairs.

17

Gareth met Sean Lebuin, now washed and dressed and looking more like a man than a ghost loosed from hell, coming down the corridor toward the hall as he came out. "She went toward her room," he said pleasantly as they passed.

"Many thanks," Gareth muttered, barely noticing.

"Or are you looking for Tess?" Gareth stopped and turned back, the hair rising on the back of his neck. But Sean had gone into the hall.

In the tower bedroom, he found Kyna still watching over Sean's sister. She was huddled on her stool beside the hearth, her conjurer's bones spread out among the ashes on the floor before her. She turned to him as he opened the door, and he saw her wrinkled cheeks were streaked with tears.

"What is it?" he asked softly, going to her at once.

"Nothing," she promised as he crouched beside her. He looked toward the woman on the bed. "No, lad, she lives." The witch laid a gnarled hand against his cheek, turning his face back to hers. "Have no fear," she said, her smile turning her eyes to little more than dimples in the deeply tanned folds of her face.

"Why do you weep, Kyna?" he said, putting his hand over hers.

"For what I know will come." She drew his face down to hers and pressed a kiss to his forehead. "But I have known it always, lad. We need have no fear." She let him go and turned back to her bones.

"Kyna?" But she didn't answer, muttering a chant under her breath. He smiled. "Good night," he murmured, kissing her forehead as well.

He found Roxanna already stripped to her shift to wash, her hair loose on her shoulders. "You shouldn't be here," she said, turning to face him with the soaking wet cloth still held against her throat. Rivulets of water glistened on her dusky skin, reminding him sharply of the first time he had seen her, kneeling naked by a tiny fire, sluicing water down her back.

"You like to be clean, do you not?" he teased, moving closer. He took the cloth from her hand and soaked it again in the basin.

"Should I not?" He lifted her hair from the back of her neck, wrapping it around his fist. "You are betrothed to someone else," she pointed out as he bathed her neck and shoulders, wetting the edge of her shift.

"Stop it." He would not argue with her anymore, not tonight. Tomorrow the earth might crack open and hell itself might rise. But tonight she was his. He pulled her hair gently, drawing her head back. "So beautiful," he murmured, kissing her throat.

She bit her lip, biting back a sigh as he drew her closer, his desire impossible to ignore against the softness of her hip. She tried to turn her head to kiss his mouth, but he still held her hair. "Gareth . . ."

"Hush." He slid the shift from her shoulder and squeezed water over her breasts, making her shiver. "Let me do it." He pushed the cloth under the shift into her cleavage, lifting each plump breast in turn to bathe the tender crescent underneath. She reached back for him, clutching at the tail of his rough linen shirt as his mouth moved to her collarbone, his hot, sweet breath scalding her skin.

He let go of her hair to wrap his arm around her waist, drawing her tighter against him, and his breath came short as she wriggled closer still. She raised her arms over her head as if in a dance of surrender, twining one hand around his neck as he bent to kiss her mouth. "I love you," he said, smiling down on her.

"When I allow it," she answered, smiling back. Her lips were parted, swollen and pink from his kisses, and he had no choice but to kiss her again, harder and more deeply, plunging his tongue into her mouth. He drew the shift up over her legs as he dipped the rag again, and she gasped as it touched her inner thigh. "Sweet Allah," she murmured as he drew the rough, dripping cloth slowly upward. He smiled, hooking a booted foot around her bare ankle to draw her legs farther apart.

She rose up on tiptoe, the hand around his neck now clutching at his hair. Kissing her again, he barely brushed the cloth over her sex before taking it away.

"You know, I saw you," he said, dipping it in the warm water again. "That first night, when you thought I was dead."

"What?" she said breathlessly, gasping as he brought the cloth under her shift again, bathing the swell of her stomach. "You saw me . . . ?"

"Saw you bathing." Bending slightly to reach between her legs, he passed the cloth over the sweet swell of her behind, squeezing it again to let water run down her thighs as he straightened up. "I've wanted to do this ever since."

She laughed, one bare foot standing on his as she arched away from him. "You should have done it," she said, then let out a tiny shriek as he crushed her close again. "In faith, you are an excellent servant."

" 'Tis well," he said, laughing low against her skin, pressing a kiss to her cheek. "I wish to be." He brought the cloth back to the cleft of her sex again, rougher this time, and she moaned, twining a leg around his, trusting him to hold her. "Is this right, princess?" he asked her. She arched herself against the cloth as he scrubbed, shameless in desire, making his own breath catch short. "Do I do well?"

"Oh, yes." Every muscle in her body felt swollen and taut, aching for his touch, but it was luscious torture, much too sweet to stop. "You are perfect."

"Then tell me that I am your servant." He let the cloth fall to the floor, touching her with his bare hand.

"Yes," she promised, nodding. She ran a hand along his arm, lacing her fingers with his where he touched her. "So warm . . ." He slipped two fingers tenderly inside her for a moment, and she cried out, wrapping her hand around his wrist. "You are my perfect slave."

"Then tell me you love me." He turned her toward him, sweeping her off her feet into his arms. "Tell me, Roxanna."

She touched his face, the longing in his blue eyes making her feel weak. "I love you." She raised up in the cradle of his arms to kiss him, his forehead, his eyelids, his mouth. "I love you."

"My angel . . ." He carried her to the bed, kissing her feverishly, all games and fears forgotten. Looking straight into her eyes, he moved inside her, and she smiled, her breath coming out as a sigh. All through their joining, he watched her and she watched him, their gazes never wavering. When her climax finally rose and broke, she laughed, her legs wrapped around him as she arched up to meet his thrust. He joined her, wrapping his arms around her as he came.

Rolling to his side, he still held her to him. He kissed her sweetly, drawing her lower lip into his mouth, and she caressed his hair, burying her fingers in its silk. "You must leave me, darling," she said softly as he kissed her cheek. "It is almost dawn."

"What of it?" He didn't want to let her go or ever move again.

"It isn't safe." It had been too long since she had fed; she couldn't risk hurting him now. She kissed him, tasting his tongue with her own. "Besides, you are meant to live in daylight," she said, turning her head for a moment to break the kiss. "Your clan will be looking for you."

"Let them look." But he knew she was right; she could see it in his eyes. He framed her face in his hands. "I love you."

"I love you." She didn't want to let him go. She wanted to snuggle against him, feel safe in his arms as she slept.

"Someday," he said as if he had read her thoughts. "Someday your curse will be broken."

She smiled. "Someday." Kissing him one last time, she pushed him away.

"I will see you tonight." He laid his hand on her arm like a bracelet, drawing it down as he rose until he held her hand. "Sleep well."

Upstairs, Kyna had fallen asleep sitting up on her stool, her head leaned against the fireplace. He drew her multicolored mantle higher on her shoulders, tucking it around her, touching her cheek for a moment to make certain she hadn't caught a chill. With the wounded girl using his bed, he wasn't quite certain where he was meant to sleep—the hall, he supposed. But late as it was, he wasn't quite ready for sleep. The room was stuffy, thick with the smell of Kyna's potions. He went to the window and opened the shutter to take a deep breath of fresh air.

The sky was breathtaking, streaked in the east with the first pink stripes of dawn, glowing green in the north and west with the shimmering winter lights. When he was a boy, his uncle, Jamey, had told him these were the spirits of dragons vanquished by long ago knights and exiled to the sky. He had waited every year as the autumn grew colder in fearful anticipation of their return. "I have come home, dragons," he murmured now, bracing his hands on the window frame. "Did you look for me?"

The woman on the bed stirred and sighed, calling out a word he couldn't quite make out. "Siobhan?" Her color seemed to be improving, he saw when he moved closer. Her eyelids no longer looked so bruised, and her lips were pinker. "Did you say something?" he said gently, touching her cheek. "Did you call for Sean?"

She said the name again, and it might have been Sean. But in truth, it sounded more like Simon. She turned her face toward his hand, then turned it abruptly away, mumbling too softly to be understood.

"It's all right," he soothed. "Are you thirsty?" He filled a cup with water, then lifted her gently in the crook of one arm to hold it to her lips. "That's it . . . one more sip."

Suddenly she convulsed in his arms, knocking the cup away. "Sean!" she cried out quite distinctly, grabbing his wrist. She stared at him, a look to chill him to the bone, her green eyes shockingly bright. "Not Sean . . ." Her voice trailed away into a rasp as she went limp again, her sudden strength draining away.

"Siobhan!" He lay her back down on the pillows. "Siobhan, what is it?"

"No," she murmured, closing her eyes again. "Not right." Her fingers closed around his sleeve as if to hold him there, as if she had something more to tell him. But she said no more.

He considered waking Kyna, but there seemed to be no point. If the girl rallied again, 'twould likely be more of the same. Lifting her hand to his lips in sad salute, he left her to sleep.

Roxanna wrapped the blankets more tightly around her, willing herself not to think of anything but Gareth, the sweet bliss she had felt in his arms. Safe behind two bolted doors, she let herself listen to the heartbeats of the living souls above her, most of them slowing with sleep. *I love you,* she had promised, returning Gareth's pledge. She couldn't take the words back now. She smiled, breathing in his scent that still lingered on her pillow. Cursed or not, she was happy. Her love might be his ruin; hell might have them both. But tonight they had loved and confessed it. Whatever else might happen in the future, nothing could take that away.

The drowsiness of dawn was taking her; she could

feel her body growing heavy. She let her mind drift to the individual heartbeats . . . Kyna, slow but strong; the red-haired girl, weak and erratic. Those a bit more distant were harder to separate, gathered together into families. What a sweet notion, she thought with an inward smile. She couldn't have opened her eyes if she had tried. Further still she felt more than heard a single heartbeat, growing slower . . . slower . . . Feeling alarm, she tried to stir, but she was already too far gone. The heart was barely beating now; with every beat, she waited, certain it would be the last. Someone was dying, not in pain, not in violence, but dying just the same. The laird, she thought, a tear escaping down her cheek. May God keep him . . . The last heartbeat slipped away.

Her perception drew back into the thick of the others as if for comfort. She was truly sleeping now. But she felt something else, a distinctive pulse that was more than a heartbeat. The feeling was familiar but not comforting; suddenly she felt cold. Kivar . . . she felt Lucan Kivar. She tried to wake herself, to make herself move, but it was hopeless. Still struggling, she sank into the black of dreamless sleep.

18

By midday, the laird's body had been brought down from the tower and laid in state in the chapel. Tess held her breath as she leaned close to wipe the dead face with a cloth, the eyes held closed with coins bearing the mark of the English sovereign. The laird's right hand was laid on the hilt of his sword, and Tess lay her own over it, the cold, hard flesh making her shiver. 'Twas strange to think that he was gone. She touched the signet ring he wore, the symbol of his rule. Her father should have worn this ring. It should be him who stood now among the elders of the clan, receiving their condolence, hearing them speak to him in a new, hushed tone as if he had turned into Merlin in the night. Not Gareth. Not the son of the Englishman who had usurped her father's place. She slipped the ring from her grandfather's finger and warmed it in her fist.

"Is there a priest near enough to come?" Gareth was asking.

"Not quickly enough for the funeral," Brian answered. "But we will send for Father Joseph even so. He will give the laird a blessing when he comes, and he can marry you and Tess."

"Oh, good, you got the ring," Grace said to Tess. "I didn't know how I would make myself do it." Tess opened her eyes and her fist, barely hiding her annoyance. "You must give it to your cousin," Grace said gently, touching her arm.

"Of course," Tess said briskly, turning to the men. "Here, cousin." She put the ring in Gareth's hand and closed his fist over it. "This belongs to you."

"Thank you." He looked over at Duncan, still just holding the ring, not putting it on. "Brian . . ." He looked back at Tess. "Tess and I are not to be married." All of the men except Duncan and his father looked shocked. "Tess was promised to Duncan long before I came home," Gareth went on. "My grandfather wanted a match between us to satisfy the clan—"

"And so it would," one of the other men said, and several others murmured their assent.

"But it would not satisfy Tess," Gareth said, looking at his cousin. "I cannot sacrifice her happiness to make myself laird. If the clan cannot accept me for myself, they need not have me."

Liar, she thought. *You just don't want me*. "Did you know aught of this, Tess?" Brian asked her.

"Of course." Duncan was looking at her now, smiling, and she made herself smile back. "We did not want to dispute Grandfather when he was so ill. There was no need to upset him."

"Speak not of the laird as if he might have been a peevish child," one of the other men scolded.

"Speak not to my lady cousin like she might be a servant," Gareth said angrily, turning on him. "She knows our grandfather's worth better than any of you and cares more for his dignity. Who is it who has cared for him this long year past? Was it you?" The man mumbled something, hanging his head. "No." Gareth turned back to Tess and offered her his hand. "She will not be my wife, but she is my kinswoman. If I am to be laird, I would have her given all proper respect."

"Gareth, every man here supports your claim and will fight to defend it," Brian said, putting a hand on his arm. "We swore as much to your grandfather long since." He looked around the circle until every man nodded his assent. "And no one doubts Tess and Duncan deserve every happiness." He did not wait for approval of this. They despised her, just as they had despised her father. If she were to be turned out with the cows and pigs, no one but Duncan would care. And if his precious friend, Gareth, were the one to do it, he would not say him nay. He might go with her and wallow in the mud and chew cud on the hillside, but he would never fight back. "But we are not the whole clan," Brian went on. "I have no doubt we could bring the others around in time, but can we afford the dispute? Now that the old laird is dead, the other clans will be watching, ready to drive us from our lands if they think we are weak. And there's the other reason to think of. . . ." Several men mumbled a protest at this, as if they didn't want to speak of any other danger to the clan, and Grace clasped her hands in prayer. "We must be united if we mean to defeat the wolf."

"The wolf is naught but a legend," Duncan protested.

"No," Gareth said. "I wish that were true, but it isn't. I thought the same, that in their old age, my grandfather and Kyna had conjured up a phantom in their minds and convinced themselves it was real. But I know now that it is real. Sean and Siobhan were attacked by the wolf; Siobhan lies near death now from the attack. And Lady Roxanna has seen him as well." At the mention of his foreign whore, Tess couldn't stop herself from letting out a snort. "The wolf is real, and he is coming for the clan," Gareth finished as she covered her face with her hands, disguising the snort as a sob.

"All the more reason to keep peace," Brian said. "I do not say you must marry Tess, but I see no harm in continuing to pretend you will, at least until this threat has passed."

"Now that the laird is dead, the people who have doubts will push for a marriage," Duncan pointed out.

"He's right," Gareth agreed. "I love Tess as my cousin. But I will take another as my wife."

"The Lady Roxanna, you mean?" one of the other men said with a laugh. Gareth had the innocence to actually look surprised, as if he hadn't all but fallen at her feet before the whole clan the night before. "I hear tell she is a princess, lad. Why should she have you?"

"Still, if she did, it might impress the other clans," Duncan said. "If we let it be known that we are led by a French-trained knight who has returned with a captured princess for his wife, the McLeans might well hesitate to come calling."

"And if she knows aught of the Wolf as the laird believed, she could help us fight him as well," another man said eagerly, and several of the others hurried to agree. Tess could not believe her ears.

"We should give her all those papers the laird had squirreled away in his room," another man suggested. "If she is a scholar, mayhap she can make sense of them where the laird could not."

"Kyna trusts her; that much is certain," Duncan said, meeting Tess's eyes. Of all of them, he should know best how little she cared for what Kyna believed.

"Aye, she does," Brian agreed. "The old laird did as well." He turned to Gareth. "Are you certain she will accept you?"

"Aye," he answered with a grin. "Pretty certain."

"Speak to her privately, then," Brian said. He looked around the circle again, including every man in his instruction. "Until you have her answer, we will continue to say you mean to marry our own Tess."

"And when he jilts me for Lady Roxanna, Duncan can be chivalrous and save me from the veil," she couldn't stop herself from saying, her voice thick with the bitterness that always betrayed her.

"When Lady Roxanna bewitches him, you can be released to marry your true love," Duncan said before anyone else could speak.

She met his eyes, seeing hurt and anger there behind his smile. "Aye," she answered, smiling back. "That will be the truth."

"Are we agreed, then?" Gareth asked.

"We are," Brian said, his answer echoed by the others. "Put that ring on your hand, and we are done."

Gareth hesitated for a moment, as if he still weren't certain that he should. He knows he has no place here, Tess thought; he knows that for him to call himself the laird is a blasphemous crime. But he would do it anyway. "As you will," he said, putting the ring on his finger. "We are done."

She hung back as the others filed out of the chapel. They would go into the hall and put Gareth in his grandfather's chair. People would come and look at the corpse for barely a moment, then hurry to the hall to curry favor.

"Will you not come inside?" Duncan said, startling her—she hadn't even noticed he had not gone with the others. "Come." He gently disengaged her hands from the twisted cloth and kissed each one. "Leave the dead in peace."

"Duncan!" His father had come back to fetch him. "You must come now," he said, his quick glance taking in their joined hands with a frown. "The gossips are watching like hawks."

"I will follow you," Tess said, dropping Duncan's hands before he could drop hers. She smiled at his father, her cheeks aching with the effort. "But not too close behind."

As soon as they were gone, she left the chapel by the back door, heading down the hill away from the tower to the tiny house the laird had given her father. She had not lived there since Jamey died and her mother ran away, but she would not allow anyone else to live there either—the one indulgence she had been allowed. She had not been inside for months, not since the laird had taken ill. She didn't realize someone else had.

"Bastards," she breathed, looking around the main room. Nothing was broken; all the furniture was still neatly in place. But every drawer and cupboard had been opened and left bare. All of her father's books were gone, all of his scrolls, even his lute. She went into the bedroom and found the bed stripped to its bare wooden frame, the chest at the foot standing open and empty. "All of it," she said aloud as if there were someone there to hear. "They took all of it!" She had seen the scrolls and books in her grandfather's tower room, had even recognized some of them as having been her father's. But it had never once occurred to her that every single scrap of writing he had ever collected could be taken from her without so much as a word.

"Tess?" a man's voice called from the front room—

Sean Lebuin. "Tess, are you all right?" She had seen him in the tower hall earlier, obviously flirting with a girl of barely sixteen, and she had smiled, knowing the truth of him at last. He was a scoundrel, a rogue—all his advances toward her had been no more than reflex. But now he was here, coming into her father's bedroom, looking at her with his pale blue eyes as if he cared about her. "I just heard your grandfather has died," he said. "I am sorry."

"Do you think I mourn him?" she demanded. She was done pretending, done trying to be what she could not. No one thanked her for it; nothing she could do would ever be enough. "I hated him, hated what he would have made of me—I hope he is roasting in hell right now, burning in the very center of the fire." He should have looked shocked. If she had said such a thing to her cousin or even to Duncan, they would probably have fainted. But he was smiling—no, he was laughing at her. "Go away," she ordered, pointing toward the door. "Leave me alone."

"I will not." In one motion, he crossed the room and caught her pointing hand, drawing her into his arms. She opened her mouth to protest, and he kissed her, pinning her hands behind her back when she tried to struggle free. "You don't want me to leave you alone," he said, his voice more a growl than human speech, making her shiver to the marrow of her bones. "You've been alone enough already."

"Yes . . ." He kissed her again, and this time she

arched up to meet him, relaxing in his grip. "I tried to kill him," she confessed as he drew her closer, sheltering her in his arms. "I saved every penny I could steal until I had enough to hire mercenaries." She wrapped her arms around him, resting her head on his shoulder, and he just held her, not trying to kiss her, not trying to make her stop talking. "There were six of them. Why didn't he die?" He stroked her hair, so soothing, but still he didn't shush her or say a word. "Duncan said they found their bodies and two graves—both of his friends were killed, and he was badly wounded—I saw his wounds myself. What could have saved him?"

She felt his laughter as a low rumble in his chest. "I can guess, little one." He pressed a kiss to her brow. "But what does it matter?" He drew back until he could turn her face up to his to kiss her mouth. "Why is this cousin of yours so important?" he asked, stopping long before she wanted him to stop. "I heard them say he would be the new laird—"

"That is why," she said with a frown that was almost a snarl.

"But why?" he asked. "I thought he had just arrived here. Why should he be made the laird instead of some other member of the clan?"

"Because he bears the mark of the wolf." She withdrew from his arms, and he allowed it. "It's ridiculous—a stupid legend. He has two clusters of marks on his arm, just here, just like my idiot grandfather. So now the elders believe he can save them from some demon they believe is coming after the clan. It's all Kyna's nonsense—"

"No." His smile was so wicked, it was almost a leer. "Not nonsense." He held out his arm to her, pushing up his sleeve. "Show me again where your cousin has his marks."

"Right here." She reached out and touched his skin. "The shape of a cross at the bottom, the shape of the Chalice at the top . . ." She stopped, her voice drying up in her throat. Everywhere she touched him, his skin seemed to bubble up as if he had been branded from the inside—she even smelled the burning flesh. "Oh, sweet Christ . . ." The burning stopped, leaving a mark exactly identical to Gareth's.

"Not exactly." She looked up to find a pale light glowing in his eyes, a light not of the world.

"You . . ." She had caught hold of his sleeve, she suddenly realized, was clutching it in her fist. "You are the wolf."

His answer was to kiss her until she could no longer catch her breath, crushing her in his arms. She should be frightened; she should scream for help, she thought. But who would care if a demon should take her? No one but the demon. "So now you know," he said, breaking the kiss. "Will you tell your cousin?" He brushed a kiss across her brow. "Will you help them destroy me?"

"No." She laughed aloud, every nerve tingling with happiness as she pressed him close again. "I swear I will not."

"My darling . . ." He squeezed her tight again, kissing her cheek. "No mercenary can kill the scion of McKail, no matter how many stolen pennies he is paid," he said, holding her head to his shoulder. "Not when he has a vampire to save him."

"A vampire—?"

"But do not worry, little one." He put a hand under her chin. "I promise you I can." He kissed her again, and she melted in his arms, drawing him down to the floor.

19

Roxanna was barely awake at sunset before Gareth was pounding on her door. "Peace, for pity," she called to him, staggering to her feet. She wanted to see him, desperately, but she had slept badly, haunted by nightmares, and she was hungry. She hadn't fed since sunset of the night she and Kyna had brought the others to the castle. To wait much longer could be disastrous.

"Roxanna, open the door," Gareth demanded, pounding again.

"I said wait!" She loved him, but she wouldn't be ordered about like a servant, particularly in such an ill temper. Muttering rare oaths in her native tongue, she donned one of the gowns that had been left for her and yanked her hair out of the collar.

"Where were you?" he complained as soon as she opened the door.

"Where do you think?" she grumbled, turning her back on him. "I was here, of course." She picked up her borrowed hairbrush and went to work on the knots in her hair.

"I was calling . . ." Gareth had been waiting all day to see her, a thousand different powerful feelings bottled up inside him, waiting to be poured out. At the very least, he had expected to be greeted with a smile.

"Yes," she said testily, tugging on a particularly stubborn tangle. "I heard you." She plaited her curls into a messy braid and tied off the end with a ribbon. "Is the sun even down yet?"

"Only just." The hurt in his voice finally penetrated her temper, making her turn around. He was sitting on the side of her bed, looking so forlorn and confused, she almost had to laugh.

"Darling . . ." Leaving her toilet, she went to kiss him instead. "Forgive me," she said, framing his face in her hands to cover it with kisses. "I slept badly." She kissed his mouth as he drew her into his lap. "And I missed you."

"Yes, I can tell." But he couldn't stay angry, not when she was giving him exactly what he wanted. He drew her closer, and she wrapped her arms around his neck, pressing herself against him. "Angel . . ." He kissed the back of her neck under her braid. "My grandfather is dead."

"Oh, no." She kissed his cheek. "I felt it . . . this morning, just after you left me, just before I fell asleep." She drew back to look at his face, laying a hand on his cheek. "I am so sorry."

He held her hand against his face, turning his head to kiss her wrist. "So we have to be married, now," he explained. Her face had gone completely blank, but he thought nothing of it. She had been fond of his grandfather, and she did not show her sorrows easily. "Other than the elders and Duncan and Tess, everyone still thinks Tess and I mean to marry," he explained, shifting her off his lap so he could face her. "If I should break our betrothal without good cause, there could be dissension in the clan. I could even be challenged for the title of laird."

"So don't break it," she said.

"Angel, I must," he said with a laugh. "This is my clan, but most of them barely know me. They will never accept me as laird without a fight unless they know I am settled, that I mean to stay and make my family here. But as Duncan pointed out, you are a princess," he went on. "If they know I have won you, they will trust me to lead them."

"So I am an acceptable second choice." For one nightmare moment, she sounded exactly like Tess.

"You are my first choice, my only choice, and everyone will know it." He fell to his knees before her, only half in jest. "Roxanna, angel, I beseech you. Will you marry me?"

"Gareth," she protested, taking her hands from his and rising. "No!" Had she not already told him she would never marry him? The very idea made her tremble. "I can't." She walked away, pacing the room.

For a moment, he was so shocked, he could hardly speak. "What do you mean, you can't?" he demanded at last. "Of course you can."

"Is that true, in faith?" she said, turning back to him. "And how can I? I am a vampire, Gareth, cursed, a demon."

"But no one else knows it but me," he pointed out, getting back to his feet.

"And how long do you think that will last?" He is genuinely shocked, she thought, aghast. "If your clan wants you to marry, will they not also expect you to have heirs?"

"And so I will have, someday," he said stubbornly. "We will have, together." She laughed, shaking her head. "Do you not mean to break this curse of yours?"

"Yes!" Nothing had changed since the first time she had told him what she was. He still believed defeating Kivar was no more than a trifle, easily done, a minor complication to be solved before the future as he saw it could begin. "But just because I mean to do it doesn't mean I will."

"You said yesterday that you believed in me," he pointed out, struggling not to lose his temper. She had been afraid of Lucan Kivar for years; he could not expect her to give up her fears so quickly, no matter how dearly she might love him.

"Of course I do—"

"You said I was your champion." She just needed for him to remind her that he meant to save her, to break her curse, he thought. She was falling back into the old despair, and he could hardly blame her. But she would come around.

"Oh, sweet Allah." She was starving; she could barely think at all. But he expected her to conjure up sweet words to promise him yet again that he was worthy, when any fool with half a brain could see he was perfect. "Don't be such a child," she scolded, putting on her shoes.

"A child?" As much as he was fighting to understand her, this struck him like a fist. He sat down on the bed again, the bed where he had finally made love to her exactly as he wanted. How could she have forgotten so quickly? "What was last night, Roxanna?" he asked, keeping his voice even with an effort.

"What do you mean?" Once again, she saw she had hurt him, and she felt horrible for it. But she was angry, too. Did he care nothing for her feelings? She could understand his commitment to his clan; she had been born to such obligation herself. But taken against the prospect of Kivar's return, the political marriage of the ruler of a group of peasants was hardly worth such a fuss. "Last night was us together." This time it was she who fell to her knees before him, taking his hands in hers. "Nothing will ever change that."

"Then why will you not marry me?" He sounded like a petulant child even to himself, and he hated it. But nothing she was saying made sense to him—how could she love him and still refuse to be his wife? How could she cling to him one moment and reject him the next?

"Gareth . . ." She clutched his hands more tightly, resisting the urge to make a fist and punch him in the face. "I am starving," she began again, keeping her tone even with great effort. It was not in her nature to hold her temper; in truth, she was more likely to bring down the rafters with her rage and always had been, even as a mortal. But she loved him with all her heart, and she knew she was not in her right mind. "Once I have fed, I will be able to think about this and discuss it with you as much as you like."

"But you won't marry me." She would explain why he could not have her hand the way a mother would explain why her little boy could not have one more sweet, he thought. Once she was done with the serious business of being a demon, perhaps she could be bothered to address the trivial matter of his offering her his soul. He smiled, lifting her hand to his lips with conscious formality. "Happy hunting, princess."

"Gareth!" She tried to catch his arm, but he was already gone, out the door and up the ladder to the room above. "Gareth!" She grabbed up her mantle and started after him.

"Let him go," Kyna advised, the bedroom door slamming behind him just as she reached the top. "You have wounded his pride, my lady. You must give him time to heal before you can make him think."

So Kyna could hear every word they spoke to one another below her, Roxanna thought with an inward sigh. "You may be right," she said. "I certainly know nothing about it." Before Gareth, the only person with whom she had ever had to argue was Orlando. And even with him, she could pull rank and end the dispute if her position started to fail.

"Why do you not wish to marry him?" the weird woman asked. She was sitting beside the bed, stroking the sick woman's hand.

"Does it matter?" she countered. In truth, the very idea of describing her reasons made her sick. Every time she thought of it, all she could see was the golden hall full of English knights being slaughtered all around her, the poor duke playing the part of her groom lying dead at her feet, the dagger in her fist soaked in his blood. "I just do not," she finished, pushing the image from her mind.

"And so you need not," Kyna agreed. "But someone will."

She opened her mouth to say something sharp, but she closed it before the words were spoken. "Is she no better?" she asked instead.

"I wish I could say. Sometimes I think yes, sometimes no." She laid a hand on the sick woman's forehead. "She dreams, poor poppet, terrible things from the sound of it. But I cannot see."

"I can imagine." She had seen the way Kivar tortured his pets, particularly the ones he had no intention of making immortal. If this woman dreamed of that, her death would be a mercy. "I have to go out," she said aloud. "Is there a way I can leave the walls without being seen?"

"You needn't bother," Kyna answered. "The young

laird has given instruction to the guard that you be allowed to pass through the gates without question, in or out."

So Gareth had thought of her need for blood after all, she thought, feeling a pang in her heart. She would ease his wounded pride somehow; she would make him understand. "Thank you, Kyna." Giving the old woman's hand a squeeze, she left her to go find food.

20

The shimmering green sky cast a strange, deceptive light over the frozen grove, making the ice-covered trees seem to dance in their circle. But there was no mistaking the stench of the blood or the livid stain that had spread over the gray stone altar and into the stark white snow. "We are too late," Orlando said tonelessly, falling to his knees before the altar. "Lucan Kivar has won."

"Is it Isabel's blood?" Siobhan asked Simon, putting a hand on his arm. "Would you know—?" He nodded before she could finish and turned away, walking back toward the horses. "Oh, Simon . . ." She turned away as well, unable to look any longer.

But Tristan continued to study the altar, thoughtfully rubbing his chin. "Explain to me again how this should work," he said. "Sean bleeds Isabel onto the altar—"

"Not Sean," Siobhan said sharply. "Sean did not do this."

"Kivar then," Tristan corrected, taking her hand. "He sheds Isabel's blood on the altar—why?"

"To open the gateway," Orlando answered. "To break through the veil between worlds. The Chalice would be on the other side."

"So we believe Kivar now has the Chalice?" Orlando didn't answer; he didn't seem able to speak. "No," Tristan said, shaking his head. "No . . . we would know."

"How, love?" Siobhan asked.

"Because he would have come after us by now," her husband answered. "According to Orlando, once Kivar has the Chalice, he has unlimited power; he becomes a god. Do you honestly think if that were the case, he would just go away and wait for us to come looking for him?"

"Maybe he doesn't care about us anymore," she said.

"No," Simon said. He had been resting his forehead against his horse's flank, but now he raised his head. "He would care." He turned back to them, new hope dawning in his eyes. "Even if he believes Orlando was drowned or at least trapped at the bottom of that lake, he would still want revenge on the rest of us."

"You particularly," Tristan agreed. "And if he only needed Isabel for her blood, where is her body? Why would he take the corpse away?"

"Tristan," Siobhan scolded, glancing at Simon. "Don't call her a corpse."

"It's all right," Simon said, smiling. "She isn't dead."

"Then where are they?" Orlando demanded. "This is the place, I promise you. I remember." He climbed back to his feet, his eyes haunted by old ghosts. "The gateway beneath the Castle Charmot was real; I believe there was once a gateway in the hill under DuMaine. But this is the source. This grove was where the old gods came through to us. This is where Kivar was condemned and the Chalice was hidden." He looked around the circle. "It was all green. That village of ice was our village."

"That was a long time ago," Simon said gently.

"More than a thousand years," Orlando agreed. "So long I had forgotten the way. But if the Chalice isn't here . . ." He paced around the altar. "Kivar would think it was here, just as I did. He would try to open the gateway—he did, we see he did. He fed on these here, making himself strong." He pointed to the dead men lying in an almost perfect line from the outer rim of the circle to the altar itself, and Siobhan shivered, cleaving to Tristan's side. "Then he put Isabel on the altar and shed her blood, probably much as he tried at Charmot. If he did manage to open the gateway and tried to reach through, the force of the rift would have weakened him badly. He is still subject to the curse of the gods, even inside Sean's living body; he is forbidden to cross over between worlds. That's why he tried to send you through at Charmot, Simon, to make you fetch it for him. Now, even with a living form to give him some protection, he would still have been counting on the

Chalice to save him, to be able to lay hold of it in time before the rift was sealed. If he couldn't . . ." He turned back to them and smiled. "He would be weak," he finished. "And except for Isabel, he would be alone."

"So do we now believe the Chalice was never here?" Tristan said.

"Oh, it was here," Orlando answered. "I saw it. We just don't know if it's here now."

"And the only way to tell is to open the gateway," Simon said. "For which we need Isabel's blood."

"Or mine," Siobhan agreed. "I am from the same bloodline, remember? Except now I'm a vampire . . ."

"Or Sean's." The other three turned to look at Tristan. "If Sean really is still alive, he still has his own blood, does he not? And isn't he descended from Merlin, too?" He grinned. "Orlando, is it possible this demon of yours is stupid enough to have not figured that out yet?"

"It's possible," Orlando said. "But I doubt it. He could not have kept possession of Sean for so long if he weren't part of his own bloodline. That's why he tried to take possession of Siobhan first."

"He wants to keep Sean's body," Siobhan said. "He didn't bleed it because he wants to keep it."

"And perhaps Sean is fighting him," Simon said, reaching for her hand. "His quarrels with Tristan aside, your brother is a good man, is he not?"

She smiled. "Oh, yes. If it were possible to fight, he would fight."

"So where have they gone?" Tristan said. "We followed tracks to get here, but they were so trodden over, I couldn't tell if anyone came back the same way."

"They must have," Simon said, bending closer to the ground as he moved around the altar. "There are indentations here in the snow, as if someone was kneeling." He touched the snow with his gloved hand, careful not to touch the bloodstain, as if he thought it could burn him. "Does anyone else smell that?"

Tristan looked around at the corpses. The ice had preserved them well enough to escape notice by a mortal, but to vampires, the stench was horrific. "Unfortunately, yes."

"Not that," Simon said, shaking his head. He lifted a handful of snow to his nose. "I have smelled this somewhere before . . . Orlando, the night I was made, there was another vampire, a woman. Do you remember?"

Orlando smiled. "Of course."

"She turned herself into a vapor, and you put her in a bottle." He sniffed the snow again. "The vapor smelled just like this."

"Sacred gods," Orlando said, hurrying to him. "It cannot be." He fell to his knees beside the vampire. "Yes . . . she was here." He looked up at Simon. "I dropped the bottle. Isabel said I should release her, that I shouldn't let her be taken by Kivar, even as a vapor, so I dropped the bottle on the road. Someone must have opened it. . . . Roxanna is free."

"Someone must have gotten quite a shock," Tristan said sardonically.

"But not an entirely unpleasant one," Simon agreed. "She is beautiful."

"She would have been ravenous," Orlando said. "If a mortal opened the bottle, 'tis likely she killed him on sight."

"Lovely," Tristan said. "So generally speaking . . . is this a good vampire or an evil one?

"She is good," Orlando said.

"She certainly seemed to me to be," Simon agreed. "I would never have known how to fight Kivar at all if she hadn't told me."

"Maybe she found the Chalice," Siobhan suggested. "Maybe she vanquished Kivar, or at least managed to save Isabel." She offered a hand to Orlando, helping him back to his feet. "Could you two follow her scent?"

"I think so," Simon nodded. "Not on horseback, but whoever was here was on foot in any case."

"We can lead the horses," Tristan decided. "These corpses are fresh; they can't have gone far." He put an arm around Siobhan and kissed the top of her head. "We may save your damned brother yet."

Gareth stormed into the room at the top of the tower and slammed the door shut behind him. The books and scrolls had all been packed into baskets to be carried down to Roxanna, and the snow had been swept out the windows and the shutters fastened. Otherwise, it looked just the same as it had when his grandfather left it, down to the dirty plates and cups on the table. Suddenly the very sight of it made him furious. Roaring the worst oath he could think of, he grabbed the edge of the table and shoved it over with a crash, sending dishes sailing in every direction.

She had refused him. He had offered her his heart, his very soul, and she had recoiled as if he were holding out a snake. She had taken him to her bed easily enough—indeed, she had fucked him before she even knew his name. But marry him? Never—she had said as much. He might as well have been some doxy in a tavern for all their joining mattered to Her Royal Highness Roxanna.

But that was wrong. It wasn't Roxanna who had wronged him. She was frightened; she needed his help, not his anger. If he truly loved her . . . he flung open the shutters, breathing in the cold night air.

The dragon lights were even brighter tonight than they had been the night before. The whole sky seemed to be shimmering green and blue. Looking down, he could see the entire village far below, surrounded by the wall. Watching the gate, he saw a dark figure pass through into the forest beyond—Roxanna on her way to hunt. He watched her move like a shadow off the roadway into the trees, unconsciously gripping the wooden windowsill so tightly splinters broke off in his hands. She was going to hunt. The beautiful, delicate woman he loved would go out into the forest and kill for blood, not because she was evil or because she wanted to do it but because she had no choice. Gareth knew her; he knew her true nature. She was his angel, his love. She would never have chosen such a life. But Lucan Kivar had given her no choice. Because of Kivar, she was a monster.

He felt as if he had just been doused with a barrel of ice-cold water. Ever since the night Roxanna had first told him she was a vampire, he had believed he understood her, that he knew what this curse of hers meant. He had seen her slaughter half a dozen men with no weapon but her hands and teeth, had he not? But even with his memory restored, the events of that night were like a dream, something he might have imagined. He had been dying in agony, barely able to see, much less think. When he had first seen her transform herself into the cat, he had been too shocked to truly see it. Indeed, he had fainted like a maiden with the vapors.

"No wonder she doubts me," he muttered. He wanted her to marry him, to trust him to free her from this curse, when he himself could hardly face it. He picked up a flagon of wine that was spilling itself in the rushes, a casualty of his temper, and drank a long swallow, sitting down hard on a chair. When Roxanna said she had to feed, she didn't mean she had to go down to the kitchens and have a bowl of stew. She meant she had to kill some living creature by drinking its blood. The food that she took was still alive. And sometimes, it was human.

His own stomach rolled with revulsion. How quickly after a kill had he kissed her? He let out a bitter laugh that made him sound like a lunatic as he pushed that happy thought away. Somehow, he had willfully allowed the reality of who—and what—he loved escape him almost completely. I am doomed to live under a curse, she had told him. Not to worry, he had blithely answered; I will break it for you. Stay with me and be my wife, and I will make it all come round in the end. 'Twas a testament to her love for him that she had not laughed in his face.

"But she does love me," he said aloud. "And I love her." He did love her with all his heart, no less now than an hour before. Nothing he ever saw her do could change that. She had cared for him; she challenged him; she had the quickest mind and the most tender heart he had ever known or heard tell of in his life. And murderous demon or not, she was still so beautiful that every time he looked at her, she stole his breath away. He couldn't give her up, vampire or not. But she was right, the idea that they could simply be married like any other pair of mortal sweethearts was absurd.

But he could save her. He finished the wine in the dregs of his flagon and tossed it in the general direction of the rest of the fallen crockery. Let someone else clean up the mess, he thought. He had problems enough of his own. He had to find this demon, this Kivar, and punish him for what he had done. He had to win Roxanna's freedom, to bring her back into the light. He was chosen to do it, the scion of the clan, and he would not fail. His rage reborn as new resolve, he got up and headed downstairs.

Roxanna straightened up into her own human form, wiping any telltale smudges of blood from the corners of her mouth with one delicate fingertip. She snapped a twig from an evergreen as she passed and chewed it idly, cleaning her teeth for good measure. The snow was lovely, she thought, much deeper than the thin ice that had clung to the mountains near her birthplace in the coldest winter months. Being so near the desert, they had rarely had real snow, even in the most bitter cold. But she was glad of the thick sheepskin boots someone had been kind enough to leave for her in her new room. She retrieved her damp mantle from the ground as well and wrapped it around her shoulders.

What to do about Gareth? She could have laughed if she hadn't felt so sad. In all her life, she had never fretted over anyone, king nor commoner, the way she seemed to spend every waking moment fretting over him. Sometimes she thought finding him was a punishment for every evil she had ever done. But mostly she knew he was a reward she could never deserve.

He was furious with her—she had handled his proposal badly. Like any Christian knight, he believed he had offered her the ultimate gift, the ultimate acknowledgment of her worth to him. To have it spurned was a terrible insult. She would have to tell him the truth. Every time she thought of their marriage, all she could think of was her nightmare, the dream of her last night in the palace of the caliph when Kivar had offered her as bride to his kill. Orlando said that dreams often had meaning, and she did not have to be a wizard to guess the truth of this one. If Gareth were to become her husband, it would mean his death. That she would not allow.

She was so caught up in her memory that for a long time, she barely noticed the smell. The caliph's palace had reeked of it from his first night in residence, no matter how deeply the bodies were buried or how much sweet perfume was burned. But walking through the crisp, clean night, she slowly realized it was real. Something was dead in this forest. Something murdered by Kivar.

She followed the scent, tearing through a thicket of thorny vines until she found the body. It was a young girl, barely sixteen from the look of her—she had seen her in the village. Holding a hand over her mouth, she leaned closer and saw the marks upon her neck, not neat but ragged, as if torn by human teeth rather than a vampire's fangs. But the smell was unmistakable. Every vampire left a trace of himself on every victim, which any vampire who knew him well could sense. Kivar had often disguised himself to tease her, fooling her with some new form or another, and many times, she had not known it was him until he revealed himself. But his victims could not be disguised. This kill belonged to Kivar.

She stumbled back into the clearing, queasy and faint. Kivar was close, close enough to have killed one of McKail's clan within sight of the castle, maybe that same night. The body certainly couldn't have been dead much longer than a day. Poor child, her kin would be looking for her. She would have to tell Gareth so he could arrange for the body to be found—she didn't dare report it herself. She would have to tell him Kivar was close . . . but if he were coming for the clan, why would he hide in the woods?

"What is your game?" she called out to the darkness. "What do you want?" But of course there was no answer. Wrapping her mantle more tightly around her, she started back to the castle.

Gareth was standing in a corner of the hall with Duncan when Roxanna came in, her hood fallen back and her hair wild about her face, as if she had been running. "I have to talk to you," she said to Gareth, ignoring Duncan completely. "Right now."

A small group of people had noticed her entrance and were now watching, bemused, Sean Lebuin among them. He caught Gareth's eye and smiled, and once again, Gareth got the distinct, angry impression that they would never be friends. "In a moment," he said to Roxanna. "Go and wait—"

"We may not have a moment," she cut him off in

her most princesslike tone. She did manage to spare Duncan a glance, but it was so brief, it was more an insult than an acknowledgment. "It cannot wait."

"Go on, then," Duncan said, the corner of his mouth curled in a sardonic smile. He had been pressing Gareth for news of his engagement, suggesting that Roxanna was taking much too high a hand in the debate. Now here was proof of his argument. "You are required."

"Duncan!" But his friend was already gone, and the others quickly turned away as well. Only Sean Lebuin seemed inclined to linger, his arms crossed on his chest. But suddenly he blanched and turned quickly to follow the others. Turning, Gareth saw Roxanna glaring after him with a look to freeze any man's blood.

"I'm sorry," she said, her manner relaxing as she turned her attention to Gareth.

"Are you truly?" he retorted. He had all but forgiven her for refusing him, but he didn't care to be ordered about like one of her servants even so.

"Yes." She put a hand on his arm, and suddenly he saw the genuine fear in her eyes. "I will beg your friend's pardon on my knees if you wish it," she said. "But you must come and listen to me now."

"What is it?" he asked, his anger and Duncan both forgotten, at least for the moment.

"Kivar." He had put his hand over hers, and she clasped it tightly. "Lucan Kivar has come."

21

He took her to the top of the tower, the only place he was reasonably certain they would not be overheard. She walked to the open window as he was bolting the door behind them. "Sweet Allah," she murmured, looking down the endless drop from the cliffs to the sea. She closed her eyes and took a step back as Gareth closed the shutter.

"Do high places frighten you?" he said, amused in spite of all.

"Not usually, no." She couldn't begin to explain the strange sensation she had felt looking over that edge, as if she were somehow two people at once, poised between two points in time. In truth, it was all she could do to stop herself throwing her arms around him and clinging for dear life. But that was foolishness; there was a real threat to be faced. "I smelled him in the forest," she said, opening her eyes. "Lucan Kivar—"

"You smelled him?" Gareth repeated, faintly aghast.

"Yes . . . I have a stronger sense of smell than a mortal would have," she explained. "And hearing, for that matter—someone in the courtyard is talking about us."

"What are they saying?" he said, not quite certain he believed her.

"Trust me, you do not wish to know." No one in her life had ever dared to call her the name some laughing Scotsman had just attached to her, and his companion seemed to think Gareth quite clever to have "bagged" her. "Or you might, but I don't." She turned her back on this as well. "I followed his scent, and I found a body in the woods," she went on. "He has killed someone from your clan, a young girl."

"Kivar has killed her," he repeated.

"Yes." She crossed her arms before her, fighting a shiver. "I know it sounds insane, but I am certain. I have always been able to sense him through his kills." Because I shared them so often, she thought but did not say aloud.

Gareth watched her look away as if she feared to meet his eyes. "Who was it? The girl, I mean."

"I don't know—I'm sorry. She was young, with light hair, very pretty—"

"Aislinn." He had heard the girl's mother complaining earlier that she had gone out looking for a missing sheep and failed to return as promised. "I believe she is sixteen."

"Was," Roxanna corrected, her tone flat and cold. "She is dead." She suddenly noticed that a table had been tossed onto its side and dirty dishes broken all over the floor. "Would she have left the walls alone?" she asked, sitting in the one cushioned chair with her legs curled beneath her.

"Her mother said she went after a sheep." He sat down across from her on the side of the high, carved bed.

"You will have to find her tomorrow by accident." She found the idea of the poor child lying alone in that thicket all night surprisingly upsetting. The girl was nothing to her, really, no more than any of the other poor souls she herself had murdered for food or just for sport. But somehow, this one had touched her demon's heart. "I would have brought her back myself, but I couldn't think of any way to explain why I was there or how I could have found her." She looked up to find him staring at her strangely, as if he didn't quite believe what she was saying. "I am not entirely heartless, Gareth," she said, surprised.

"I know that you are not." He took her hand in his, and she felt it was cold, not at all like his usual touch. "Roxanna, I saw you," he said, meeting her eyes with his. "I saw you go into the woods . . ." He was pale, she suddenly realized.

"Gareth, what is it?" He sounded very young, she thought, not like himself at all.

"Nothing, really." He looked at her with a ghost of his usual smile. "I know you are a vampire," he said. "I just never . . ." He broke off, getting up. "I never really understood what that meant until I saw you."

"I know." She folded her hands in her lap, resisting two conflicting instincts, one to rise and comfort him, the other to leave him in fury. "I knew you didn't understand." She smiled grimly. "You could never have asked me to marry you if you had."

"That's not true," he said, turning around. "I love you, Roxanna, just as you are, vampire or not. That is why I want to marry you, why I want you to share my life." He knelt before her and took her hands. "But I know now why you say you can't."

"I don't just say it, Gareth." She leaned forward into his arms, holding on with all her might, her head on his shoulder.

"I know," he promised, holding her close. He drew her down from the chair into his lap. "We will destroy him, angel. Whatever it takes to save you from this curse, we will do it."

He sounded so certain, so sincere, and she longed to believe him. "Gareth, I'm so scared." Never in her life had she confessed such a thing to anyone, even as a tiny child. By the time she could walk, she had known that fear was weakness and she must not be weak. But with this man, all of her defenses were destroyed. She might as well confess her heart as not. "I knew he would come. Even if Sean had not told me he was in the grove of ice, I would have known it. Only Kivar could have killed so many and just left them there, as if they were nothing. But when I saw that body, that poor little girl . . ." His arms around her felt so strong, she could almost forget he was mortal, a fragile, living thing. "I don't know how to destroy him," she confessed. "Orlando said the Chalice could do it, but I don't know where that is—I never believed it was real."

"I know," he repeated, stroking her hair. Demons, chalices, destiny—none of this felt so real to him as the weight of his love in his arms. "You are certain it was Kivar you sensed. There can be no mistake."

"None." He believed her; that was something—everything, really. Somehow, in spite of everything, he trusted her. And he sounded calm. But then, he didn't really understand. He had never seen Lucan Kivar.

"So what does he look like?" he asked as if reading her thoughts. "If he is close enough to kill Aislinn under our very noses, why have we not seen him?"

"I cannot tell," she answered. "He could look like anything or anyone. We destroyed his true body, Simon and I." She trembled at the memory, but this time, she did not try to push it away. She told him of her last night in the caliph's palace, of the making of Simon, her vampire brother, and Orlando, the wizard who believed Simon could save them all. She told him of the farce of a wedding where she was forced to play the bride, trembling as she told it.

"The vampire court attacked the knights like wolves on a flock of sheep," she said, making her voice calm. "When Simon fought back, Kivar attacked him himself. He drank his blood, then gave his own blood back to him to drink—that is how a vampire is made."

"Charming," Gareth said, looking sick. In truth, she thought he was to be congratulated for hearing this tale with such calm. He had held her in his lap and silently listened, never betraying so much as a shiver.

"But Simon never stopped fighting," she went on. "He cut off Kivar's head, and together we stabbed him through the heart. His body melted into filth, as if he were destroyed."

"But he wasn't?" Gareth said, his first interruption. His thoughts were obvious—if beheading, stabbing, and dissolving didn't constitute death for this demon, what exactly would?

"Apparently not," she said with a wry smile. "Orlando said then that Kivar was not gone, that his evil could only be destroyed by the power of the Chalice."

"So Simon, poor lad, becomes a vampire, and Kivar gets away with no body of his own." He didn't sound as if he doubted her, only wanted to make the matter clear in his own mind. "And my Roxanna gets trapped in a pretty cut glass bottle?"

"Orlando did it," she said. His Roxanna . . . she laid her head against his chest and smiled.

"So I have him to thank," he said with a grin. "Though I suppose I should be angry with him for your sake."

"No," she said, shaking her head. "I let him do it. I wanted to die, but he convinced me to go into the bottle instead." She closed her eyes, remembering her despair. "I meant to face the sunlight and burn away to nothing. That is one way a vampire can die—the other is to be stabbed through the heart with a stake and beheaded, as we tried to do to Kivar. But he is more than just a vampire."

"Why would you want to die?" He made her turn to face him. "Roxanna?"

"To escape being a monster," she answered. "I told you; I didn't believe in the Chalice. I didn't believe I could be saved. I just wanted it all to be over." He looked horrified . . . but no. There were tears in his beautiful blue eyes. "When I came out of the bottle and realized Orlando was gone, I meant to do it again," she confessed. "I was standing on the cliff over that hovel where we stayed, waiting for the sun to come up."

"But you decided to save me instead," he said with a teasing smile.

She smiled back. "I wish I could say that was true," she said, hugging him close for a moment, her arms around his neck. "But in faith, it was Kivar." She laid her head on his shoulder. "I smelled him then; I found another body. That was when I knew he was still alive and here, in your Highlands. I swore I would find him." She drew back and touched his cheek. "But I found you instead, and I loved you." He kissed her, and she opened her mouth to his, melting against him again. "And now, I don't want to care about Kivar," she confessed, the sweet sound of his heartbeat making her want to cry. She could not bear it if something should happen to him; she would lose her mind, shrivel to a husk, and die. "I could almost give him his Chalice if he would just leave us in peace."

"But he won't." With every word she had spoken, Gareth had become more certain that his grandfather was right. She had not come to him by accident. He kissed the top of her head. "You know he won't."

"I know." She turned her face against his throat, and he could feel her cold tears on his skin, breaking his heart. "Now do you see why I cannot marry you?"

"No," he said, stroking her hair. "In faith, I do not." She looked up, mouth open to argue, and he kissed her. "We were meant to be together," he said softly, almost a whisper. "How can you not see that?"

"I do see it." She seemed very young as she looked up at him, all her pride dissolved. "But I see my father's hall. I see Kivar. . . ."

"I see him, too." He cradled her cheek in his hand. "I am not your poor, doomed Crusader, blundering into a nest of demons unawares. I have you to tell me how to fight him. I have the blood of my ancestors." She touched the markings on his arm, and a shiver of desire rippled through him. "You say you are not a Christian, but I am." She looked up at him, confused, and he smiled. "We are meant to face this evil together." She closed her eyes for a moment as if the very thought was appalling, but for once, she didn't tell him he was wrong. "I cannot believe that we are meant to fail," he said, caressing her cheek. "We will destroy the wolf, and you will be free."

She smiled, her eyes still closed, and he kissed her. "My dear one," she said, wrapping her arms around him. He seemed so certain, so calm in his belief that things were meant, that the world was not a thing of chaos but of order, a place where their love might prevail. How dearly she longed to believe he was right. "If your Christ brings us through this together, I will be glad to hear of Him."

"I will fetch a priest myself," he promised, his smile clear in his voice even though she couldn't see it. "Perhaps he can convince you to marry me in the bargain."

"There is no need." She drew back and put her hand to his mouth before he could speak. "I am convinced." His smile was so sudden and so complete, she almost laughed aloud. "If you are fool enough to want me, I will marry you."

"Angel . . ." He gathered her into his arms again and kissed her doubts away.

He made love to her with luscious deliberation on the high, carved bed, bringing her to sweet release over and over again. But when he finally joined her, he collapsed, exhausted, his head pillowed on her breast. "I'm sorry," he mumbled, his night beard rough against her skin.

"Don't be stupid," she scolded softly, running her fingers through his hair. "You have barely slept in two days." She traced the stitches still in his back, his wound barely healed. "Go to sleep."

"No," he protested. "I'm awake." But he didn't move,

wrapping his arm around her instead and snuggling closer.

"Oh, aye," she said with a soft laugh. She bent and kissed his forehead as he answered with a snore.

She drew the blankets up around them, wide awake herself but content to stay. Who knew how long she would have to hold him, now that Kivar had returned? Every instinct inside her led her to despair, to believe they must surely fail. But Gareth saw things differently. He saw her curse broken, saw them growing old together in this tower. His faith gave him a vision so beautiful she could barely imagine it. "He believes in You," she prayed in a whisper to the God she barely knew. "It would look quite bad for You if You should let him fail." This was blasphemy, she suspected, but she didn't care. If they were meant to cross the world to find one another, if Kivar's evil were theirs to defeat, the power that decreed it surely owed them His guidance. Even if she were a heathen and a vampire besides. If Gareth was right, if they could win and she could be free of the darkness, she would happily be neither ever again. "He is Yours, not mine," she whispered. "You must keep him safe."

22

Tess listened as her cousin made his announcement over breakfast. "Lady Roxanna has agreed to be my bride," he said, his happiness plain on his face. "She is a princess in her country, and I am proud to have her for my own, and for the clan." A smattering of applause greeted this, as if the wench's royalty were assured by nothing but his saying it was so. But several of the women, at least, had the decency to glance in her direction, though no one caught her eye. "But only because my beautiful cousin, Tess, will not have me." He turned his wretched smile on her now, so like his mother she could have spit in his face without a moment's shame. But she did not; she made her face smile back. "All here know of her affection for Duncan, and his for her. She would have done her duty to the laird, our grandfather, and for that, no one can fault her. But I would prize her happiness more highly than duty."

"Particularly since you've found a princess with an angel's face," one man said just loudly enough to be heard, earning himself a barely suppressed general laugh.

"Tess did our grandfather the courtesy of obedience," Gareth said, turning a frown on the man that would have done the old laird proud. "But she loves Duncan. Can any man or woman in this hall say this is not so?"

Duncan's mother actually opened her mouth, the old cow. But seeing Duncan's face, she closed it again. "What does the lady say?" Brian asked, turning to her.

"Duncan knows my love for him," she answered. She had always liked Brian; he and his wife would have taken her in as one of their own if the old man had allowed it. She looked over at Duncan, standing near the archway. He was still handsome to her. But after Sean, he seemed smaller, a lesser creature—a dog instead of a wolf. She was glad Sean was not in the hall; she might have laughed out loud. "Is that not enough?" she asked, returning Duncan's smile.

"More than enough," he answered, coming to take her in his arms.

Gareth watched his cousin kiss Duncan, his pulse returning to its normal rate. That much at least was settled. Roxanna had taken the books and papers his grandfather had collected down to her room an hour or so before dawn, promising to stay awake as long as possible deciphering them. She even had a beginner's knowledge of the ancient language that the oldest of the scrolls was written in, from her tutor, the wizard Orlando. Perhaps she would find some clue that would tell them where the Chalice was hidden and how to banish this demon back to hell for good. In the meantime, she had promised to marry him, and the clan seemed pleased. He had only one more pressing task to manage while she slept.

"Brian," he said, catching his older cousin's arm as the clan went back to their breakfast. "Do you fancy a hunt?"

"Oh, aye," Brian answered with a grin. "Needing a bit of fresh air, are you?" The man sitting next to him snorted over his mug, but his wife gave him a sharp rap to the back of the head. "We'll go as soon as we eat," he finished with a slightly less leering smile.

"Good." Roxanna had told him exactly where the dead girl's body could be found. If they took hunting hounds to that clearing . . . he pushed the thought away for the moment. He would face it when he had to, not before.

Tess allowed Duncan to kiss her until the people around them turned away, some of them snickering but all of them apparently appeased. "Duncan," she said, bracing a hand on his chest to break the kiss. "Will you take me here before the entire clan?"

"I would," he answered. "If you would allow it."

"I would not," she retorted, but she smiled, feeling dizzy. Everything was changing, even Duncan—what was to become of her? What was she meant to do? "But I like that you would," she said with a giggle, leaning close to kiss him one last time on the cheek.

"Tess," he protested as she left his arms.

"I have to take Lebuin his breakfast," she explained, ducking away from his grasp. "Kyna has gone out to find mushrooms or something for his sister, and he cannot leave her alone." She picked up a tray from the table. "Besides, don't you have better things to do?"

"Other things," he allowed, returning her smile. "But not better."

She took the tray to the tower bedroom and found Sean sitting beside his sister, a strange, sad look on his face. "I thought she was better," she said, setting the tray on the table. They were lovers; she ought to have felt easy with him. But in truth, seeing him now, she found her heart beating faster, like a child who has stumbled upon something private between adults.

"She will never be better," he answered. He brushed the backs of his fingers across his sister's cheek, and the wounded woman flinched, jerking her head away with surprising strength.

"I'm sorry." She put a hand on his shoulder, not certain if she should. "I know you love her very much."

She saw him smile, but he did not look around. "You think so?" He lifted Siobhan's hand as if to kiss it, but the palm was turned up, not the back. He pressed the kiss to her wrist, and Tess gripped his shoulder harder, tense with shock as he sank his teeth into the woman's flesh. The woman on the bed arched upward, her mouth opening as if to scream, but she made no sound, and Tess, her own hand flying to her own mouth, could make none either. After a moment, he lifted his head, and she saw his mouth was smeared with blood. "Who do I love?" he asked, still not looking back at her.

"Your . . . your sister," she managed, her tongue so dry she could barely form the words. "Siobhan."

He licked the wound his teeth had made in the other woman's wrist, and the skin seemed to grow back together, closing the gash without so much as a scar to mark where it had been. "Her name is not Siobhan. It is Isabel." He turned to her then, and she took a half step backward in fear. But her hand was still on his shoulder as if of its own accord. He turned and wiped the blood from his face on her sleeve, and her knees went weak as his tongue flickered for a moment on her wrist.

"But you love her," she persisted.

He looked up at her and smiled as if he were happily surprised. "No," he promised, taking her hand in his. "I love you." He drew her down to him and kissed her mouth, his hand on the back of her neck. She returned his kiss, laying a hand on his cheek, and he moaned against her mouth.

The door latch rattled, and Kyna muttered something from outside as they heard a thump. Tess sprang back and turned just as the door opened.

"You've dropped your basket," she said, hurrying to help the old witch pick it up again.

"Careful," Kyna chided, as Tess swept up a handful of moss like the trash that it was.

"Forgive me," she said, making herself smile. Her legs felt like water, and what felt like a flock of butterflies was dancing in her stomach. But she straightened up and handed the basket over without so much as a shiver to give herself away. "Is it important?"

The old witch looked at her as if seeing her for the first time. "Aye," she answered slowly with a nod.

"May I help?" Kyna would sooner cut off her own fingers than let her help her with her messes, she knew. Behind the old woman's head, she could see Sean smile and shake his head as if she were being very naughty.

"No, child." For the first time since she was a very little girl, the witch was smiling at her. "Go and leave us in peace."

"As you will."

"Tess?" Sean called as she started to go, and she stopped, careful not to turn too quickly. "Where will I find your cousin?" he asked as Kyna went to her cauldron. "You said he sent you to fetch me."

"How should I know where he will be?" she asked, covering her smile with insolence. "Look where you found him yesterday." She glanced over at Kyna, but the old witch was already engrossed in her conjuring. "Good-bye." Turning on her heel, she left, closing the door behind her.

The hunting party had barely been out an hour when the body of young Aislinn was found. "Holy Christ," Brian swore, leaping down from his horse. She was lying in the brush in what looked like perfect repose, one arm up and the other folded over her stomach.

"Is she hurt?" Caleb, Duncan's father, asked, climbing down to join him. Duncan had been invited along himself, but he had declined for reasons he'd kept to himself.

"She is dead," Brian answered, crouched beside her. He spoke sharply to the dogs who were sniffing and whining around them, and they fell back, keeping to their pack as if they were afraid.

"Dead?" Caleb echoed. "How?"

Gareth tore his eyes from the dead girl's face with an effort. "Could she have frozen to death?" he asked, climbing down as well.

"Less than a mile from the village?" Brian said. "Not likely." He turned the girl's head, revealing a horrible gash in the side of her throat. "I would call that a clue."

"A wolf," Caleb said with a heavy sigh. "So close already . . . it will be a perilous winter."

"A wolf that didn't eat her," Brian said. "A wolf who closed her eyes when he was done." He looked back at Gareth.

"What are you suggesting?" Gareth said.

"Sweet Mary and Joseph," Caleb said, crossing himself. "It is the demon. Kyna's vision was true."

"So it would seem," Brian agreed, standing up. "In any case, we must take her home." He took off his mantle and laid it over the girl, preparing to pick her up.

"Wait," Gareth said. "I will do it." If he was meant to

vanquish Kivar, he should at least have the stomach to face his crimes. 'Twas strange, he had seen the dead a hundred times before in battle. But the most bloated corpse on the most gore-soaked battlefield in France had never sickened him like the sight of this innocent girl arranged as if she were sleeping. Folding the mantle tenderly over her face, he lifted her in his arms. "She's so light," he said, thinking aloud before he could stop himself.

"She is a child," Brian answered, his tone uncharacteristically flat. "Let us take her to her mother."

Tess had found Sean waiting for her when she walked into her father's old house. Before she could ask him any questions or even speak at all, he had swept her into his arms and crushed her mouth with his, making love to her as if it might kill him to stop. But now he was quiet beside her, his golden head pillowed on her stomach where she lay on the dusty bed. "Who are you really?" she whispered, twisting a lock of his hair around her fingers. She knew she should be frightened, that as soon as she had seen him hurt Siobhan, she should have run away to Duncan or even her cousin to tell them the truth. But she couldn't. Demon or not, she could not make herself betray him.

"I do not know." She hadn't expected an answer; in truth, she had thought he might be sleeping. "I swear, little one, sometimes I do not even remember." He sounded so sad, she wanted to cuddle him close like a child. He had said he loved her, and she wanted desperately to believe it, so much she was afraid she might love him in return. "I am lost," he said, holding her hand against his cheek. "I have always been lost."

"Not always." She felt breathless, much more frightened of the words she meant to say than the evil she had seen him do. "I have found you now." She expected him to answer or at least look up at her, but he didn't. He wrapped his arms more tightly around her and kissed her stomach, but he didn't say a word. "What do you want?" she asked him. "Why have you come?" He let out a mocking little snort of laughter as his answer. "Not me, I know," she said, biting back her hurt. "I know you didn't come for me."

"No," he admitted. "Not just for you."

"Then what?" Not just for her—then he did want her. "I can help you." At least he didn't laugh this time. But could she truly betray the clan? "I know things," she said, trembling in horror at what she meant to do. "I know where to find things."

He sat up so quickly, she nearly fell out of the bed. "What things?" he demanded, every trace of drowsiness burned from his blue eyes.

"Tess?" Duncan was calling from the door of the cottage. "Tess, are you here?" He came into the bedroom and froze, all color draining from his face.

"Duncan, get out," she ordered.

"How could you?" he demanded, coming toward her. "I love you—"

Before the words were spoken, Sean was on him like a rabid beast, ripping out his throat. She watched with her fist pressed to her mouth as he drank Duncan's blood, nearly tearing his head from his shoulders. Then he drew Duncan's own sword and cleaved what was left of his neck in two, stabbing him through the heart for good measure. "What things?" he repeated, rounding on her, his voice like the snarl of a wolf.

"Things that belong to the clan." She felt as if she were dreaming; this couldn't be real. "Things that can help you. If you are . . ." But she could not doubt it anymore. Sean was the wolf. There was a choice before her, a terrible choice. Duncan was dead. Nothing she could say would save him now; grieving would not bring him back. "I can show you where to find them." She reached for the demon before her, touching his blood-smeared cheek. "It is hidden in a cave, but I can find it. I followed them, my grandfather and Brian—my father . . ." She saw love in his eyes behind the demon's fury, the same sadness in his voice that she had heard before when he had told her he was lost. "My father said I should follow them and find out where they went," she finished. "He said someday I would need the treasure they were hiding."

"My precious little one . . ." He drew her into his arms and pressed her close. "Never in all my years . . ." He kissed her, and she tasted blood, Duncan's blood, on his mouth. "I love you." He kissed her again, her mouth, her cheek, her eyelids, framing her face in his hands. "You will rule them all, my love," he promised. "I will make you a queen."

In the tower bedroom, Kyna was dozing by the fire, her conjurer's bones clutched in her fist. Her visions had failed her; a veil of darkness had fallen over her magical sight. But the visions would return. They always did.

"Simon!" The girl on the bed was sitting straight up, her eyes wide open, green and staring as if into the face of the devil himself. Her fists were clenched so tightly, Kyna saw blood seep between her fingertips as she hurried to her side. She had screamed like a thing possessed, one single word. But when Kyna touched her, she sank against the bed again, collapsing like a rag dropped to the floor.

23

Gareth was surprised at how quickly the dead girl's parents wanted her buried. Before the afternoon was halfway done, the clan was gathered in the churchyard. "Where is Tess?" he asked Brian in a whisper as the body was lowered into the grave.

"I was wondering the same," Brian murmured back. "And Duncan . . . have you seen him since we came back?"

"No," Gareth answered. "I saw him down at the kennels just before we left. He wanted to thank me for giving him Tess, and I wanted to ask him to come with us." He paused, bowing his head as the oldest man in the clan said a prayer in the absence of a priest. "When he turned me down, I got the impression he had business with her," he finished when the prayer was done.

"No doubt," Brian said with a ghost of a smile, his first since they had found the girl in the woods. He looked back over his shoulder toward the cottages at the foot of the hill. "I thought so."

"Thought what?"

"Jamey's old house. There's smoke coming from the chimney." The crowd was breaking up, most of them heading for the tower. "If he took her there, 'tis likely they know naught of what has happened."

"I wouldn't want to disturb them." Sean Lebuin was watching them, he suddenly realized. Their English-born kinsman was standing just outside the churchyard, looking directly at Gareth and Brian, his strange, haunted smile on his face.

"Disturb them my arse," Brian grumbled. "That girl ought to be thrashed, and Duncan with her." He clapped a hand on Gareth's shoulder. "But we'll settle for giving them a start." Lebuin raised his hand and waved, then turned away, headed for the tower with the others. "Caleb!" Brian called. "Come and help us find your son."

Walking back into his uncle's house for the first time in fifteen years was so strange, for a moment Gareth didn't even smell the stench of blood. "Sweet Mary and Joseph," Caleb said, pushing past him. "Duncan!" He moved quickly toward the tiny bedroom, Gareth and Brian close behind.

But the sight of what was inside stopped Gareth in his tracks. He couldn't speak; he couldn't even breathe. Duncan was dead—more than dead. He had been slaughtered, hacked to pieces. Tess was sitting on the floor beside him, her head bent as if she hadn't heard them come in, her hands red with his blood. Caleb reached out to lean on the mantel and missed it, collapsing to the floor. "Holy Christ," Brian managed to say at last. "Tess, love . . . what happened?"

She looked up, startled, her face red and swollen from weeping, her eyes haunted and lost. Then she turned her gaze on Gareth, and her expression cleared. "Ask him," she said, pointing at him with one bloody finger. "He did it."

Gareth was so shocked, he couldn't speak. "No," Caleb spoke for him, still sitting on the floor, his legs sprawled out before him, tears streaming down his face. "It cannot be."

"It isn't," Gareth said, recovering his voice. Why would she say such a thing? "Tess, you know I never—"

"You did!" she insisted, her voice rising to a scream. "You found out what we did, that Duncan hired the brigands who murdered your true kin, the English."

"Tess, no," Brian said.

"He did!" She looked down at Duncan's body, fresh tears in her eyes. "He did it for me, because I begged him, because he loved me." She looked up again. "He loved me!"

"Aye, Tess," Gareth said, feeling cold. "He did."

"Your whore discovered it," she said, facing him with brazen calm. "Everyone knows 'twas she who saved you from dying, too. She told you we did it, and you kept silent, waiting. You asked Duncan to meet you here; you didn't know I was hiding, that I would see you."

"Tess, Gareth was with me and Caleb, hunting in the woods," Brian said.

"After," she said with a twisted, bitter smile that made her look so much like her father, Gareth felt sick. "I don't think he meant to kill Duncan, he just . . ." She broke off, all color draining from her face. "He just seemed to go mad." Caleb had climbed back to his feet. "Duncan said he wasn't sorry the English were dead." She raised her eyes to Gareth's again, her voice drained of feeling. "He said he wished they had killed you, too. That you would be the ruin of the clan."

"You know that's a lie," Gareth said, so shocked and furious he could barely speak. "Who did this, Tess?" He took a step toward her, his voice rising to a shout. "Who killed him?" Before he could reach her, Brian and Caleb had grabbed him. "Let me go!" he roared, fighting back. "She's a liar!"

"Peace, lad," Brian ordered, wrenching his arm behind his back.

"You cannot believe—"

"We must hang him," Tess said, standing up. "He hates us all for what was done to his father and his cousin—he's an Englishman. If we let him live—"

"Tess, enough!" Brian shouted. The shouting had brought three other men from outside, all of whom froze in shock at the sight of Duncan's body. "We will sort this out," he continued more calmly. "Help the girl." One of the newcomers hurried forward and offered Tess his hand.

"Brian, what has happened?" another asked. He looked at Gareth, still being held. "My laird?"

"My son has been murdered," Caleb said. "Lady Tess has accused the laird." His tone was flat, and he held Gareth fast. But he didn't seem to want to hurt him, and he didn't join Tess's plea for a hanging.

"Tess, tell us the truth," Gareth demanded. "You know I didn't do this. Duncan deserves true vengeance. As much as you hate me, you can't deny him that."

For a moment, he thought she would do as he asked. She opened her mouth as if to speak, her lower lip trembling with tears. Then her eyes turned cold. "You did this," she answered. "It was you."

"No!" He broke away from the men who held him and lunged for her.

"Stop him!" she screamed, recoiling and tripping over Duncan's body, falling to the floor as Caleb and Brian caught Gareth again. "Now do you believe me?" she demanded, her eyes wild. "He meant to kill me!" She scrambled back farther, one hand slipping in the pool of blood.

"She's a liar!" Gareth shouted over her, fighting to break free.

"Of course she is," Brian said in an urgent whisper in his ear. "For Christ's sake, lad, be still."

Tess had frozen, staring down at her bloody hands. "Sweet God," she mumbled, her eyes gone glassy with shock. "No . . ."

"Stop it, lass," one of the other men urged, crouching beside her. She looked up at him and swooned, falling into his arms.

"Take her to her room," Brian ordered, still keeping a firm hold on Gareth. "Have two of the women help her wash herself, then put a guard on her door."

"What of McKail?" another man asked.

He means me, Gareth realized. They were all staring at him, some just looking miserable, but some unmistakably suspicious. "I will find out who has done this," he said, relaxing in Brian and Caleb's grip.

"Perhaps you know already," one of the men was brave enough to say.

"That's enough from you," Brian said, fixing the man with a scowl, and Gareth was relieved to hear nearly all of the others protest as well. Only this man and one other seemed to believe Tess's tale. Caleb was silent. "The laird will stay in his tower until the murderer is found," Brian went on. "Locked in, if it will make you feel better." Gareth moved as if to protest, and Brian gave his arm a warning wrench. "Now go, bring help to move the body—and keep Grace away."

"Yes," Caleb said softly, his voice rough with grief. "She must not see this."

As soon as the other men left, Brian and Caleb let him go. "I can't let you just lock me up," Gareth said.

"It won't be safe for you otherwise, Gareth," Caleb said before Brian could answer. Gareth turned to him and found him pale but calm, his face still stained with tears. "Too many will believe her."

"But you do not?"

He smiled. "Duncan did not hire brigands to kill you," he answered. "Do you believe me?"

"Of course." Duncan is dead, he thought, grief twisting his heart in its fist.

"Then you know why I believe you." He was looking past Gareth to his son's slaughtered body, his jaw set hard.

"Come," Brian said. "It shouldn't take long to find out who had the stomach for a deed like this."

"Do we even have to ask?" Caleb said. "It is the wolf." He turned to Gareth again, his eyes haunted. "He has returned."

"All the more reason I need to be free," Gareth pointed out. The demon was inside the gates, and apparently Tess was in his thrall. The last thing he wanted was to be shut up in the tower. "And Roxanna," he began. "She isn't safe—"

"We'll put a guard outside the sickroom, too," Brian said. "Now, come, and for God's sake, don't struggle. I'm too old for this as it is."

Roxanna awoke at sunset, half sprawled across the table among the scattered scrolls where she had fallen asleep. She straightened up slowly, moaning softly at the ache in her shoulders. Vampire or not, she could think of very many more comfortable ways to sleep.

From what she had been able to gather, the Clan McKail were the last remnants of the clan that had spawned Lucan Kivar in the first place. His mortal mother had been one of them, his father one of their ancient pagan gods. As a young man, he had stolen the Chalice, a sacred vessel of these gods, and used it in blood rituals of his own devising, creating the first vampires of this line with their magic and his own blood. When he was cursed and banished to the other side of the earth, these vampires had apparently been destroyed if they had supported him in the battle or returned to mortality if they had fought against him. Most of the mortal survivors had left the Highlands, led by Merlin, Kivar's son from the time before he stole the Chalice. But some few hardy souls—the vampires who were saved—had remained to guard the gateway to the immortal world and the Chalice that served as its key. Kivar had apparently made many vampire minions, the first vampires of his line. The ones who had fought alongside him had perished when his gods banished him to darkness. But those who had fought against him had regained their mortality. She knew from her own experience with Kivar that there were other vampire clans from other parts of the world that had nothing to do with the Highlands or the Clan McKail. But this was the only tale of possible redemption she had ever heard. If it was true, Gareth and his clan were descended from ancient vampires. And she could be mortal again herself, just as Orlando had promised. Now all she needed was the location of the Chalice itself. But she could find nothing in the scrolls.

She had been rereading the tale of the ancient vampires' salvation when sleep had taken her, half frightened to let herself believe it. Now she rolled up the scroll and tied it with trembling fingers. She had to show Gareth, to find out what he thought. She had to tell him that maybe he was right.

She found Kyna opening the shutters when she opened the trapdoor, letting in the crisp night air. "Aren't you worried she will take a chill?" she asked, looking down on the woman in the bed, lying still as death.

"I fear it is too late to fret about chills, my lady," Kyna said, coming to join her. "I was hoping the cold might wake her."

"Kyna, I don't understand," Roxanna said. "When we found this girl, you seemed so certain your potions could revive her."

"And so they should have done," the witch said. "But every time she begins to rally, she fails again." She drew the blankets back, and the woman shivered.

"Kyna, don't," Roxanna protested. "Look at her; she's freezing." She tried to pull the blankets back up, but Kyna stopped her.

"She woke for a moment earlier," the weird woman explained. "Screamed like a banshee, eyes wide open."

"Poor child," Roxanna said. "What did she say?"

"One word—a name," Kyna answered. "Simon."

Roxanna froze, her hand suspended over the sick woman's where she was reaching to take it. "Simon?"

Could it be the same man? Could this girl have seen her vampire brother, maybe even seen Orlando? "Has Sean mentioned anyone by that name?" she asked.

"No one," Kyna answered. "I asked him earlier, and he said I must have been mistaken, that they knew no one named Simon."

"But you are certain it was Simon that she said." She lifted the girl's hand between her own. It felt cold, even to her vampire's touch.

"Quite certain."

"Siobhan." She had brought the girl back to the clan to question her, but it had seemed cruel to use vampire persuasion on her when she was so weak—the strain could kill her. But now she had no choice. If this girl knew Simon, she would surely know Orlando. She would know where they had gone. "Look at me, Siobhan." The girl's eyelids crinkled, her brow drawn in a frown.

"Poor lamb, I doubt she can," Kyna said with a sigh.

"I said look at me!" She gave her a sharp slap, gripping her hand tighter with her other hand. She didn't want to hurt her, far from it. But she had to know the truth. "Siobhan!"

"No," the girl whispered, turning her head on the pillow. "I'm not . . ." The whisper faded away, too soft for even Roxanna to hear.

"It's all right, dear one," Roxanna said soothingly, using vampire persuasion but leaning close to stroke her brow. "Tell me about Simon." The girl made a sound as if her heart were breaking, a kind of sobbing sigh, and the vampire's own heart ached for her. "I know, dear one, I know." Even so close, she could barely hear a heartbeat. "Tell me about Orlando."

Suddenly the girl's green eyes snapped open. "Father," she whispered, barely as loud as simple breath. She searched Roxanna's face as if she were trying to place her in her memory. "Your . . . you are Roxanna."

"Yes!" The green eyes were closing; the girl was losing consciousness again. "Siobhan!" But it was no use; she was lost to dreams again. She was still holding the other woman's hand between her own, and she drew it closer, pressing a kiss to her wrist. "Sleep well . . ." Suddenly she stopped, her flesh prickling with cold. "Allah save us," she whispered, the name burning her tongue.

"What is it, my lady?" Kyna asked. "Do you know this Simon?"

"Yes." She sniffed the girl's skin, feeling sick. Lucan Kivar. She had smelled him on the girl when she first found her, but that hadn't surprised her. He had attacked her, after all. But she had been in this room for days now, with Kyna bathing her every few hours to cool her fever. The scent should have faded by now. She leaned close again and sniffed her throat. The scent was there as well, but much more faint.

"Who is he?"

"Another vampire." And this girl loves him, she thought but didn't say. Nothing but love could have made her make that sound at the mention of his name.

She straightened up. "I think I know why she isn't getting any better," she said, turning to Kyna. "Bar that door behind me. Let no one come inside but me and Gareth."

"My lady?" Kyna said, confused. "What is it?"

"Just do as I say." Kivar wasn't just close; he was inside the castle. "I have to go speak to the laird."

Gareth paced the tower room, trying to stay calm. The sun was down; Roxanna would be waking. Brian had promised to keep her safe and explain what had happened as soon as she woke, but Brian had his hands full already, keeping the clan from erupting into war within the walls. A flattering majority of his kinsmen were convinced Tess was lying or at least confused, and many of those were incensed at her confession that she and Duncan had plotted to murder Gareth before he ever reached the castle. The problem was, even among his supporters, opinion was scattered. While his friends were working their way through knots of rumor, his enemies, though they were much fewer, were absolutely united. They believed Tess's story without question, believed he had plotted the ruin of the clan from the beginning, believed she had acted against him in the best interests of the clan, believed he had slaughtered Duncan in a fit of temper worthy of a demon.

For that was the unspoken terror underneath all the debate. Every adult in the clan knew something of Lucan Kivar, even if it was only a whisper of a myth. They all knew Gareth had been summoned home because of the mark on his arm. They knew Kyna had prophesied disaster, the return of a terrible demon who would seek to destroy the clan entirely. Now people were turning up dead, two in one day. Everyone was afraid. Most of them were expecting him to do something to save them, though no one had a clue just what. The rest thought he was the monster they feared. Brian said there was even a rumor that Sean Lebuin bore the same mark he had, that he was the true prophesied champion of the clan.

These happy thoughts were interrupted by the sound of someone outside the door. He turned, expecting Brian, but the lock was not turned. He heard what sounded like a woman's whispered oath, then a strange white mist began to waft from under the door. A familiar perfume filled the air, making him feel dizzy, like he had drunk too much wine. Then his vampire love stood before him.

"Gareth!" she said, running to his arms. "Brian told me." She kissed his cheek. "I'm so sorry."

"You . . ." He drew back to look at her, still stunned. "How did you do that?"

"Do what?" She looked back at him for a moment as if he was daft. "Oh, that," she said, comprehension dawning. "God's beard, Gareth, you saw me come out of a bottle you could carry in your pocket. You're surprised I can come under a door?"

"I just . . . never mind." He took hold of her shoulders. "I was worried about you."

"About me?" She looked poised to scoff at him again, then her manner softened. "I am fine," she promised, hugging him close.

"I am glad." He was hugging her so tightly, she thought her ribs might crack, but she was a vampire; she would mend. "So Brian told you. Our friend Kivar has apparently come inside the gates."

"It's worse than you know," she said, drawing back again, holding his hand instead. She told him about her conversation with the girl Siobhan. "Kivar has been feeding from her here, inside the castle," she finished.

"That's impossible," he protested. "Surely someone would have noticed a demon wandering the tower—"

"Would they, in faith?" she interrupted. "How many of your kin have noticed me?"

"They know you're here," he pointed out.

"Yes, and whoever Kivar is, they have seen him, too," she answered.

"Whoever Kivar is?" he asked. "What are you talking about?"

"He can change," she explained. "Orlando said he could take the shape of anyone. And we destroyed his original body; if he lives, he lives as someone else." She sat back against the edge of the table, the sheer impossibility of their task making her feel weak. "He could have been here when you arrived."

"And the people who believe Tess may well believe I am him," he agreed, sinking into a chair.

"But Tess has seen him." She stood up again, a sudden thought occurring. "Or she is him."

"What? No," he said, shaking his head. "I have known Tess since she was a child; trust me, she is my cousin—"

"That body is your cousin, yes," she cut him off again. "But why would an ordinary girl care so much if you should come back and take your grandfather's place as he wanted?"

"Because her father hated mine," he said, still unconvinced.

"Or because she knows you are destined to destroy her." In truth, she had taken very little notice of Tess since she arrived. Every time she thought of her, it was as a rival for Gareth's love, not a possibility she cared to consider. But the more she thought about her now, the more her theory made sense. "I have to talk to her," she decided, heading for the door.

"No," Gareth protested, going after her. He caught her by the arms. "I still think you're wrong, but what if you're right? You can't just confront her, not alone."

"I have no intention of confronting her," she answered. "And I would take you with me, but you seem to be locked in." She looked back at the door and frowned. "Idiots . . ."

"Brian means to keep me here for my own protection," he said, inclined to agree. "He believes he can discover the murderer more quickly with me out of the way."

"He can't discover the murderer at all," she said. "But I can." She rose up on tiptoe and kissed him briefly on the lips. "I will be right back with the truth and the key to let you out."

"Roxanna, I said no." She was dissolving in his grasp, melting back into a mist. "Roxanna!" She slipped back under the door the way she had come. "Bleeding whoreson . . ." He banged on the door with his fist. "Come back here!" He grabbed the handle and rattled it hard on its hinges, but it wouldn't budge. "One of these days, I really am going to spank you," he muttered, listening to her light little footsteps running down the stairs.

24

Roxanna rounded the corner from the narrow wooden stairs to the corridor and nearly crashed headlong into Sean Lebuin, headed the other way. "Good evening, my lady," he said with a smile, catching her elbow to steady her before she fell.

"Good evening," she answered, rather breathless. She had been so lost in her own thoughts, she hadn't even sensed him until she was on top of him. For the first time since coming to this castle, she had a clear plan of action. Unlike Siobhan, Tess was well enough to talk. With her vampire powers, she knew she could make her confess whatever she knew about Kivar. And if the girl were possessed by the demon herself, Roxanna was fairly certain she could drive him out. But in the meantime, she had to calm down and keep her wits about her.

"If you were headed for the hall, I would advise against it," he said, letting her go. "Tempers are running high."

"I don't doubt it." She hadn't really spoken to this

man since she had brought him from the frozen grove and abandoned him to the mercy of the clan. But she had noticed he seemed to adapt to his new surroundings quite well, for all he was obviously worried for his sister. "But I wasn't going to the hall."

"Good," he nodded. He stepped aside to let her pass. "Good night."

"Good night." She started down the corridor toward the broader stairs.

"My lady!" She turned to find him coming after her. "Forgive me," he said, catching up. "I just . . ." He stopped, his pale blue eyes searching her face.

"What is it?" she asked, trying not to sound as impatient as she felt.

"You're very beautiful," he said with a wry smile. "But I just wanted to thank you." He touched her cheek as if she might have been some precious jewel he feared was not quite real, and something in his eyes was strangely familiar. "For helping me." The men she had deigned to invite to her bed when she was still a mortal princess had often looked at her so, as if they could not quite believe their luck. "I always knew you would," he said, his smile tender and sweet. "From the very first moment I saw you."

"Did you, in faith?" Perhaps she had been too quick to decide he was well. The ghosts of his ordeal were still clear in his eyes. But the way he was touching her was making her uncomfortable, and she had urgent business to attend. "Then I am glad I did not disappoint you." She took his hand from her cheek, giving it a comforting squeeze before she let him go. "Good night."

He made a courtly little bow that looked rather strange with his rough clothes. "Good night." She could feel his eyes still on her as she hurried for the stairs.

Tess looked down at the short silver sword, her heart pounding with excitement. All through the ordeal of accusing Gareth and being brought to her room, she had managed to conceal it in her skirts, a tangible symbol of her terrible secret. Sean had given it to her, his first lover's gift. She belonged to him now, not to the clan. "What do I know about fighting and swords?" she had asked him.

"Do not worry, little one," he had answered, kissing her. "It is in your blood. When the time comes, you will know." And so she would. Sending the brigands after Gareth had been almost like a game, murder from a distance. But this was real. Duncan was really, truly dead, and she was really lost. She laughed, clapping a hand to her mouth—there was a guard outside. But she couldn't help it. She had never felt so frightened or so free.

Roxanna was surprised to see the guard standing outside Tess's door—perhaps Brian was not such an idiot after all. "Well met, my lady," he said with a courteous nod.

"Good evening." Still, this was a complication she hadn't been expecting. "I need to speak with Lady Tess," she said.

"I don't think the laird would like that, my lady," the guard said, looking wary. "He was dead set on your safety."

"I'm sure I will be safe." The man seemed bright enough, but not so bright he could resist a vampire, she thought. "It was the laird who sent me," she went on, bringing the demon's purr into her tone. "He wanted me to make certain Tess was resting."

"That was kind of him," he said with no trace of irony—he was hypnotized.

"May I have the key?" She held out her hand and smiled as he fished it from his pocket. "Thank you." She started to open the door, then stopped. "Will this open the door to the laird's room, too?"

"No, my lady," he answered, holding up a second key. "You'd need this one for that."

She nodded. "Of course. Will you go and let him out, please?"

His expression clouded a bit. "I'm not certain I should."

"Why not?" she countered quickly before he could gather his wits. "I fear I may need him." She put a hand on his arm. "Do you believe the laird killed Duncan?"

"No, my lady," he said with great feeling. "I know that he did not."

"Then he should not be imprisoned, should he?" she said.

"No," he agreed, setting his jaw. "He should not." Without another word, he turned and started for the stairs, the key held in his fist.

She unlocked the door quickly and opened it to find Tess dropping something on the bed and throwing a mantle over it. She could tell the girl was surprised to see her—indeed, she looked on the verge of fainting dead away. "May I come in?" she said, pausing on the threshold.

"All right," Tess answered, stepping back. Her heart was pounding, Roxanna noticed, and she was pale as milk. "What do you want?"

"I wanted to see if you were all right," she answered as she turned to face the girl again, though in truth, she began to doubt her theory. If Kivar had taken possession of her, surely she would not have been so frightened. "Brian told me Duncan was murdered."

"As if you care." She backed toward the bed, one hand behind her. "It was your lover who killed him."

"No, Tess, it was not." For the first time, it occurred to her that perhaps Tess really had seen someone who looked like Gareth murder Duncan, that perhaps Kivar had taken Gareth's shape. He had always loved such tricks. "Duncan was Gareth's dearest friend," she continued, meeting the girl's eyes with her own. She looks like Siobhan, Roxanna thought, surprised. The woman

Kivar had attacked had those same green eyes. "Gareth would never have hurt him."

"You would say that." She was now backed up flush against the bed, as if she expected Roxanna to attack her at any moment. "You are Gareth's witch."

"You don't have to be afraid of me, Tess." She considered using her vampire's persuasion, but with the other woman in such a state, she doubted she would need it. "Why should I want to harm you?"

"You want me to lie," she said. "You want me to tell them that it wasn't Gareth."

"I want you to tell me the truth." The rhythm of Tess's heart was slowing; she was calming down. "The man who murdered Duncan. Did you actually see him?"

"Of course I did." She sat on the edge of the bed, her hands behind her.

"What did he say?" She felt her voice deepening after all, the demon's trick creeping into her tone. "Why did he want to hurt Duncan?"

"To protect me. Duncan . . ." She broke off, her eyes going wide. "What are you doing to me?"

"The man who killed Duncan was trying to protect you?" Roxanna pressed on. "Why?"

"I didn't say that," Tess insisted, her voice rising. "You made me say it."

"You're right," Roxanna admitted. "I can force you to tell me the truth."

"No." She drew a sword from the blankets behind

her, a short silver blade. "You can't force me to do anything," she said, gripping it in both hands. "No one can force me."

"Tess, your sword cannot hurt me," Roxanna said, surprised but hardly frightened. "I can help you—"

"You don't want to help me," Tess cut her off, sounding more confident by the moment. "No one wants to help me but him."

"Who?" Roxanna said, taking a circling step around her, looking for a way to take the sword that wouldn't hurt the girl.

"The wolf," she answered with a beautiful smile very much like Gareth's. "He loves me."

"No." She could hardly believe her ears. She had considered that Tess might have seen Kivar; she had thought she might even be possessed by him. But it had never occurred to her that the stupid girl could be helping him willingly. "I promise you, little one, he does not."

"Liar!" She lunged so quickly, Roxanna had no time to react. Before she could move, Tess had plunged the blade directly into her stomach.

"Sweet Allah . . ." The pain that should have been little more than a sting was agony, a bolt of freezing fire. She grabbed the girl's wrist and shoved her back, yanking the blade from her stomach in the process. But her flesh didn't heal. This was no ordinary blade.

"He does love me," Tess insisted. "I can give him what he wants."

"Tess, listen to me. . . ." The pain was getting worse; her legs seemed to melt beneath her, making her crumple to the floor.

"I told my grandfather I knew where it was." Madness glittered in her eyes. "I followed him; I saw it. He told me I was a silly girl, that I didn't understand." Roxanna tried to stand, and Tess struck her again, a clumsy blow across the shoulder that felt as if her arm had been cleaved off with an ax. "But he was the one who didn't understand. The wolf will save us."

"Fool." Pain and shock had completely destroyed any desire Roxanna might have had to be discreet. With the strength she still had, she lunged for the girl, grabbing her by the throat with both hands. "What have you done?"

"Leave me!" She flung Roxanna away as if she were a mortal girl. Somehow Tess had the same strength as Gareth, the same power to fight back. Roxanna changed her form and lunged again, this time as the cat, and was stabbed, this time through the heart. "You are a devil," she said softly as she backed away, her heartbeat like thunder in the tiny room. Roxanna transformed again, back into her human form, but she could not rise. Her body was heavy, dead weight. *I am dying*, she thought, appalled. "You will not have my place," Tess was saying, her voice distant and distorted. She tried to answer, but her mouth was full of blood, as if she were a mortal still able to die. *Gareth!* she thought, the whole world going black.

Tess looked down at the woman curled and bleeding on the floor. Had she truly changed into a beast? She dropped the sword, her hands shaking too violently to hold it. "You will not," she insisted. "It is my place, my right. . . ." There was blood on her hands, a spatter of crimson specks all the way up her arm. She scrubbed at them furiously as if they burned her.

The door opened behind her, and she turned, appalled. But it was Sean. "Oh, dear . . ." She ran to his arms, burying her face in his shoulder. "Hush now, little one," he said, laughing.

"I killed her," she said, shaking all over.

"Not quite." He put her gently from him and crouched beside the woman lying on the floor. "You would have to take her head." He picked up the sword she had dropped.

"Do it, then," Tess ordered. For a moment, she thought he would obey. He raised the sword as if he meant to do it.

Then he dropped it. "No," he said, reaching down to touch Roxanna's cheek. "I should . . . but I cannot." He raised his head as if he heard something. "But we must hurry," he said, standing up. "Your cousin is on his way."

Gareth had just given up banging on the door and started to pace the room instead when he heard the key turning in the lock. "Thank God," he muttered, heading toward it. "Brian—"

But the man who opened it was not his cousin but one of the younger men of the clan. "I know you did not kill Duncan," he announced as soon as he saw Gareth.

"I am pleased to hear it," Gareth answered, confused and a little wary. The man looked determined but entranced, a warrior walking in his sleep.

"Your lady told me I must let you out," he explained. "She said she might need you."

"She was quite right." Another day when he had more leisure to consider it, Gareth thought he would find Roxanna's ability to turn a grown man's will to pudding rather upsetting. But just then, this demonic gift of hers was rather helpful. "Take me to her."

Tess's bedroom door was closed, and Gareth raised his fist, prepared to smash it to splinters if necessary. But as soon as he banged it once, it swung open. Tess was nowhere to be seen, but in the far corner was a pile of clothes and blankets with a familiar, booted foot sticking out of one side. "Roxanna!" he said, running to her and falling to his knees beside her.

Brian appeared in the doorway, huffing for breath. "What in Christ's holy name has happened here?" he demanded. "What are you doing downstairs?"

"Never mind that," Gareth ordered, barely glancing at him before he drew back the blankets. Roxanna's eyes fluttered open.

"It's all right," she managed as he lifted her upright in his arms. "It is healing."

"Healing?" Looking down, he saw the entire front of her gown was soaked with blood, along with her right sleeve. "Angel . . ." He unlaced one side of the gown and drew it back to reveal her blood-soaked shift. Her stomach had been punctured just above her navel, and a deep gash had been slashed into her shoulder. "Who did this?"

"Tess." She leaned her head against his shoulder, groggy and weak with both pain and relief.

"Holy God," Brian muttered.

"I left her," the other man said, appalled. "I can't believe I just left her. . . ."

"It's all right," Brian said, clapping a hand on his shoulder. "Go make a search party and find her."

"Tess?" Gareth echoed, barely hearing them as the guardsman left. "How? I thought you couldn't be wounded. I thought because you—" He broke off, remembering Brian too late.

"So did I," Roxanna answered. "I don't know how she did it. She had a sword." She opened her eyes and saw Brian as well. "She is helping Lucan Kivar," she went on, seeing no help for it now. "She said she had something he wanted, that she told your grandfather she knew how to find it, but he wouldn't listen to her."

"The Chalice, no doubt," Brian said grimly. He knelt down beside Gareth and took his own look at her wounds. "She stuck you right well, didn't she, my lady?" He smiled at her, ignoring Gareth's look of shock. "But you should be whole in a few more hours." He patted her cheek and straightened up again.

"What do you know about this?" Gareth demanded.

"Only what I can guess, since no one saw fit to confide in me," his cousin retorted. "You should put her on the bed; that floor can't be comfortable."

Roxanna smiled at him in spite of her pain. "You knew I was a vampire."

"Suspected until now," he answered with a nod. Gareth picked her up and laid her on Tess's bed. "Kyna said at least one of you would come to fight the wolf." He patted her hand, but his brow was drawn with worry. "So little Tess has taken up with the demon."

"What about this sword?" Gareth demanded. The fact that Brian was taking the news so well that his fiancée was a vampire was a comfort, no question, but the stab wound in her stomach was still rather upsetting.

"The ancients gave the people swords to fight the wolf in the first battle," Brian explained. "Tess must have come by one of them somehow—probably stolen from the Chalice cave, since you say she knows where it is."

"The Chalice cave?" Roxanna asked.

"Aye," he nodded. "The lairds of McKail have kept the Chalice there for centuries, ever since the first whispers of the wolf's return. Tess followed your grandfather there when he said he was sending for you. She thought she could blackmail him with the knowledge, keep him from bringing you here. He told her if she tried to take the Chalice, it would strike her dead." The corner of his mouth quirked in a bitter grin. "I'm reckoning she decided he was lying."

"So Tess knows where the Chalice is," Gareth said.

"I never said that," Brian corrected. "I said she knew where it was." His grin widened. "Your grandfather moved it, of course."

Roxanna knew this conversation was extremely important, but somehow, she couldn't seem to stay awake long enough to listen. "Moved it?" she mumbled, reaching for Gareth's hand.

"It's all right," Gareth soothed, kissing her brow.

"She'll sleep through the rest of the night and most of tomorrow, I would think," Brian said. "They say the cursed ones could not help but sleep in the daylight hours." He reached out with one gnarled finger to touch a lock of her dark hair. "I never thought to see one."

"Get a good look now," Gareth answered. "She won't be cursed for long."

His cousin nodded. "May God in His mercy will it so."

Gareth touched the tender flesh around the gash in Roxanna's shoulder again, comforting himself that the wound was indeed getting smaller. "So McKail moved the Chalice?"

"Aye," Brian said with a nod. "Good thing, too, as it turns out, wouldn't you say?"

"I would." He lifted his love and took off the bloody gown completely. "So where did he put it?"

Brian laughed, a bitter little snort. "I wish I knew."

Gareth gaped at him for a moment. "You mean you don't know?"

"Did I not just say I didn't?" He got up from his chair. "Now, the next order of business is finding Mistress Tess, I suppose."

Gareth turned back to Roxanna, caressing her cheek. She was sleeping peacefully now, but what if the guardsman hadn't come for him? What if she had been left here, wounded and helpless, until sunrise? She could have been burned to a cinder. "I don't want to leave Roxanna," he said. He knew he should go after Tess at once, but the idea of leaving his vampire love alone while she was still so helpless made him feel sick. They were meant to face Kivar together—everything Kyna had foreseen and every instinct in his soul told him as much. "How far is it to this Chalice cave?" he asked.

"Less than a day on horseback," Brian answered. "A day and night on foot, at least."

"Find out if Tess stole a horse." If she had, he would have no choice but to go after her now. But if not, he would wait until Roxanna was awake. "And find out if anyone went with her."

"You think it was someone from the clan?" Brian asked.

"Roxanna believes Kivar has possessed someone

here," Gareth explained. "She thought it might be Tess herself."

"Ah, Christ," Brian muttered, turning away. "Poor, stupid girl."

"Forgive me if I don't feel sorry for her," Gareth muttered.

"Ah, Gareth, she never had a chance." Suddenly, his cousin sounded very, very tired, but when Gareth looked back at him, he smiled. "You will find it, lad," he promised. "The old laird was right. It is your destiny."

Gareth only nodded, too worried to argue, and waved as Brian left. Where could his grandfather have hidden this Chalice? And what was he meant to do with it if he found it? He pulled the blankets up to Roxanna's chin, smoothing her hair on the pillow. Then he lay down beside her, wrapping an arm around her waist. She sighed in her sleep, and he drew her closer, kissing her shoulder. "Sleep well, angel," he murmured. "I will be right here."

A few times, Tess was afraid she might be lost. It had been nearly two years since she had come to these caves. But when she saw the first of the rough paintings on the walls, she knew she had it right. "Do you understand these?" she asked the man who held her hand. "Sean?"

He was staring at a portrait of a man with long red hair and a long, trailing beard, the image slightly misshapen by the shaping of the wall. "Don't call me that."

His words were harsh, but his voice was tender, a caress that echoed along the stone walls. "My name is Lucan Kivar."

"It is beautiful." At her words, he turned to look at her. "I will give it to your son."

He lifted her hand to his lips. "Go on," he said, smiling back at her. "Show me the way."

She led him through an even more narrow series of caves, passing through a chamber hung with swords and shields, artifacts of the ancients of the clan. "These are like my sword," she said, touching one as she passed.

"Yes." He was breathing faster, following her more closely, and a tingle of desire rippled through her, making her want to turn and kiss him, devour his mouth. But he would not wait, she knew. Gareth, champion of the clan he hated, could be coming for them even now.

"Not much farther now."

They turned a final corner into the Chalice cave, its wall slick with moisture that gleamed and flickered in the light thrown by their torch. At its center was a round stone table, and on the table stood the cup. "There," she said, pointing.

"Yes." He dropped her hand, moving forward like a man in a trance. "I had forgotten." He held out his hand toward the cup, but did not touch it. "So much, little one . . . I have forgotten so much. But I will be restored." His hand closed over the stem, and she let out her breath—she hadn't even realized she was holding it. “So beautiful.” The light glimmered on the polished carvings, sparkled on the jewels set on its rim. He turned back to her and smiled. “My love.” He held out his hand to her, drawing her close as she took it. “My only love,” he repeated, kissing her hair.

“What now, Lucan?” she asked, pressing her cheek to his chest. “What must we do now?”

“We must open the gateway.” He turned her face up to his and smiled. “We must remake the world.”

25

Roxanna dozed and dreamed all through the day without ever really resting. Several times she heard someone knocking on the door and Gareth conversing softly with the visitor, but she couldn't rouse herself enough to know who it was. Kyna came and cleaned her wounds at mid-morning; she felt her bony little fingers prodding her, making her wince, but before she could completely form the desire to protest, the weird woman was gone. Sometime in the late afternoon, she slowly became aware that Gareth had left her, and that was worrisome—where had he gone? But Kivar was surely still a vampire; he couldn't possibly have taken any action in the daylight. This thought swirled into the chaos of her dreams, making her toss and turn.

At sunset, her eyes snapped open at last. She was alone in Tess's little room, and the wounds in her arm and stomach were completely healed. She looked down at the ruined shift that was her only garment and grimaced. The gown she had been wearing was gone.

With a sigh of resignation, she began to rummage through Tess's trunk.

Gareth barely knocked on the door before coming in. "I thought you might be awake," he said, closing the door behind him.

"Do you know what I wish for with all my cursed soul?" she said, emerging with another woolen gown and linen shift. "My own clothes." She sniffed the fabric—clean, but not her own.

"When we are married, I promise, you will have more gowns than you could wear in a month, all made just for you." He sat on the edge of the bed and watched her strip out of the shift she was wearing and toss it aside like a rag, surprised and charmed as ever by her utter lack of modesty.

"That alone is reason enough to wed." She caught him watching her and stopped, planting her hands on her hips. "Shall I dance?" she asked, raising an eyebrow.

"Would you?" he answered with a teasing grin. Even now, with the world on the verge of crumbling around them, his smile could make her breath catch short. "I think I would enjoy that very much."

"I am certain you would." She moved closer, arms raised in a graceful curve. Just out of his reach, she stopped, swiveling her hips as her mother the harem slave had taught her, and his eyes went wide. "But no," she said, dropping her arms. "Perhaps when we are married."

"I'm not certain I can wait." He pulled her to him where he sat, catching her hair to gently draw her mouth down to his kiss. "How fare your injuries, my lady?" he asked softly, his hands on her hips.

"Well enough, sir knight." She kissed him again, framing his face in her hands, and shivered as he moaned softly against her mouth. She kissed his brow, nuzzled his hair aside to kiss his cheek, and his hands slid up the curve of her waist and around to her back, pressing her closer. "Wait," she protested, bracing her hands on his shoulders. "We have no time for such as this."

"I know." He bent his head to her breast, drawing the nipple tenderly into his mouth.

"Gareth . . ." She buried a hand in his hair, catching her breath as warm waves of desire rippled through her. They should stop; she knew he knew it as well as she did. But she didn't want to stop. She wanted to be with him now, this moment, while she still could, while there was no one to snatch her from his arms. She climbed onto the bed, kneeling over him as he suckled one breast, then the other. When he raised his head, she kissed him deeply, settling into his lap. "Be quick about it," she ordered, her hands laced behind his neck.

"Aye, princess," he said with a breathless chuckle. "As you will." He entered her roughly, making her gasp, and she clenched her thighs around his hips and rocked, finding a rhythm to match his attack. He wrapped his arms around her, the wool of his tunic scratching her delicate skin, but his words were tender whispered promises of love against her cheek that could have brought her to climax by their sound alone. She leaned farther forward, grinding the most sensitive center of her want into his thrust until they exploded together. Shivering and spent, she pressed her cheek against his throat, the throb of his pulse both soothing her and making her heart ache. He was alive, her mortal love, so fragile and so strong.

"I love you," she whispered, holding him with all her strength.

"I know," he promised, kissing her shoulder. "I know." He took her gently by the wrists and urged her back, extricating himself from her embrace but keeping her in his lap. "You are mine," he said, meeting her eyes with his for a moment before he kissed her mouth. "No one will take you away from me." He smiled. "Trust me, princess."

"I do," she promised, smiling back. "You are my champion."

Later he led her out into the hall where most of the clan seemed to be assembled. All of them were staring at her with avid interest. "They know you are a vampire," Gareth explained, leading her to a chair.

"Are you mad?" she said, her head snapping up as she gaped at him in shock.

" 'Tis not so dire as that, love," Brian said with a grin. "It's not as if we've never heard of such a thing before."

A murmur passed around the room at this, and some of them laughed, albeit rather grimly.

"It seems the Clan McKail is descended from Kivar's first vampires," Gareth explained.

"I know," she said. "I mean, I did not know until I read it in your grandfather's papers. . . ." She looked around the hall at all their faces, some barely more than toddling infants, some seemingly old as the tower where they sat. But all of them were beautiful. There was a glamour about them, a flawless beauty to their skin, a sparkle in their eyes—she had seen it in Gareth the first moment their eyes met, and these others had it, too, to lesser and greater degree. "But that was centuries ago," she finished, reaching for Gareth's hand.

"Millennia," he agreed, sitting beside her. "Most of the old tales have been forgotten by all but the council."

"But we know enough," a woman she recognized as Duncan's mother said. "We know you have come to help the laird." Her husband stood behind her with his hands on her shoulders, and she reached back and put her hand on his.

"Tess has gone," Gareth went on. "She has taken Sean Lebuin with her—or he has taken her."

"Sean?" Roxanna said, confused. "Why?"

"We can only guess," Brian said with a grim smile. "Someone—some body is harboring the demon."

"No," Roxanna protested. "Surely not—I would have known."

Before she could say more, one of the guardsmen

from the gates came running into the hall, spear in hand and helmet knocked askew. "My laird, we have visitors," he announced. "Two men, a lady, and a dwarf." He glanced at Roxanna, a more furtive version of the same look she had received from everyone else. "They would speak with you, my lady."

"A dwarf?" she said, standing up. "Did he tell you his name?"

"Aye, my lady," he said, straightening his helmet as he gave her a respectful nod. "He says he is called Orlando."

Gareth was hard pressed to keep up with Roxanna as she sprinted through the village to the wall. "Open the gates," she shouted as soon as she was within hearing of the guard. "Hurry!"

"Do it!" Gareth called, catching up. He put an arm around her shoulders as the guard scrambled to obey.

Three horses rode in, led by a huge, jet black destrier. Almost before it stopped, a small figure leapt down from the saddle at great peril to his bones. "Orlando!" Roxanna cried, a most uncharacteristic shriek, and ran to meet him, falling to her knees and into his arms.

"My beloved," the dwarf was saying, hugging her close. "I am so sorry." He caressed her hair, kissing her again and again. "I beg you, please forgive me."

"No need," she promised, kissing him back.

The black horse's other rider had climbed down

more slowly. He was a tall, well-made knight in armor, with long black hair and a face that, minus the three days' beard and the desperate sorrow in his eyes, would have been beautiful. He smiled at Gareth and winked before turning to the two hugging before them. "Well met, my lady," he said, raising his voice to be heard.

"Simon!" With one last kiss to the dwarf's grizzled cheek, she scrambled to her feet to embrace the knight. "Well met, warrior," she said, pressing her cheek to his shoulder. "Thank Allah you have come."

Gareth, feeling the first twinges of a jealous fit, turned as the other two riders dismounted, and his eyes widened. The woman was exquisite, a fine-boned beauty with jet black hair and huge blue eyes. But it was the man who surprised him—he recognized him. "Lord DuMaine," he said, moving forward to greet him, a well-dressed giant with the careless grace of a lion. As a mere knight, he had never met the king's cousin personally, but he had seen him often from a distance.

"Tristan," he corrected with a smile, clasping Gareth's hand.

"Gareth," he replied.

"My laird, the gates are closed," one of the guardsmen said with a bow. "Shall I send ahead for food to be set out?"

Gareth looked at the flawless faces of the new arrivals, like Roxanna, too perfect to be real. "I don't know," he said, quirking an eyebrow at Tristan. "My lord?"

"Orlando can always eat," the woman beside the nobleman said with a laugh. Tristan put an arm around her shoulders and drew her close.

"My wife," he explained. "Siobhan, Lady DuMaine."

"Siobhan?" Gareth and Roxanna said together. Roxanna let go of Simon to come back to them, exchanging a look with her love.

"Yes," the lady answered, her smile fading to a more curious look. "Why do you ask?"

"Forgive us, my lady," Gareth said. "But you are the second visitor to come to us with that name."

"A lady named Siobhan is lying ill inside," Roxanna explained. "I brought her here, along with her brother, Sean." This new Siobhan gasped, her hand going to her mouth. "I believe their family name is Lebuin."

"Sean," the woman said, looking to her husband.

"Is he still here?" Tristan asked.

"Where is she?" The knight named Simon caught Roxanna by the shoulders, making Gareth reach for his sword. "This other woman named Siobhan—"

"Inside the tower," Roxanna said. "Come, I will show you—" But he was already gone, running for the tower.

"Not Siobhan," Orlando explained. "Her name is Isabel, and she is his."

"I will show him," Roxanna said, giving Gareth's hand a final squeeze before running after the other knight.

"Sean Lebuin is gone, my lady," Gareth said to the

real Siobhan. "He left last night with my cousin, who is apparently helping a demon named Lucan Kivar."

"Good lord," Siobhan said, looking away as Gareth saw a scarlet tear streak down her cheek. "He was here last night."

"We knew we couldn't be far behind him," Tristan said gently, drawing her to him again. "Who is your cousin, Gareth?"

"Her name is Tess," Gareth said. "You were following Lebuin?"

"Kivar has possessed him," Tristan explained as Siobhan let out a small, despairing sound against his shoulder. "We are following Kivar."

Roxanna stood between Kyna and Orlando, watching Simon kneel at the bedside of his love. "Simon, I'm so sorry." He was thinner than she remembered him, and his angel's face was drawn with grief. "I can't believe I didn't realize."

"It is not your fault, beloved," Orlando said, patting her hand. "Inside the living man, he was beyond your sight."

"Isabel," Simon said as if he hadn't heard a word. "Rest, darling." He leaned close and kissed her cheek, and she sighed as if she were trying to answer him. "I am here," he promised, encircling her in his arms. "I won't leave you ever again."

Gareth had come in behind them with the others, and Roxanna turned to him, hiding her face in his chest and biting back a sob. She could imagine only too well how Simon felt, watching his mortal beloved waste away, powerless to stop it.

"Can she live?" Tristan asked softly.

Kyna looked back and shook her head. "We don't know," Gareth answered. "But it doesn't seem likely."

Siobhan moved forward and put a hand on Simon's shoulder. "You could do as Tristan did for me," she suggested gently. "You could make her a vampire."

"No," Simon snarled, turning on her with such fury, she took a step back. "Don't touch her!"

"We will not," Tristan promised, coming forward to pull Siobhan back. Roxanna saw the other vampire woman was stung, but she understood Simon. As dearly as Tristan and his bride seemed to love one another and happy as they seemed to share their immortal life, she could not imagine bringing such a curse to Gareth, even to save him from death. "Come," Tristan went on. "Let us leave them in peace."

"Would that we could, warrior," Orlando said. "But the crisis has come." He turned to Gareth and Roxanna. "Tell us all you know about Kivar."

26

Within the hour, Gareth and Roxanna had heard all the important details of the journey that had brought the others to the Clan McKail and told their own tale in return. Brian had come in with the serving woman who brought food, and he had been pressed into service to tell his part of the clan's story as well. "So you are absolutely certain the Chalice was moved after this wretched girl found it?" Orlando demanded.

"Aye," Brian answered, giving Gareth a quizzical look.

"But your laird never told you where he put it," the dwarfish wizard finished. "Idiot."

"Orlando," Roxanna scolded, putting a hand on Gareth's arm. "The important thing is that the Chalice is safe from Kivar, at least for now."

"That would be the most important, yes," Tristan agreed. "But I for one would like to have this over."

"Kyna's prophecy said it would be," Gareth said. "All her portents say I am meant to fight Kivar now."

"You?" Tristan said, not bothering to hide his smile. "No offense, sir knight; I'm certain you are very skilled. But the rest of us are immortal—"

"Which is why we will be useless." Simon hadn't spoken in so long, they had almost forgotten he was still there, sitting on the bed across the room. Still cradling Isabel against his chest, he turned to them. "Don't you remember what Isabel said at Castle DuMaine, what she discovered in the chronicles? No vampire can defeat him." He turned his sad, dark eyes on Gareth. "Only a mortal can use the Chalice."

"No one can use it unless we find it," Orlando said, shuffling again through the same stack of papers he had been scanning for an hour, the scrolls Roxanna had read the night before. "There is nothing here."

"My grandfather was not an idiot, whatever you might believe, Orlando," Gareth said. "He would have put the Chalice somewhere safe."

"Aye, lad, he would," Brian agreed. "Death might have caught him unawares, but I doubt it. He must have left you a clue, something he knew Mistress Tess would never find." He rubbed his chin thoughtfully. "He almost never left that tower lookout the last two months of his life," he mused. "And he was quite keen you should have that room when he was gone."

"We took all the scrolls and papers out of there already so Roxanna could read them," Gareth pointed out.

"Perhaps the clue we want isn't written on a paper," Roxanna said. "We should go and look." She loved Orlando dearly and was thrilled beyond measure to have him restored to her. But she was accustomed to his wizard's ways. Gareth, she feared, might twist off his head like a chicken's if he goaded him any further. "Come, love," she said, getting up.

"We all must go," Orlando said, getting up as well. "Come, Simon."

"Nay, wizard," Simon answered, his attention returned to the woman still unconscious in his arms. "I will not."

"Warrior, you must," Orlando began, but Gareth put a hand on his shoulder, forcibly steering him back.

"Bring Isabel with you," he said. "It can't hurt her, and the air might do her good."

Simon looked for a moment as if he might refuse, then he nodded. "As you will."

At the foot of the last stairway, Roxanna drew Gareth aside. "You must forgive Orlando," she said softly as Brian led the others on, Simon carrying Isabel in his arms. "He means no harm."

"I know he does not." He took her hands, trying to put his feelings into words when he could hardly make sense of them himself. "What is he to you?"

"He was my teacher," she said, frowning. "I told you." She smiled. "Surely you are not jealous."

"I am, but that isn't why I asked," he retorted. "The things he said about my grandfather . . ."

"Darling, he didn't know him," she said. "He says rude things to everyone, about everyone."

"He has no right," he said stubbornly.

"I do not dispute you," she answered. "But sadly, that won't stop him. You should have heard the things he used to say to my father, the caliph—'twas a miracle he was not skinned alive." She laid a hand on his chest. "But my mother loved him very much, as do I, and he loves me."

"That much is obvious—"

"So for my sake, you must let him say what he likes and ignore him," she finished. "Your people are not all overfond of me either, you know."

"That's only because they don't know you yet," he said with a ghost of his usual smile.

"We shall see," she answered, smiling back. "In the meantime, I will let them stare at me as they like, and you will bear Orlando." The others were out of sight. "He has pursued Kivar for all his life," she said more soberly. "He knows more about the demon than anyone else."

"That may be what worries me," Gareth grumbled, but in truth, he felt better. His grandfather had been much like this Orlando, quick to speak his mind and damned be any thought of giving offense. "I will not quarrel with him," he promised. "But my first loyalty will always be to you."

"As mine will be to you, my love," she answered with a nod. She rose up on tiptoe to kiss him. "Now come. They are waiting."

Simon transferred Isabel to the high, carved bed, and they searched every inch of the tower room, even sweeping the rushes out the windows to crawl over the flagstones of the floor. But they could find nothing. "Isabel found writings at Charmot that were carved into the walls," Simon said. "She put a piece of parchment over the rough spots and rubbed it with charcoal, and the writing showed up white."

"Sadly, these walls are stacked stone," Siobhan said, running a hand over the wall. "It looks like a bigger version of the druid's tower at home—the one you took down, Tristan." She made a droll face at her husband. "I told you it was bad luck."

"What about the ceiling?" Gareth said, looking up. But the stones were stacked and mortared to come together into a point twenty feet above them.

"I doubt the old laird would have climbed the wall like a spider to leave you a message," Brian said. He looked out of the open window. "I have never seen them so bright," he mused. "The winter lights, I mean."

"I have," Orlando said with a grimace. "But only once."

"What about these?" Roxanna said, touching one of the bedposts. "What are these carvings?" Each post was square, but the corners were rounded. On each side was a rough figure of a person in a pagan style somewhat out of step with the newer shape of the bed itself. Two of the figures were rather shockingly depicted as male; the other two had rounded protrusions just under the arms that could have been meant to be breasts. All of them had their arms raised over their heads, and crooked lines extended from each of their hands into a more complex design that sloped into a point where the posts narrowed above them. More curving lines were carved into the rounded corners. "Give me that parchment," Roxanna said. "And a piece of charcoal from the fire." She wrapped the parchment around the post and rubbed until the design was transferred. "Look at this." She took it to the table and carefully tore it into four sections, lining up the points.

"Bloody hell," Gareth swore, looking over her shoulder. Put together this way, the figures stood in a circle, the curving lines from the corners forming the twisted trunks of trees. The jagged lines coming from their hands came together at the center like bolts of lightning striking the writhing figure of a wolf.

"Two men and two women," Tristan said. "Simon, me, Siobhan, and Roxanna."

"Or Abraham, Isaac, Rebecca, and Mary the Mother of Christ," Gareth retorted. "There is nothing in that drawing to show these figures are meant to be vampires, assuming it means anything at all." He touched the smear of charcoal with his fingertips, remembering the drawing Brian had made on his forearm. "Maybe it's us," he mused, touching each figure in turn. "Me . . . Tess . . . Sean, and Isabel."

"Of course," Siobhan said, coming to join him. "All four of you are still mortal, and all four of you have the blood of the wolf."

"Except that Sean is possessed, and Tess is now his minion," Tristan pointed out. "I don't envision either of them offering much help when the time comes."

"That bed has belonged to the laird of the clan for longer than anyone remembers," Brian said. "But as it's made of wood, I doubt it's as old as the wolf."

Roxanna opened her mouth to say she agreed with Gareth, but she was cut off by a sudden fit of coughing from the bed. Isabel was fighting against Simon as if for dear life, gasping horribly for breath. "Kyna, help her!" Roxanna ordered.

"I fear I don't know how, my lady," the weird woman said.

"We can't just watch her choke to death," Gareth snapped. In truth, the girl wasn't choking; she wasn't turning blue. But something was happening—she looked as if she were fighting back a demon none of them could see. Gareth snatched up the tarnished silver cup lying in the corner with the rest of the dishes he had broken in his temper days before and filled it with water. "Simon, try to make her drink this."

At a loss for a better solution, Simon took the cup. "Drink, darling," he pleaded, pinning her down and holding the cup to her lips. At first, water sloshed over her chin as she tried to jerk her mouth away. Then suddenly she relaxed, drinking deeply. "That's it," Simon said, weak with relief. "Just a little more." She put her hand on his, tipping the cup until the last dregs of the water poured into her mouth.

"So thirsty," she mumbled, wiping her mouth with the back of her hand. "I was so thirsty." She looked up to find them all staring at her in shock. "Simon?" A smile broke over her face, her cheeks slowly blooming pink with life. "Hello," she said, laughing, as he took her into his arms.

"The Chalice," Orlando said, staring at the cup. "That is the Chalice."

"God save us," Kyna said, crossing herself as she hurried to the bed. "My lady, how do you feel?"

"A bit dusty," Isabel said with a laugh from over Simon's shoulder. "And I must look appalling."

"You look beautiful," Tristan assured her with a grin. "Just ask your husband."

"I don't think he can speak," Siobhan said.

"The Chalice," Orlando repeated, his face turning red as a berry. "Here, flung among the crockery, the Chalice of the gods." He gave the pile of broken plates a vicious kick, sending shards of pottery flying. "Merlin was a fool!"

"Peace, Orlando," Isabel scolded. Simon drew back to look at her face, and she smiled at him. "Kiss me, why don't you?"

Simon dropped the cup to do just that, and Gareth picked it up, nearly as incredulous as the wizard. "This can't be the Chalice," he said.

"It must be," Brian said. "Nothing else could have cured her."

"But McKail drank from it," Gareth protested. "I saw him myself, more than once." He turned it in his hand, a dented, misshapen thing, thick with black tarnish, its carvings stained and worn so smooth they could hardly be seen at all. "He died, if you'll recall."

"He had been sick for years," Brian pointed out. "He was dying when he wrote to you, summoning you home." He took the cup and looked at it as well. "Perhaps he only stopped drinking from this when he knew you were here to take his place."

Gareth thought back to his last conversation with his grandfather in this room, when the laird had ordered him to marry Tess. He had drunk from the cup like a man thirsting to death when Gareth had said he would not be the laird. "Holy Christ," he muttered aloud.

If Roxanna had been a Christian, she would likely have said the same. She had sunk into a chair, unnoticed by the others, her legs dissolving beneath her. "It is real." She turned to Orlando. "The Chalice is real."

"Did I not promise you as much?" he answered, his fit of temper passing as he smiled at her.

Simon and Isabel had finally broken their kiss.

"Have you told her the truth, Orlando?" Isabel asked. "Have you told Roxanna who she is?"

All the color drained from Orlando's face, a fact not lost on Gareth. "What truth?" he said, going to stand behind her chair.

"Darling, what are you talking about?" Simon asked Isabel.

"Orlando must tell it," she insisted, getting up from the bed as if she had just awakened from a restful sleep. She put a hand on the wizard's shoulder. "She deserves to know."

Roxanna suddenly felt dizzy and too warm, as if the room were too crowded. I don't want to know! she wanted to scream, but she didn't know why. *I always knew you would help me,* she heard inside her head. *From the very first moment I saw you.* When the words had been spoken in truth, she had thought it was Sean Lebuin speaking, that they meant nothing. But it had been Kivar. "What is it?" she said, her own voice sounding weak and far away. Gareth touched her shoulder, and she grabbed his hand, holding on as if for dear life.

"Nothing of consequence, taken in all," the wizard answered, giving Isabel an unmistakably irritated look. "You know how dearly I loved your mother," he said, taking Roxanna's other hand. "I loved her better than you know." He smiled, touching her cheek. "You are not the caliph's daughter, beloved. You are mine."

"Yours?" she echoed.

"My daughter." There were tears in his eyes, but his

smile never dimmed. "You are not truly a princess."

For a moment, Roxanna could not speak. Her mind was spinning, a thousand different puzzles falling into place inside her head. She was not the daughter of the caliph but of this wizard, her Orlando. She was born not of the union of a tyrant and his slave but of the two people who had loved her best, who she had loved. She let go of Gareth's hand to hug the wizard tight.

"Are you disappointed?" Orlando asked with a shaky laugh. "You made such a good princess, after all."

"I don't care," she promised. "But wait . . ." She looked at the others. They were all smiling, but the other vampires looked uneasy. Both Tristan and Siobhan were looking at Isabel, who nodded. "I read in the old laird's scrolls that you were the son of Kivar," she said, turning back to Orlando.

"And so I am," Orlando answered with a nod, taking her hand between his own. "Before Lucan Kivar first stole the Chalice and became a true demon, he fathered two sons on two different women of his village. One, the daughter of the ugliest, most thick-headed lout in the clan, gave birth to a beautiful child she named Merlin. After Kivar was defeated by his people and banished by the gods, Merlin chose a mortal life and led those who had survived untainted by the demon away from these mountains. It is from him and offshoots of his tribe that I believe both Isabel and Siobhan are descended, and perhaps Simon as well."

"And Sean," Siobhan added.

"And Sean," the wizard agreed. "Kivar's other mortal lover was the most beautiful woman in the village, the daughter of a priest. But the son she bore was stunted and misshapen, a dwarf. Kivar hated this child from the moment it was born; he even tried to smother it in its crib. But against his will, he had given this dwarfish monster the immortality of the gods." His grip on her hand tightened. "His name was Orlando."

"You," Roxanna said with a nod. Now that the terrible truth was out, her fear was fading, replaced by a cold, sickening calm. "And I am your daughter. The demon is my grandfather." She stood up and turned away toward the window, unable to face their eyes another moment. "He called me daughter," she said, looking out on the green-gold waves of light that danced on the dark sky. "Does he know?"

"No," Orlando answered. "If he had suspected, I am certain he would have told me. He could not have resisted torturing me with the truth."

Gareth watched all of them staring at his heart's beloved as if she were the monster. "Why should it be torture?" he demanded. He followed her to the window, putting his hands on her shoulders and turning her to face him. "What difference does it make?"

"What difference?" she asked, swaying in his grasp as if she might be about to faint. "Kivar is a monster—"

"Aye, love, he is," he interrupted. "And all of us here must call him family." He framed her face in his hands.

"Did you not hear the wizard? All of them but Lord DuMaine are descended from Kivar's other son—"

"But not so closely," she protested.

"The Clan McKail was made by those he cursed," he continued. "We're all of us tied to him, one way or another. That is why we are the ones who will finish him."

"He is right, Roxanna," Isabel said. She let go of Simon's hand to come and join them at the window. "My mother dreamed before I was born that I would kill the Wolf. Simon was cursed to the dark on the far side of the world, but somehow, he found me. Tristan and Siobhan were bitter enemies, but now they are together, joined by love and demon blood. You were born a princess in the Urals, but you have pledged your soul to a Scotsman." She smiled. "All of us are meant to be here. All of us are meant to fight Kivar."

"Not you," Simon said.

"All of us," she repeated, turning back to him. "I'm tired of being kidnapped." She was smiling, but her eyes were serious. "It is time for this nightmare to be done."

Roxanna waited as the others filed out, Isabel leaning heavily on Simon. She caught Gareth's hand as he moved to follow and held him back. "Orlando," she said. "Will you wait a moment?"

The wizard stopped and turned back as Brian and Kyna went out. "Of course."

Siobhan looked back and smiled. "We will see you all downstairs," she said, steering Tristan toward the door and closing it behind them.

"So," Roxanna said when they had gone. "You are my father." She held out her free hand to Orlando, who took it between his own. "Why did you not tell me?"

He bent and pressed a kiss to her hand. "Ah, beloved," he said with a sigh. "What would have been the point? To claim you as my own would have meant your death and your mother's as well."

"But I would have known." She took her hand from his and put it under his chin, turning his face up to hers. "I would have been glad," she told him, smiling even as her eyes filled with tears. "All my life, I have loved you so much." Letting go of Gareth, she fell to her knees and hugged the wizard tight.

"Thank you," Orlando said, stroking her hair as his own tears stained her cheek. "Thank the gods that you are safe. I did not want to leave you—"

"I know," she promised, drawing back. "I knew that you must have had no choice." Sitting back on her heels, she reached for Gareth's hand again. "But if you are my father, you must give us your blessing," she said. "Gareth means to save me from my curse and make me his wife."

The little wizard looked up at Gareth, fixing him with an assessing eye. "And is this what you wish, my love?"

"More than anything." Gareth helped her to her feet again, and she twined her arm in his. "He is my choice."

"And you, McKail?" Orlando said, trying and failing

to conceal his smile. "Is this true? Do you mean to marry my daughter?"

"Yes." Gareth touched Roxanna's cheek. "She is all I want."

"Then may the gods be praised," Orlando said, taking Gareth's other hand. "All is as I wished." He looked back and forth between them, his eyes warm with love. "My blessing is yours."

27

Roxanna was shocked at how quickly Tristan DuMaine managed to organize an army from the men of the Clan McKail, including putting them on horseback and arming them with as many demon-ready swords, like the one Tess had used to wound her, as could be found. "Apparently Tess took the bait," Gareth said, coming back to her in the courtyard after a brief conversation with the men who had gone to fetch the swords. "The fake Chalice is gone." He unbuckled the scabbard that held his usual broadsword and hung it over the pommel of his saddle, replacing it with one of the smaller blades. "I'm surprised Kivar didn't know the difference."

"Isabel said he kept forgetting things before they reached the grove," she answered. "Perhaps he doesn't remember what it looks like." Isabel had told her a great many things, including what it was like to have one's life's blood spilled on the altar in the grove. She watched Gareth buckle the front of his chain mail vest with a rising sense of panic. "We should wait until tomorrow night," she said. "It's too late now; by the time we reach the grove, it will be close to dawn."

"Kivar and Tess could be there now," he pointed out.

"But they don't have the Chalice—"

"But if we are going to destroy Kivar, it must be done there." He had been skeptical about the need for troops until Tristan had described the demon soldiers Kivar had called up from cracks in the earth to attack them at Castle DuMaine. Now he wished he had his English lord's garrison and a few thousand mercenaries to keep them company. "Besides," he went on, fastening his broadsword to his saddle, "if we do what we mean to, it shouldn't take long." He turned to her and smiled. "And afterward, you won't need to fear the dawn."

"You make it sound so simple." She couldn't stop thinking about the last thing Kivar had said to her, that he had always known she would help him. Perhaps the help he meant was bringing him Gareth, the laird of the clan he so despised, to slaughter. "I don't want you to go," she said, catching his arm. "I forbid it."

"You forbid it?" he echoed with a grin. "And to think Orlando believes you are not really a princess."

"I am not jesting, Gareth." In her mind, she saw him as he was when she first found him, his body broken and torn. "I can't bear it," she said, shaking her head.

"I have to go, angel—"

"What if Tristan was right?" she interrupted. "Those people in that carving—what if they are meant to be us, the vampires only? You and Isabel could be risking yourselves for nothing."

"If that were so, why am I here?" he said gently, touching her cheek. He has changed so much, she thought. Less than a week before, if she had suggested he stay behind, he would have been angry, would have been certain her fear meant she thought he was a weakling. Now he understood she was simply afraid. "Why am I not in France with Lord Emory? Why did Kyna have her vision? Why did the Clan McKail remain behind to guard the Chalice and the gate?"

"I don't know," she admitted miserably, leaning on his chest.

"For better or worse, this is meant," he said, holding her close and trying not to smile. If nothing else, he had lived long enough to hear her confess there was something she didn't know. "Truth be told, I would rather leave you and Isabel behind. Siobhan . . ." He looked over his shoulder to where Siobhan was practicing with her bow, striking her target with deadly accuracy every time. She still hoped to save her brother, though even her own husband seemed to think it was impossible. "I want Siobhan to go," he admitted. "But you and Isabel could wait here."

"You need not even think it," she retorted. She let him go with an effort, stepping back from his arms. "I am not such a bad fighter myself, you know." She took his hands in hers. "You were right before. We are all tied to this quest." Simon and Isabel were coming out into the courtyard, and from the look of grim determination on the lady's face, it was obvious they had just had a similar discussion. "May your Christ be with us."

"Amen," he said, kissing her nose. "I will even share Him with you." He lifted her onto the horse, scolding it softly when it pranced at having a vampire on its back, then climbing on in front of her.

"It is time," Tristan called, mounting his own horse as their troops did the same. "Let's go."

Gareth drew Roxanna's arm more tightly around his waist and wrapped his reins around his fist. "Bar the gates," he told Brian, leader of those left behind to guard the clan. "If we do not return—"

"We will know what to do," his cousin promised. "God be with you, lad."

"Amen," Gareth repeated, crossing himself for good measure. He took a last, long look at the tower. In truth, he still trusted his own theory about the meaning of the carvings on the resting place of the laird, and though both Simon and Tristan refused to even consider it, both Siobhan and Isabel had told him privately that they were inclined to believe it, too. Two men and two women . . . himself, Isabel, Tess, and Sean Lebuin. Four mortals of the demon's blood, brought together in the sacred grove with the Wolf between them. Clucking again to his horse, he brought it around and moved to the front of the column, leaving the tower behind.

Tess stood beside the altar, her face turned up to the glowing winter lights. It had taken them most of the night to walk there through the frozen hills; dawn would be breaking soon. "In the clan, we are forbidden to ever come here," she said, turning in a circle. "We are told this place is cursed."

Lucan smiled. "It was the same when I was young," he answered. "But I was conceived here." He unwrapped the cup and set it on the ice-covered stone. "My mother came to pray for her true love." His accent had changed completely; the English inflection of his host was gone, replaced by the lilting brogue of the clan, thicker than her own. He looked up at her and grinned. "And so he came."

"She told you this?" The air was getting warmer; the ice was melting from the circle of trees, dripping like rain all around them.

"She didn't have to tell me." He took a knife from his belt. "I am a god, little one. I remember." He bared his forearm and slashed the blade along the vein from the heel of his hand to the elbow, spilling a thick gush of blood into the cup.

"Lucan!" she cried, reaching for him across the altar, and he grabbed her wrist.

"Do you trust me?" he said, holding her fast.

"Yes," she answered, tears rising in her eyes. "Wait!" she said as he raised the knife again. "What will happen?"

"The veil between worlds will be destroyed," he answered. "With the power of the Chalice, I will defeat the ancient ones, curse them as they have cursed me, make them mortal and watch them die." His smile was beautiful and terrible at the same time, making her heart beat faster. "All of their power will be mine, not in some blessed afterlife, but here, in the world of the living," he said, touching her cheek.

"And will I be with you?" she asked. "When you have dominion over all, will you still love me?"

"Yes," he promised. "You will be my queen."

She smiled. "Then do it." She held her breath as he slashed her arm as well, spilling her blood into his. Some of the drops fell on to the altar itself, and the ice melted faster, the branches of the trees rustling with life.

"We are one," he promised, his free hand caressing her cheek.

Suddenly, she heard the sound of hooves—horses galloping toward them. Looking back, she saw a line of torches coming closer. "It's Gareth," she said, her heart beating faster. "They have come for us."

"It doesn't matter, little one." He lifted the cup, now brimming with their blood, and offered it to her. "Drink, and we are safe."

Closing her eyes, she took a sip of the blood, bile rising in her throat. Smiling, Lucan withdrew the cup and took a long swallow of his own. The torches were closer, circling around them. "Is it happening?" she asked. "Are we safe?"

He looked down at the cup in his hand, his face twisting in a snarl of rage. "Little fool!" He flung it down on the stone altar, spilling their mingled blood, and grabbed her by the shoulders. "Where is it?" He flung her down on the altar, raising the knife as if to plunge it into her heart. "Where is the Chalice?"

"You have it," she protested, horrified.

"No!" Suddenly his arm wrenched back behind him as if some invisible force were yanking him backward, the knife falling from his grasp. "No," he repeated, a guttural growl, and a cloud of what looked like black gnats poured from his nose and mouth as he fell backward, letting her go. "Run, Tess," he said, writhing on the ground, the voice of the Englishman again. "For Christ's sake, run!" He screamed as if in agony, the black cloud swarming back into his mouth.

"No!" she cried. "I will not leave you!" The ice was cracking all around them; the trees were bursting forth with leaves, their branches intertwining, roots racing across the ground. She scrambled down from the altar to reach him as the riders broke through the circle of trees.

"Rise!" he shouted, arching upward from the ground. "Rise and defend me!" The ground cracked open, narrow gorges spreading outward from the altar, and with a rush of hot, vile wind, gray-green figures rose from the cracks, the shapes of rotting corpses armed with swords.

Gareth's horse reared in terror. "Hold on!" he shouted to Roxanna over the din of shrieking demons and cracking earth. He thought he heard her try to answer, but he couldn't make out the words. "Don't let go." A phalanx of demons was rushing toward them, floating just above the ground, and he drew his ancient sword, muttering a prayer as he kicked his horse and charged. They did not yield, but the sword seemed to hurt them—he cleaved the head from one, and it collapsed, melting into mist. The others grabbed for his horse, tearing at its flesh with rotten fingers, and it reared again. He felt Roxanna slipping and grabbed for her arm, but she was fighting as well, striking out with her own sword as she slid to the ground. "Roxanna!"

"Go!" she shouted, hacking her way through another mass of demons. "Go for Kivar!"

He wanted to stop her, to protect her, but there was no time. Another demon leapt for him, and he stabbed it through its rotting face.

"Gareth!" he heard Isabel shout from somewhere ahead of him. Roxanna ducked to dodge another demon's charge, slashing its legs to bring it down, then stabbing it in the throat.

He wheeled his horse around and saw the rest of his troops fighting back the demons. Siobhan was already afoot, shooting them neatly through the head with arrows, and Tristan and Simon looked like reapers, hacking their way through the throng. But with every one they destroyed, a dozen more seemed to rise from the cracks. Isabel and Orlando were running for the altar at the center of the grove, dodging between the combatants, Isabel with a bundle clutched to her chest.

"Gareth!" she shouted again. "Come on!" Kivar seemed to be standing on the altar, holding Tess by the arms.

"Bloody fucking hell," he swore, kicking his horse.

Roxanna beheaded another demon, wrenching its hands from her arm where it had been trying to drag her to the ground. The snow was melting, she realized; grass was growing around her feet. Looking up, she saw shining figures standing in a circle just outside the trees, tall, beautiful men and women with gleaming golden hair and robes of purest white. "Help us!" she shouted, stabbing another demon. But the ancient spirits did not move, only watched, their beautiful faces drawn with sorrow.

"Lucan, let me help you!" Tess was pleading. She had drawn the sword that he had given her, ready to defend him as well as any demon loosed from hell. A woman with long black hair, armed with a bow, was coming toward them, shooting every demon in her path. "Tell me what is happening!"

"Your cousin is doing what you could not," he answered with a laugh that made his handsome face look ugly. "He is bringing me the Chalice." He grabbed her hand that held the sword and forced the point under her chin. "But first you must open the gate."

"Sean!" the woman shouted. "Sean, stop this! Fight him!" Lucan cut a shallow gash in Tess's throat, ignoring her. "Sean, you must fight!"

"Do it," Tess said, meeting his eyes with her own. "I love you. I don't care."

The ugly snarl faded from his face. "I love you." He turned the point of the sword from her throat to his chest and shoved, plunging it into his heart.

"Kivar!" Tess screamed, grabbing for him as he collapsed onto the altar, gushing blood.

"Sean!" Siobhan screamed, rushing forward.

"Finish it," he said, still clutching Tess's hand. "You have to finish . . ." He let out a howl of agony as his body arched up, the demon inside of him still fighting for control.

"What is happening?" Tess demanded, blinded with tears. "Leave him alone!"

"Take care of Tess," he said, grabbing for Siobhan. "She didn't . . ." He broke off, his eyes rolling white as the black mist swarmed around his head again.

"I will," Siobhan promised, weeping tears of blood. "I promise." Closing her eyes, she raised her sword.

Gareth saw Siobhan about to kill Kivar. "Wait!" he cried, leaping down from his horse. Isabel was huddled on the ground, trying to defend the bundle she carried from a trio of demons, and he fought them back. "Where is Orlando?" he asked her.

"I don't know," she answered, raising her head.

"Come on." He grabbed her hand in one hand and the bundle in the other, pulling her with him toward the altar. "Siobhan, wait!" he called. "Don't kill him!"

Siobhan froze, the sword still raised. "Of course." Sheathing the sword, she grabbed Tess. "Take Sean's hand," she ordered. "Do it!"

"Gareth, take her other hand," Isabel ordered as Tess struggled in Siobhan's grasp. "Siobhan, take the cup."

The man on the altar let out a roar of fury as Isabel grabbed his other hand. "Hurry, Siobhan!" Gareth said, grabbing Tess's hand with bone-crushing force. They now formed the circle of four, two men and two women, around the altar. "Don't let him break free!"

Siobhan brought the sword down on her brother's throat, cleaving his head from his shoulders. "You bitch!" Tess screamed, trying to twist free of Gareth's grip to reach her. A black mist was pouring from Sean's throat as his headless body staggered backward toward the altar. "What have you done?"

"All of you, cover your nose and mouth," Siobhan ordered, dropping the bundle to grab Tess by both arms and drag her back from the circle. "Don't let the mist inside!" Blood flowed from her brother's throat as from a fountain over the stone altar, and suddenly the grove burst into midday sun.

The demons dissolved like puffs of smoke, and all four vampires collapsed to the ground, screaming in agony. "Holy Christ," Isabel said, grabbing Gareth's arm. "We are killing them."

"Give me the cup!" Behind her, he could see Roxanna, his angel, clawing at the ground like some wounded beast at bay, as if to dig her way to darkness, and Tristan had transformed into a great, golden mastiff, howling as he burned. "Isabel, give me the goddamned cup!"

"Yes," she said, coming back to herself to tear through the wrappings of her bundle. "Take this as well." She handed him the Chalice and a wooden stake, then froze, looking over his shoulder. "Oh, dear God," she said, crossing herself. "Gareth, look . . ."

He turned to see a huge black shape rising over the altar, as tall and broad as the tower of a castle. "Go to Simon," he ordered, reaching behind him to push Isabel away. "Stay back." Orlando was standing between him and the cloud of black, his arms upraised.

"Do you have it?" he shouted over his shoulder.

"I do," Gareth said, hooking the cup in his belt to draw his sword.

"Then remember your promise." He turned to face Gareth and smiled. "Remember how you love my daughter." He turned back toward the cloud as it drew together, focusing its strength. "Come to me, Father!" the dwarfish wizard shouted. "I am here!" The black mist that had been rushing toward Gareth suddenly plunged downward, encompassing the dwarf.

"Orlando!" For a moment, the darkness disappeared. Then the tiny figure on the ground began to grow. His clothes split and fell away as his shape changed, his flesh darkening. Thick black fur sprouted from his skin, and still he kept growing, changing, his face elongated to a snout, his spine twisted, legs becoming haunches, lips drawn back over curving yellow fangs as he grew bigger still, a wolf the size of a horse. Gareth gripped his sword more tightly, willing his heart to stop beating so fast. This monster was his destiny; he must kill it and save his love and his clan or die in the attempt.

He charged just as the creature turned, plunging his sword into its throat. But the wolf wrenched free, snapping at him with his teeth, tearing through his chain mail vest to rip flesh from his shoulder. "Brave little mortal," it mocked him, a voice inside his head. "Tasty, too." It licked its chops as Gareth turned to charge again.

"The stake!" Isabel shouted. "Use the stake!"

This time, instead of striking, Gareth dropped into a crouch just as he reached the wolf, raising the stake as it leapt over him and plunging it into its heart. A huge paw swiped across his head, knocking him sideways so hard he saw stars and opening his cheek to the bone with its claws. But instead of springing back at him, it rolled to its side with a howl of pain, the stake still buried in its heart.

Staggering back to his feet, Gareth raised the sword again as the wolf scrambled up, its tongue lolling between its teeth as it drew closer. "Well done, maggot," it whispered, malice glittering in the lamplike yellow eyes. "But how long do you think you have to finish me?" It lunged, and Gareth leapt back. "How long before your love is burned to ash?"

"Long enough," Gareth said with a snarl of his own, refusing to be distracted. He struck again at the creature's throat with his sword, slashing through the thick fur, and the wolf knocked him off his feet, the two of them rolling together toward the altar. The wolf grabbed his shoulder in its massive jaws, and he screamed in pain, clutching his sword with all his might and will. It slung him up on the altar and snapped at his throat, but somehow he was faster. He brought the sword up between them, plunging the blade up through its jaw into its brain. "Taunt me now, Kivar," he said, twisting, the creature's claws scrambling madly, ripping at his legs. He got his feet underneath him, still holding the sword hilt in both hands, and the wolf fell back on the altar, still writhing in pain. Thick black blood poured from the wound, soaking its fur, then rising in a fountain. The Chalice, he thought. Use the Chalice. Still holding the sword in one hand, he snatched the Chalice free of his belt and held it to the fountain of black blood.

"No!" he heard the voice of Kivar shriek inside his head, and the ground trembled underneath them. The blood still poured into the Chalice, but it did not overflow; it seemed to be drinking it, consuming the demon's evil as it bled. The form of the wolf started shrinking, dissolving into the fountain of blood, and still the Chalice drank it in, consuming every drop. As quickly as the thing had grown, it disappeared, the last of the blackness rising in droplets from a gash in the corpse of Orlando, lying on the altar, and disappearing into the cup.

"Thank you, Christ," Gareth muttered. He looked down into the Chalice, but it was apparently empty. He staggered a half step sideways, his ears ringing and his shoulder burning like molten iron, then fell to his knees. "Forgive me, Orlando," he said, reaching for the dwarf and collapsing to the ground.

Roxanna rolled over, the fire that had been consuming her a moment before suddenly snuffed out. She opened her eyes to find the blinding sunlight fading, the bright blue sky turning dark. She sat up and saw the shining figures on the outside of the circle fading into pearly mist. One of them, a man with red-gold hair, raised a hand and smiled in farewell for a moment before he was gone. His father, she thought. That was Kivar's father.

"Gareth!" She scrambled to her feet. The true sun was breaking over the mountains, and she flinched, turning away. But the light didn't burn her. She looked down at her arm, watching the sunbeams move up to her shoulder, gasping as it reached her face. Her curse was broken. Her stomach rumbled—she was hungry. "Gareth," she repeated, breathless with shock. "You did it." She turned toward the altar and saw him lying facedown on the ground. "Oh, no . . ."

She ran and fell to her knees beside him. "Gareth," she repeated, rolling him over to pillow his head on her lap. He opened his eyes and smiled at her, the beautiful smile that had first stolen her heart. Looking up, she saw Simon scoop Isabel up in his arms, swinging her in a circle. Tristan was crouched beside Siobhan near her brother's body, holding her as she cried, with Tess lying on the ground beside her, holding her hand, her eyes empty with shock. "You are hurt," she said to Gareth, caressing his cheek.

"Aye, lady, I am." The sunlight fell upon them both, shining golden on his light brown hair. "But I fear Orlando is worse."

"Orlando?" She had not seen her father since the demons had first attacked. She had been fighting back-to-back with Simon, then the sky had exploded into daylight. Now she turned toward where Gareth was pointing and saw the little wizard's body lying on the altar of stone. "No . . ."

"I'm sorry, angel," Gareth said, squeezing her hand.

"Don't say that." She rose slowly to her feet, easing Gareth gently back to the grass. "He will be fine." She took a slow step toward the altar. "He is immortal, remember?" She touched the grizzled cheek, an aching knot rising in her throat. "He raised the first beams of the heavens and dug out the cellar of the earth." Tears welled in her eyes, spilling down her cheeks, but she was not blinded; the world did not turn red. She touched them and looked down to find her fingertips wet with saltwater, not blood.

Gareth climbed back to his feet, accepting Tristan's offered hand until he found his balance. "He called the wolf into himself," he said, reaching out to touch Roxanna's shoulder. "If he had not . . ." She turned before he could finish, hiding her face in his chest as she cried.

"He saved us," Simon agreed, putting a hand on her back as well.

"He destroyed Kivar, just as he swore he would," Isabel said.

"No." Tess had not made a sound since the moment the grove had burst forth into daylight. Now she clamored to her feet, breaking free of Siobhan to move toward the altar. "He is not destroyed." She stood over the beheaded corpse of Sean Lebuin, livid spots of color rising in her death-pale cheeks. "He is a god." She turned her gaze on Gareth, the wild light of pure madness in her eyes. "You are nothing!" she screamed, lunging for him.

"Nay, lady," Tristan said, catching her easily. "Enough." He lifted her off her feet with one massive arm and pinned her hands behind her back with the other. "What will we do with this, then?" he asked dryly as she shrieked and twisted in his grasp.

"Tess!" Siobhan said sharply, moving to face her. "Stop it!" She slapped her hard across the cheek.

"You," Tess said, her eyes narrowing. "You killed him!"

"No, I did not." From the look on her face, it was obvious Siobhan's temper was more than a match for Tess's. "Kivar killed him," she said, her face scant inches from the other woman's. "Just as he would have killed you, and all of us."

"No," Tess insisted, but some of her fire seemed to drain away. "Lucan loved me—"

"Kivar loved what he thought you could give him, nothing more," Siobhan cut her off. "Even if you had managed to survive his great ritual, he would probably have wrung your neck the moment it was done." Tess shook her head, but she didn't seem able to speak. "But my brother, Sean, did love you," Siobhan went on more gently. "He saved you. Did you not hear him order you to run away? Did you not see him fighting the demon?" Tears were streaming down both their cheeks, Tess's and Siobhan's. "Did you not see Kivar hold the sword to your throat, you stupid, stupid girl?" Siobhan demanded. "Did you not see my brother turn it on himself?"

Tess seemed to go limp in Tristan's grasp, a sob escaping her open mouth. "Yes," she admitted in a voice so ragged with tears she could barely be understood. "I saw him." She slumped back against Tristan as if in a swoon, but she continued to cry. "I saw him. . . ."

"I promised him I would take care of you, and so I will," Siobhan finished. She looked up at Tristan, a challenge in her eyes as if she dared him to object, but he only nodded. "But trust me, Tess." She drew her dagger and held it under the other woman's nose. "The very first time you make the slightest move to hurt me, or my husband, or my friends, I will break my promise and cut your throat myself."

Coming from any other noblewoman, Gareth thought this might have been an idle threat. But from Siobhan, he knew it was a promise. He looked down at

Roxanna, still snug against his side, and started to tell her as much. But somehow, he couldn't seem to form the words. The world seemed to be wavering behind her, the turf rolling like waves under his feet. The next thing he knew, he was crashing to the ground.

"Gareth!" Roxanna cried, falling with him.

"I am well," he promised. Somehow lying flat on his back made it easier to speak. "Well . . . perhaps not well." The sunlight on her hair was beautiful, he thought.

"We must take this poor knight home at once," Simon said with a smile. "It would be a sorry thing to let him perish after all he's done."

"I won't die," Gareth promised Roxanna, reaching up to touch her cheek. "Not if you nurse me back to health."

"And so I will," she promised, bending down to kiss him. "For you are my champion."

28

Roxanna walked out of the tower into the blazing August sun. The procession of two carriages, four wagons, and three dozen mounted knights that would escort their friends home to England was already assembled, crowding the courtyard and spilling down the village street. She rose on tiptoe, craning her neck to search for Gareth in the throng, one hand straying unconsciously to the swell of her pregnant belly. But her husband was nowhere to be seen.

Isabel emerged from the smaller of the two carriages, her face flushed and her red hair escaping from its braid. "We packed too carefully," she said, accepting Roxanna's hand to climb down. "Clare has lost her doll."

"Tristan will find it," Roxanna answered with a grin. "Or if not, she can play with the baby instead."

A heavy snow just after the destruction of Kivar had made it impossible for the others to leave the Clan McKail for months, and in truth, they were all glad they had stayed. Gareth had spent the first month recovering from his injuries—both Kyna and Isabel had suggested he drink from the Chalice in hope of a magical cure, but after having seen the wolf consumed inside it, he adamantly refused, and even Roxanna had agreed with him. Besides, she had rather enjoyed nursing him herself.

"Have you seen my husband?" Roxanna asked Isabel now.

"Not lately, but he was in the chapel, saying goodbye to Tess," her friend answered. Roxanna's opinion of this must have shown on her face, because Isabel laughed. "Stop worrying," she scolded, squeezing Roxanna's hand.

Tess's recovery from the grove had taken much longer than Gareth's. Her wounds healed quickly enough, but her spirit seemed to be broken, and in truth, few in the clan seemed to care. But Siobhan refused to give her up. She had promised her brother to take care of her, and she was determined to do so, whether Tess liked it or not. She shielded her from the wrath of the clan, even drawing a sword against her own beloved husband when he suggested she might be past saving. (Though Tristan intimated that this was not quite as unusual as saner folk might imagine.) And slowly, Tess began to trust her. Siobhan spent long hours telling her about Sean, the man he had been before Kivar possessed him, and in time, Tess believed that perhaps it was Sean that she had loved. When it became apparent that she was pregnant, Siobhan had insisted this was a good thing. She had convinced Tristan that not only must they stay until the baby was born, but they must take Tess and the child back to Castle DuMaine with them afterward—that was why they were only leaving now, in August.

"I'm not worried," Roxanna insisted now. "After all, she's only tried to kill me once and Gareth twice."

"That is true, alas," Isabel said, feigning a sigh. "But I think Gareth can defend himself, don't you?"

"Let us hope so." The child was beautiful, she had to admit, and Tess did seem to have mellowed dramatically since his birth the month before. But she had insisted on christening him Sean Lucan Lebuin, and not even Siobhan had been able to change her mind. And as he grew, a series of small birthmarks on his arm had begun to look hauntingly familiar. "But I can't say I'm sorry to see her go."

"I don't blame you in the slightest." Isabel sat down on a mounting block.

"Are you all right?" Roxanna asked, instantly alarmed. "Shall I fetch Simon?" The darkest blot on their contentment that winter had been when Isabel suffered a miscarriage just after Christmas. Now she was pregnant again, but she had told no one but Roxanna and Siobhan for fear Simon would not let her travel.

"I am perfectly fine, I promise." Tristan's little daughter, Clare, ran between them, chasing after a puppy and giggling like a fiend. Tristan had sent for her at the first thaw, and she had quickly become the whole clan's pet. Her stepmother came running from the same direction, obviously in pursuit.

"Clare!" Siobhan called, stopping beside Isabel and Roxanna. "Where are your shoes?" Lady DuMaine was dressed for the journey in a tunic and breeches with a sword at her hip. "We will be leaving soon!"

"I'll find them!" Clare called back happily, ducking between the legs of one of her father's knights, making him smile in an addlepated manner quite at odds with his armor.

"She won't," Siobhan said with a sigh. "We'll be halfway across Scotland, her father will see that she's barefoot, and it will be my fault for bringing her up as a brigand." She looked down at Isabel. "Why are you sitting? Are you ill? Shall I fetch Simon?"

"No and no," Isabel insisted. "Did you find Clare's doll?"

"I believe Brian has it, fixing . . . something," Siobhan answered. "You know, when Simon finds out you're with child and didn't tell him, he's going to be furious."

"I mean to tell him as soon as we're well under way," she answered. She reached for Roxanna's hand again. "As lovely as you and Gareth have been, I'm ready to go home."

"I understand completely," Roxanna said, giving her hand a squeeze.

"So do I," Siobhan agreed. "Of course, I have to go

home and be Lady DuMaine, whatever that means. No doubt I'll fail miserably."

"Oh, I suspect you'll manage," Roxanna said, sharing a wink with Isabel. They had discussed it at length between the two of them and decided 'twas the royal court they trembled for, not Siobhan.

"So what of you, princess?" Siobhan said. "Are you homesick? Do you think you will ever go back?"

"No," she answered, shaking her head. In truth, she had been privately considering this question for some time. "It's very far away, you know."

"Still, Gareth would take you if you asked him," Isabel said.

"He would want to," Roxanna agreed. "But he is needed here." She looked around at the courtyard, bustling with activity. "And I have what I wanted." Clare was making another round of the carriages, her shoes now swinging by their laces over her head like a double-headed flail, and all three women smiled. "This is my home."

"Come here at once, little heathen," Siobhan called, leaving them to grab her stepdaughter up in her arms and swing her in a circle, making her shriek even louder.

"She is afraid to go home without Sean," Isabel confided. "She told me she knows she'll see him everywhere she goes."

"And so she will, for a time." She had only been with Orlando a matter of hours here at the Castle McKail, but she still saw his ghost in her memory every time she went into the laird's room at the top of the tower. "But Tristan will help her."

As if he might have heard, Tristan emerged from the chapel across the courtyard and stopped to join the fun. He took Clare from her stepmother and tossed her in the air. "Careful!" Siobhan scolded, but she was laughing, cleaving to his side.

Simon and Gareth had followed him out and came to join their wives. "Did Tess weep to leave you?" Roxanna asked her husband, arching an eyebrow.

"She is inconsolable," he retorted, draping an arm around her shoulders to draw her to his side.

"Frightened is more the word," Simon corrected with a grin. "Tristan gave her to understand in no uncertain terms what would happen if she fails to behave herself at DuMaine." He turned his grin on Gareth. "He can be quite scary when he tries."

"You can joke," Isabel said, her voice dropping a notch. "We all can and have. But the woman is dangerous. She managed to hire mercenaries to go after Gareth long before she ever met Kivar."

"Unfortunately, she is also the mother of Siobhan's last living relation," Simon answered. "In faith, Tristan would be no happier to have Sean himself in his castle, with or without a demon inside of him. But Siobhan worshipped him, and Tristan worships her."

"Which is not to say he doesn't mean to be cautious," Gareth agreed. "And Simon is right; I would not want him for an enemy."

"So," Isabel said, standing up. "Are we finally ready to depart?"

"I'm not sure," Simon said doubtfully. "Perhaps we should stay one more night—it's already mid-morning." He touched her cheek, the familiar look of worry in his eyes. "One more night's sleep in a proper bed could do you no harm."

"But waiting one more day to see Charmot might," his wife retorted, hugging him close. *You see?* her eyes said to Roxanna over his shoulder. *Imagine if he knew I was carrying his child.*

"As you will," Simon said. "We will leave at once."

An hour later, Gareth and Roxanna stood at the window of their tower room, watching as the caravan disappeared in the distance. "How long before they are home, do you think?" Roxanna asked, leaning back against him, his arms around her waist.

"A week at least," he answered. "Two if Simon has his way—he won't risk another miscarriage." She turned and looked at him, mouth open in shock. "You didn't honestly think he didn't know," he said with a grin. "As closely as he watches her? She can't sneeze and keep it a secret."

"In faith, I am glad," she said, turning around again. He was idly rubbing her stomach, and she smiled. " 'Tis passing strange. . . ."

"What is?" He kissed the top of her head.

"Getting a child so quickly when I never thought to

have one." She laced her fingers with his. "And Isabel as well . . . what do you think it means?"

"Well, I can't be certain," he said, mock-serious. "But if what Sir John told me once about the getting of babies is true, I think it would be more remarkable if you were not."

"Do you, in faith?" she retorted.

"I do." He turned her in his embrace, draping her arms around his neck. "You mean because you were a vampire," he said, touching his forehead to hers.

"And Simon," she agreed. "But you were not, and Isabel was not. But Siobhan was, and Tristan, and Siobhan is not having a baby."

"Unless we're counting Tess." She stepped down hard on his foot, making him wince. "What is your worry, angel?" he said, taking a more respectful tone. "Our clan was founded by the children of vampires, if you will recall."

"That's true," she answered. "But they stayed here in this village; they didn't scatter themselves across Britain." She caressed the mark on his arm, embellished now with tattoos in the manner of his ancestors. "Baby Sean already has this mark," she pointed out. "Surely that means something."

"Lucan Kivar is gone," he promised, the same promise he made to her every night before she went to sleep. "He will never hurt us again."

"I know." She wrapped her arms around him, curling as close to his chest as his child she carried would allow. "You destroyed him." She heard his heart beating just under her ear, and she smiled, warm with the knowledge that hers was beating just the same. "Siobhan asked me if I would ever go back to the place where I was born," she said.

"Did she?" In truth, he had wondered this himself, worried that she grieved for the world she had lost. Did this life seem small to her after her palace with its hall of gold and jewels? "And what did you tell her?"

"I told her I would not." She drew back to look at him, mortal, human tears of happiness sparkling clear in her eyes. "Everything I could want is here."

"Angel," he murmured as he kissed her, knowing exactly what she meant. They were home at last.